HE LOOKED   ,
HIS DARK EYES QUESTIONING. . . .

But there was nothing to say, really, and he knew it once he saw the love in her eyes shining bright. They had said it all already, in a language more profound than any words they might choose to speak.

She touched her fingers to the side of his face. He turned his mouth to kiss her hand, then lowered his lips to meet hers. She laced her long, slender arms around his neck; her fingertips caressed the nape of his neck as she yielded to his embrace.

This was the first time a kiss had ever been as he had dreamed it to be.
For her it was the first kiss.
It was a kiss to inspire others. . . .

HEART AND SOUL

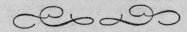

Lynn Cartier

A DELL BOOK

Published by
Dell Publishing Co., Inc.
1 Dag Hammarskjold Plaza
New York, New York 10017

Dell ® TM 681510, Dell Publishing Co., Inc.

ISBN: 0-440-13594-X

Printed in the United States of America
First printing—October 1982

For David

PART
I

CHAPTER ONE

The sun poured through the bedroom window. She opened her eyes, winced at the brightness, and pulling the covers back over her head, burrowed deeper into the pillow. It was early September, but the sun continued to rise much sooner than she thought necessary. The day would have to wait, at least for another hour, she thought dreamily, drifting back through the melodic threshold to sleep. But before she could escape the day, her dreams were interrupted by a pounding at her bedroom door.

"All right, all right," she cried impatiently. "What's the emergency?" Melissa Dennison threw back the covers from her long, slender body. Her fair skin was occasionally freckled beneath the soft folds of cotton print. In spite of the sun that flooded her room, she shivered and clutched the neck of her nightgown tightly to her. She hated mornings, when her body was slow with sleep, her mind even slower. She crossed the room resignedly. Melissa was usually cheerful, but mornings always clouded her disposition.

"Morning, sweetie." It was her roommate. Who else

could it have been? Melissa rubbed sleep from her emerald-green eyes.

"What are you so cheerful about?" Melissa asked. She stood face to face with the irrepressible grin of her closest friend. Patrice Millay was of medium height, pliantly slender, with shoulder-length blond hair and thick bangs that stopped just short of startling blue eyes, today dazzling mischievously. A white-eyelet peasant dress left bare tanned arms and legs. "And what do I owe this early-morning greeting?" Melissa inquired.

"Honey, you're impossible. Do you know what day this is?"

"No," Melissa answered. "But I'll bet you are going to tell me."

"Would you rather I didn't?"

"I don't think I have a choice."

"Sure you do. If you want to sleep through your first day of class, I—"

"My God!" Melissa was awake now. "How can I be so dense?" She cursed herself sharply. "And on the most important day of the whole year!"

"I'll fix coffee," Patrice said, following her to the door of the bathroom. "Do you want eggs?"

Melissa stripped off her nightgown. Hot water steamed from the shower. "No. Just coffee."

She disappeared behind the shower curtain, her tangled hair knotted on top of her head. From under the stream of hot water came the familiar morning swearing, more vehement today than usual.

Patrice laughed to herself as she walked to the kitchen. She removed the copper kettle from the stove

an instant before it whistled, waited for the boil to settle, then flooded the deep-brown grounds in the filter.
The air thickened with aroma. She set two heavy mugs
beside the grapefruit she had already sectioned; toast
warmed in the oven; bacon, lean and crisp, too. While
Melissa dressed, Patrice scrambled eggs for herself,
adding two more in case she could persuade Melissa.

As independent as both girls were, there were times
when they relied heavily on each other. When Melissa's
exhaustion overwhelmed her common sense, Patrice ex-
ercised her two-year seniority by forcing her to sleep
and eat. They had been friends a long time, since the
last year in high school, when Patrice had transferred to
New York City from Waco, Texas, more frightened
than a kitten caught in a dogfight. Melissa had recognized her terror and had adopted her at once. That was
four years ago, but the memory of kindness hadn't faded
at all.

At first Patrice had thought the gesture purely al-
truistic, but soon she saw that Melissa had needed a
friend as much as she had. Possibly even more. Eventually, Patrice made friends with her classmates, but for
Melissa it was different. She was two years younger,
and smarter than the rest of the class; a mere child
amid sophisticated, sometimes cruel teen-agers. To
worsen matters she was taller than all the boys, and
painfully thin. Her classmates called her Birdlegs, and
instead of satisfying their jealous taunts with tears or
anger, Melissa held her head high and retreated into the
one place she felt wholly confident: her music. Even
now, at twenty, Melissa preferred music to people. Patrice didn't blame her—life had taught her to protect

herself—but she worried that the wall surrounding her had grown insurmountably high. She divided the eggs onto two plates as Melissa slid into the kitchen.

"Gosh, thanks, Pat," said Mel, grabbing two napkins off the counter and throwing one across the table. She had dressed casually in a pearl-gray sweater and charcoal wool skirt. A blazer hung carelessly over the back of her chair. She gobbled her eggs, pausing only to sip her coffee.

"At least let your coffee cool."

Melissa squinted at the wall clock, and reassured by the hour, set down her mug. "I don't know how I can sleep so late."

But Patrice knew. She had heard the piano late into the night, her friend resolutely refining the Kreutzer Sonata she had perfected in Switzerland over the summer. "What time did you get to bed?"

"I don't know, but I think it was late."

Patrice was sure of that. It was three A.M. the last time she had read her clock. Hours later she had heard Melissa close her bedroom door. In much the same way that sleep erased all detail from Mel's mind, the piano erased all thought of time. She seldom ceased practice before midnight. Often when Patrice awoke at dawn she found Melissa buried in a difficult passage, refusing to sleep until she had mastered it.

Patrice understood. She herself had worked nearly to exhaustion the previous year, earning top marks at Columbia Law School. But she had known if she were to finish her last year of school with her health she would need a summer vacation to relax. When she had first mentioned her plans to visit Switzerland, she half-hoped Melissa would join her. But only when she mentioned an Alpine school for advance pianists did Melissa perk up and take interest. They traveled over together but separated as soon as they arrived. From the look of Melissa's pale skin, and the intensity of her eyes, Patrice gathered she hadn't seen anything of the countryside except when riding to and from the airport.

Even the vast landscape outside Melissa's dormitory window had gone unappreciated. She had seen only the landscapes her music created, often more beautiful than the great mountains and lush pastures that had distracted her classmates from their studies. While they were off visiting the local boys in the village below the school, Melissa had remained behind practicing.

The effort had not been wasted. Patrice noticed that the music that filled their West Side apartment was measurably better this fall than it had been the previous spring. She wondered if it were worth it. Could it be healthy to have no other interests? Melissa insisted that the only way to success was through complete dedication. If that were true, Melissa was certain to succeed. She watched her young friend's eyes aglow with excitement.

"Are you scared?" Patrice drawled.

"Who, me?" Mel answered too quickly. "Not on your life." Her hands waved the air nervously. "I've waited all summer for this day."

Patrice poured more hot coffee into their cups. She knew it wasn't just first-day-of-term nerves from which Melissa suffered. Today she would meet the great composer Jean-Pierre Arbour, and if that didn't make her friend nervous, nothing would. Patrice tore the last piece of toast in two and handed half across the table. Melissa accepted it absently.

"You know," she began, chewing each bite deliberately, "as impressive as the teachers were this summer, all I could think about was the fall when I would work with Arbour. I guess they served as stepping-stones—not that I would ever have said that," she hastened to add, always sensitive to people's feelings. "But Arbour is the top. He's the—"

"Eiffel Tower?" Patrice kidded, breaking into a bar of her favorite Cole Porter tune.

"I was going to say—before I was so irreverently interrupted—*Monsieur Arbour est la crême de la crême.*" Melissa's adulation was in earnest. There was no rocking her, and Patrice didn't even attempt to kid her about her French accent, usually the subject of great amusement.

"It's funny," she continued, her voice soft with feeling. "I've never met the man, but he's affected me more profoundly than anyone in the world. His work, I mean." She sighed deeply. "Not that I'll ever play as well as he, but he's inspired me beyond what I might settle for in myself." She was quiet for a minute, her thoughts fixed on the man. "Yeah, it's funny. He'll never know how important he's been in my life." She turned to Patrice, as if suddenly remembering her presence. "Imagine. Being so powerful you affect people you've never even met."

Relaxed in her chair, elbows resting on the edge of the table, her eyes shone brightly. Patrice was moved by just how young she really was. So innocent. In some ways Mel was highly sophisticated; in others, a babe in the woods, needing protection from dangers she didn't even know existed.

"Gosh! I've got to go," Mel cried, scrambling to her

feet. She gathered the books and papers she would need for class. "What if I am late?"

"You won't be," comforted Patrice, knowing Melissa needed an ear for her worry. "I'll bet you even have time to brush your hair."

Melissa looked horrified. She rushed to the mirror in the hall. "Thanks," she said, pulling her comb through her long heavy hair. "I don't know what I'd do without someone to watch over me."

"You'd look *and* play like Beethoven." Patrice watched her gather the dark hair with luxuriant carelessness and twist it into a simple knot. She opened a sterling clip between her teeth, then stuck it fast into her hair. A lock curled loose at the nape of her regal neck.

"Okay?" she asked, an uncertain smile tainting her pretty mouth.

"Very okay," Patrice assured her. Melissa had developed into a striking beauty. "If you play as well as you look today, you'll win his heart *and* his respect."

Melissa made a horrible face. "He can keep his heart," she said wilfully. "All I want are a few hours of his time—like twenty a day," she added, grinning devilishly. She leaned across the cluttered breakfast table to deliver a hug. "Save me the dishes. I'll do them tonight."

She grabbed her books and raced down the two flights of stairs. Because it was colder than she had anticipated, she pulled her notebooks close to her chest and dashed to the corner of Eighty-sixth Street, glancing north in time to signal the approaching bus. It bounded toward her, opening its doors just as she stepped from the curb smiling shyly at the bus driver.

Melissa deposited a token, squeezed her way to the rear where she grabbed a strap for balance, and remembered her blazer back at the apartment, content to warm the chair while she faced the cold September day.

A half an hour later Melissa took a seat in the first row of Michael Paul Recital Hall. The room was empty still, except for one student in the last row fidgeting with a score. Now that her seat was secured, she saw no point to sitting idle when she could use the time to practice. Leaving her books on her chair, she hurried down the corridor and took the elevator to the piano studio on the fourth floor.

It was good to be back to the familiar surroundings. After two years at the Juilliard School of Music she knew every nook and cranny; most importantly, which of the pianos in the complicated maze of studios held their tune and which lost distinction after a day's abuse. Her own favorite was the old Steinway grand at the far end of the hall. It wasn't the prettiest, or the easiest to play, but she knew the worn ivory keys like her own hand, and felt a loyalty to it. Grabbing the handle to the familiar studio door, she swung it open joyfully.

"Oh, I'm sorry," she said at once. "I had expected to find the studio empty," she explained to the man at the keyboard.

He studied her critically, angry at the intrusion.

"You were mistaken," he said curtly. He let his eye appraise her lithe figure before turning his back to her.

Melissa let the door fall closed, but she hesitated to leave. She didn't want to play another piano. She wanted to play *this one*. How long would he be? She heard no music, and when she peered through the narrow rectangular window she saw he wasn't even at the keyboard, but pacing the studio. Maybe he was nearly finished. It wouldn't hurt to ask.

"You again!" he said angrily. "What do you want?"

Melissa hesitated. He didn't frighten her. His foreign accent and his age, undoubtedly twenty years greater than that of most Juilliard students, must account for his defensiveness. She hadn't seen him before. Was he a first year student, she wondered, or a transfer? If he were just beginning his studies, no wonder he was nervous. "I didn't hear you playing . . ." she started. "And I wondered—"

"You wondered?" he challenged.

"How long you would be?" she replied calmly. "If you aren't going to play, I am anxious to—"

"But I am," he said defensively, as if to deny an accusation. "Or rather, I was intending to," he added meanly. "Until I was interrupted."

Melissa stared at him. She would never understand such blatant antagonism. She could forgive him for feeling anxious on the first day of classes, but he wasn't making it easy. "Sorry to have bothered you," she said coolly, turning on her heels to leave the room.

Instead of seeking out another room to practice in, she returned to the recital hall, no longer in the mood to play.

The room buzzed with excitement as Melissa slid into her seat. For many of Juilliard's students, summer vacation had meant travel all over the world: new stories, adventures, escapades, affairs. These were the last moments of freedom before the students settled into their rigorous academic schedules, and the talk was carefree. Gathered into one room for the only time all semester, by afternoon they would be set on their individual courses, divided into classes depending on their specialties and capabilities. They would remain that way until reevaluation at the end of the term. A few would discreetly disappear as the pressure and competition mounted.

Sara Cummings waved vaguely as she passed Melissa, stopping to chat with two handsome Italian scholarship students. Melissa heard their familiar chatter, the frivolity, and for once she regretted the inherent loneliness of first place. Thank goodness for her friendship with Patrice! At least she understood Mel's need to perfect her music, above all else, and never resented the time it took.

She glanced around the room curiously, noting the worried countenance of a disoriented freshman, the transparent mask of confidence worn by a second-year student. She wondered at the rudeness she had encountered from the student in the practice studio, but dismissed him from her mind, or tried to. Something about him held her attention. He had seemed so serious. Maybe he would provide real competition for her, but she doubted it. Previous years had proven sorely disappointing, and she had no reason to expect differently this year. Increasingly the students were confident in attitude but timid in performance. Like Indians transplanted onto reservations, they yielded to their lot as if they had no choice, as if to fight for what they wanted was beneath them. From their smug seats of mediocrity, they resented her drive, her position as first in the school. No one had given her first place; she had worked night and day to overcome the deficiencies that bonded the other students together. It hadn't made her very popular, but she was used to that.

She relaxed in her chair, looking forward to her morning instruction with mild interest. She had not yet dared to admit to herself the anxiety she felt for her afternoon interview with Jean-Pierre Arbour.

Arbour was more than a master. He was her inspiration. In those moments when doubt prevailed, when Melissa wanted to quit from exhaustion and depression, she turned to Arbour's music, to his fine composition. Passionate, moving, yet never undisciplined, his music renewed her determination and instilled a sense of obligation. To quit, it seemed to say, was worse than never to have begun. It made Melissa want to try harder, to perform better than before. Refreshed, more completely than from any vacation abroad, Melissa would return to her music, like a raven transformed into a songbird, out of doors in the sunlight. Late at night, alone with Arbour's rendition of Ravel, or Brahms, Melissa imagined what love must be like. His music held her like a loving embrace. No wonder she feared meeting the man more than a little.

She had braced herself for disappointment. So often, she knew, great musicians were impossible as teachers; they had neither patience for students nor talent for teaching. Performance was one thing. Composition was another. But to translate genius into a language comprehensible to someone less experienced—that was another thing altogether.

Juilliard was Arbour's first teaching engagement. She had wondered why a great musician would take time from his music to teach others. She had heard rumors that a concert series had been canceled in favor of his teaching assignment. Perhaps the pressure of constant travel and performance was too much? Whatever his reasons she felt fortunate. It had been a long wait, but she was ready for him.

At three o'clock he would interview her, to decide if she was worth his instruction. What if he took an instant dislike to her? What if he disagreed with her interpretation of his works? Had she been wrong to include one of his compositions in her repertoire? Perhaps she should omit it? Her style was original, which he might appreciate—unless he was an egotist. Her rendition resembled his in temperament, which he might consider a compliment—unless he hated any kind of imitation.

Suddenly Melissa was certain he would exclude her from study. Her heart raced with anxiety as she watched Sue-Ellen Frazer exchange confidences with a girl from the composition department, both petite and sure of their charms. Sue-Ellen was inferior to Melissa on piano, but Arbour might choose her instead. The girl had a head for details and knew how to display them intelligently—a trait Melissa found tiresome. But in an interview it was just the kind of slick performance that might fool Arbour.

She cursed herself for not wearing something more attractive. More feminine. She should have bought a new dress. She didn't have a lot of extra money from what her father allowed her, but certainly she could have managed one new outfit. Patrice had encouraged her. Why was she so stubborn? What greater occasion was there, after all, than an interview with Arbour?

Melissa blushed. She wasn't auditioning for his affections. If she couldn't win his respect by playing the pieces she had practiced all summer, then she didn't want it. But she knew she was lying to herself. The year would be worthless without Arbour.

"Do you mind if I sit with you a moment?" a pleasant male voice inquired, taking the seat next to her in the concert hall.

Melissa found the student she had encountered in the studio addressing her. The anger was gone from his face, turning it boyishly handsome. "Of course not," she said, shifting her books on her lap. He smiled at her, brushing his black silky hair out of his face with one sweeping gesture, but it was fruitless; it fell again, and Melissa noticed the long, thick lashes that bordered his penetrating expressive eyes. Color rose in her cheeks, and she returned her attention to the front of the class.

"I have been looking for you," he said.

"You were?" she said, turning to face him again. "Why?"

"To apologize for my rude behavior. I am miserable before noon, but they insist I be here early."

Melissa brightened with compassion. "I am awful in the morning myself," she confided. "I never schedule anything important before noon."

"They let you do that?" he asked seriously.

She nodded. She doubted he could have her flexible schedule in his first term, but he might as well know what he could look forward to. "I am sorry I disturbed you," she said. "I—I was anxious to play. I've been away all summer, and I do love that piano. Almost no one uses that studio," she explained. "I've come to claim it as my own."

"You will have to share it now," he said. "It is the best in the school—a fine old instrument."

"You know that already?" she asked incredulously. "Aren't you new here?"

"Yes," he said offhandedly. "But it doesn't take long to make a comparison." A commotion at the front of the lecture hall caught their attention. "I must go," he said nervously. "I came only to ask your forgiveness."

"That's okay," she assured him. "But you'd better stay here now. They're about to begin," she told him, placing her hand on his shirt-sleeve to stay him. "You can get your books later."

The room quieted as an impressive line of professors entered; at a slight distance the junior faculty followed; then the teaching assistants. The caste system prevailed in academia more than anywhere, Melissa thought. Or was it just more noticeable here? She glanced back at her neighbor to find him looking frightened. "Don't be so nervous," she whispered. "This part is a breeze." She smiled at him warmly, and for a moment the fear left his eyes.

She scanned the group of professors for Arbour. She had only seen one picture of him, on the back of his albums, always the same candid photograph, a view from the side, hands poised over the keyboard, his face furious with concentration. She had heard more than once that he shunned publicity.

In front of her were two or three men she didn't recognize. She singled out one, a man about fifty, slightly balding and angry-looking. She was sure he was Arbour. She leaned forward in her seat to scrutinize his face. It was funny to think such an ordinary-looking man could perform such brilliant musical feats. It just proved how faulty snap judgments could be. She wouldn't be intimidated by his angry look. Certainly he wouldn't care if she wore an old skirt or a new one. She had been silly to worry. Only the music would matter.

He would be professional, and she was always professional.

She tapped her fingers nervously on the book she was holding, wishing they'd commence. The men settled into their chairs at the front of the lecture hall. The dean greeted the faculty privately, and the assistant dean, Ms. Sagan, surveyed the room, as if looking for someone in particular, or counting heads.

"Would you mind not tapping?"

Melissa started at the words as if she had been slapped.

"Your tapping," the man beside her explained. "It is biting my nerves."

She stopped her drumming instantly. "Gosh—I'm sorry," she said, flushing deep red. She wondered at his peculiar way of talking. She glanced backward at him, settling on a view of his hands so as to avoid contact with his eyes. They were large hands, and his fingers were long and graceful. They looked strong, yet surprisingly sensitive for a male's. With practice he might outreach her own, which was a tenth, in any key. Melissa folded her own graceful hands on her lap, noting the comparison. She wondered if he noticed it, too.

The clock ticked a minute past ten. She puzzled why they didn't start. A hand covered hers—she had been drumming again. She blushed fiercely, and without a word pulled her hands into her lap and locked them there. She wasn't used to such capable hands being laid over hers.

Dean Evans caught her eye, as if he had been looking for her. She sat up straighter in her chair as he crossed the room. What if he wanted to introduce her to the assembly? Being first in piano gave her a certain status, but she knew an introduction would further alienate her from her peers. She hoped again that there would be stiff competition this year. If not, there were always the rounds of competition she devised for herself. And her tutorials with Arbour to look forward to.

She greeted Dean Evans formally, but it was to the man at her side that he spoke.

"There you are," he greeted heartily. "We have been looking for you. Will you join us in front?"

"But of course," he answered quickly, rising from his chair. He was taller than Melissa had first noticed. And more handsome. His thick black hair made a noticeable contrast to the dean's thinning gray; his strong, straight back emphasized the dean's administrative slouch. Even at a distance Melissa recognized his nervousness, also a contrast to Dean Evans's assuredness. It was no wonder, Melissa thought. She would be nervous in front of all these people if her English were that poor. Maybe she would talk to him during the semester, if there was time. It would improve her French, and he would need help to live in New York City, where people were impatient, often ungenerous, to foreigners.

The faculty grew silent. Dean Evans magnanimously addressed his colleagues, then the student body. Melissa leaned forward in her chair. It felt good to be back. The hard summer's work would now pay off. She saw no reason to vacation from what she loved best in life. So what if people thought her compulsive, obsessive, all the other unflattering words that surrounded people dedicated to their art. At least she wasn't frivolous.

She stared so hard at the fierce, rotund face she knew to be Arbour's that she forgot to listen to Dean

Evans's introductory remarks. He was introducing the
faculty already, one by one, down the line. She held her
breath as the dean introduced the stern-countenanced
professor; readied herself for instant applause—Gus-
tav Hoston—not Arbour at all! Melissa felt horri-
bly cheated, as if he had intentionally misled her. But
who, then? She inspected the line of teachers furiously,
fearful that while not paying attention she had missed
his name. But that was impossible. Who else could it
be?

The class rose to their feet in spontaneous applause
as Dean Evans signaled the nervous young man forward. Melissa numbly joined them, but she was still off
balance when the applause died down. This man who
had sat so close to her, had covered her hand with his,
was the world-renowned Jean-Pierre Arbour? The man
who had inspired her playing?

She stared at him dumbly, ashamed to recall her ar-
rogant thoughts. Tears stung her eyes in self-
admonition. In a blur she watched him reach the po-
dium. When he spoke, his faulty English translated into
poetry for her. His words were not confused, just spoken with new emphasis, with varied order, like his music. As in the subtle shifts he gave to Rachmaninoff,
Ravel, Mozart, he breathed intention into every word.
Unlike her own playing, she thought, in which she extracted feeling from each note, Arbour gave. He complemented the music with passion of his own. That
was what made him so special. So it was with his
speech. Already he had taught her more with these few
words than she had learned all summer.

Overcome with conflicting emotion, she felt both in-

timidated and inspired. She wanted to abandon her
studies as pointless in the presence of genius, and she
wanted to practice harder to acknowledge his influence
on her. She listened intently, and his words, as his music had done so many times before, calmed her; inspired her to take the next step, the greater risk. Yes,
with his guidance it might be possible to take the steps
she had always feared, always avoided.

"What I have to teach is a passion," he said. "To me,
I love nothing, if not for music. Music is our gift of
humanity, is not that true?"

Melissa nodded imperceptibly, as if he spoke directly
to her.

"There is nothing without music . . . ourselves are
not important. . . . The rest is incidental."

Melissa wanted to cry. To cheer. He spoke *her* feelings out loud, and no one laughed. They listened, to
English that would have embarrassed the poorist immi-
grant. He articulated sentiments she had never dared to
voice, not even to Patrice. She ached, his words
touched her so deeply.

The room resounded again with applause. She
watched from her seat as her classmates crowded him;
saw his eyes flicker with fear as they closed in around
him. By turn they grabbed his hand in congratulations,
the same hand that had stopped hers because she had
made him nervous. She stayed in her seat, not knowing
what to do. How would she ever face him? she wondered. With all his powers of perception, she was sure
he had been able to read her thoughts. What a beginning!

* * *

The rest of the morning had been endless. Melissa attended her music history class, selecting a seat at the rear of the room, giving her attention to the hasty character sketches she drew of Arbour. Already she had memorized the strong lines of his face.

The minutes crept by like hours and the hours refused to budge. Intending to practice during her lunch hour, she begrudged the time lost to the students who banged mercilessly at the keyboard, keeping her from the one refuge guaranteed to calm her. The unpracticed scales worsened her ragged nerves, and for the second time that day she abandoned any notion of playing.

At two o'clock, shaky from no lunch, Melissa forced herself to the coffee shop across Broadway and Sixty-sixth Street where she stewed over a BLT on toast and a bitter cup of coffee. She checked her watch against the wall clock, certain something had affected them both. At two thirty, unable to stand the wait any longer, she paid her bill, grabbed her books, and dashed back to school.

She was out of breath when she reached Arbour's studio. Pacing the corridor nervously, she ran through a mental list of things she could say to him. Should she attempt wit? She might try addressing him in French, but what if he had no tolerance for imperfection? No, she had better not speak at all. Let him address her first. Was that proper? she worried. If she thought of America as her home, then he would be her guest; as the hostess, she had better address him first. But then he was older. Her superior. Her teacher. A man. That was four points on his side, only two on hers. Oh, God, she wished Patrice were here. She would know what to do.

Then she remembered her hair. She had seen her reflection in the glass doors of the school entrance, and
most of it had uncoiled down her back. Leaning against
the door, she unclasped the barrette and brought her
comb quickly through her hair. Holding the clip open
in her mouth, she twisted two handfuls of hair into an
attractive knot. As she reached for the clasp to fasten
her hair, the door swung open, and Melissa fell helplessly into the room, landing in Arbour's unsuspecting
arms. Her books scattered across the floor, but he kept
her from falling with his sturdy hands.

He helped her regain her balance and invited her
into the room. She stopped to gather her books. He,
too, had stooped, and their hands touched when they
reached for the same book. Jean-Pierre laughed, handing her the notebook.

"Not my standard entrance," she offered, too embarrassed to be anything but honest.

"Welcome," he said simply. An amused, if somewhat
bewildered look shadowed his olive-skinned face. "Do
you play the piano as well as the book? As well as
you enter a room?" His voice was scaled with laughter
as he watched her. The abundant hair, free from its tidy
knot, cascaded over her slender shoulders, and he wondered that he hadn't noticed her beauty until now. Except her eyes. He hadn't missed the intense green light
that had beamed through him that morning. But now
she looked as frightened as a doe caught in headlights,
and he wanted to erase the fear, if he could. "Won't
you come in," he offered, stepping back against the
door to let her enter. She looked up at him gratefully,
and silently crossed the room to the piano.

Her heart pounded wildly, but in spite of her nerves

she had noticed that all signs of fear were absent from his face. And what a difference it made! He appeared more beautiful to her by the minute. She glanced around the room, trying to steady herself.

Arbour disappeared into the adjoining room, and she was glad for the respite to regain her nerve.

But after a minute she began to worry that he had wanted her to follow him. What if she did, only to find he had gone to the bathroom? No, she must wait.

From the other room she heard his deep voice: *"Voulez-vous ouvrir la porte?"*

Melissa hastened to translate, then hurried to open the door.

"Ah, you understand French," he said. He held a tray filled with teacups and pitcher, creamer, and lemon. "Do you speak my lanugage as well?"

"Un petit peu," she answered, hoping her accent wouldn't elicit his laughter as it did Patrice's.

He shook his head sadly, then smiled. "My English is bad, you have noticed, no?" When Melissa didn't answer he continued. "Your French will make me less self-conscious, if you will excuse my conclusion from so short a sentence."

"Gosh, is it really that bad?"

Jean-Pierre nodded.

"Patrice—that's my roommate—tells me I sound awful," she said. "But there's only one way to improve. And I can't practice when no one will talk to me."

"Well, perhaps we can teach each other to speak less sourly."

"It's a deal!" Melissa said enthusiastically, holding out her hand confidently.

"What's a 'deal'?" Jean-Pierre asked, covering her

delicate hand in both of his and holding it while he waited for her answer.

"That means you're on," Melissa explained.

Jean-Pierre continued to look puzzled.

This, Melissa thought, is going to be harder than I thought. "It means I look forward to our agreement," she said at last.

"Ah, bon! D'accord!" he answered, then turned to the tea tray on the table. He beckoned her to join him.

"Don't you want me to play for you?" she asked, wondering if he had misunderstood the reason for her visit.

"But of course," he said, pouring first one cup full of steaming tea, then another. "But I am nervous when we first meet. I would like to first talk quietly. Perhaps to dislodge this morning from both our minds, no?" He smiled at the memory, and Melissa felt a pang inside her stomach which she concluded to be nerves. He handed her a cup of tea. "Soon you will play for me."

She watched him inhale the steam from the porcelain cup, and she was surprised to find that his greatness didn't intimidate her, as she had feared it would.

"I am told you are first in the school?"

"In piano," she said, hoping to downplay her position. She didn't want him to expect too much from her. It would be hard enough to satisfy him. He was used to excellence. Again her thoughts drifted to the great sacrifice he was making to teach others.

"Is there any other instrument?" he said playfully, but Melissa could tell from the look in his eyes that he was serious. He had spent his life composing music for the piano. He was revered internationally as second to none for his piano playing. It made her position at Juilliard seem insignificant. "Do you have any other interests?" he asked seriously.

Melissa hesitated. She didn't want to bore him with talk about herself. She wanted to hear about his life, but she didn't dare bother him with questions. "I spend almost all my time at the piano," she admitted shamefacedly. "I've been called compulsive," she said, raising her clear, earnest gaze to meet his.

"That is good," he pronounced firmly. "It is the only way to play. You have other classes?"

"Three," Melissa told him. "This is my last year, so I've completed most of the requirements, but I have musical theory in the morning—"

"When we are both miserable." His eyes twinkled.

Melissa blushed. "When we are miserable," she agreed. He nodded for her to continue. "I was supposed to take music history as a freshman, but I was too impatient to sit still for lectures then."

"So now you pay?"

"Yes. It's not bad, but I already know most of it. And I would rather be practicing."

"How long do you practice each night?"

"Until my roommate breaks my fingers," she said, laughing, but she bit her lip in shame when she saw he didn't share her laughter. What had prompted her to take such liberties as humor with the great Jean-Pierre Arbour? She *must* remember her position. "Seven or eight hours," she said formally.

He nodded. "Now you must play for me," he said, taking her by the hand and leading her to the piano. "You will notice I have had our piano moved to my studio."

Melissa hadn't noticed, but now she saw that the

aged Steinway had replaced the newer, more prestigious piano that usually filled this studio. Seating herself at the familiar instrument, she tried to stifle her reaction. She knew he merited the best piano in the school—she wanted him to have it—but for herself she regretted the loss. It would take precious time to accustom herself to another piano.

"Do not fret, my little friend," he said softly, as if reading her thoughts. "If you are as talented as you are reported to be, the piano will be yours to use as well as mine. A deal?" he said. Melissa smiled shyly. He was making this as easy for her as he could.

Her fingers hovered over the smooth ivory keys. She took a deep breath, knowing that her future rested on the quality of her performance, and then she began to play.

She started with Beethoven's "Appassionata," the first sonata she had learned at Juilliard, but still her favorite. It was a popular piece, overplayed and often badly, but she hoped Arbour would distinguish artistry from mere skill. Besides, she needed to begin with a piece that boosted her confidence.

By the beginning of the second movement her only thought was of the music. It engaged her, like a flame to a summer forest, and exploded into the all-consuming blaze of passion the piece required. When she finished, the fire was extinguished, as by a gentle but quenching rain. Without hesitation she turned to the second of the four pieces she had prepared for her recital.

She had chosen, as contrast, a series of "Lyrical Pieces" by Grieg, as soft and melodic as the "Appas-

sionata" had been bold and driven. Superficially it was
simple enough to please a child, but she hoped Arbour
would hear the subtleties and appreciate the difficult
transitions.

For all its simplicity it was a moving piece but she
didn't dare look when she had finished to see if Arbour
had been likewise moved. If he had made the slightest
criticism she wouldn't have been able to go on.

She raced over the next selection, Debussy's "La Plus
que Lente Valse", anxious to reach the last and her favorite composition: Arbour's. Nevertheless, the third
selection went well enough, she thought. At last she felt
ready to attempt Arbour's "Nocturne Sonata."

It would be the telling piece. So much depended on
his preference for style. She was sure Sue-Ellen's bland
performance would not have offended his ear, but Melissa believed in taking risks: when it worked, it was
magic.

She followed the score to the note, but she varied the
tempo. Like an abstract painting, music could mean
something different to each viewer. Melissa understood
the risk she was taking. As the composer, Arbour knew
exactly what he intended the music to say. Not only
did she risk insult, but sacrilege, if she misinterpreted
his masterpiece. She tried to free her mind from the
worry as she hit the first chord.

As always, his music lifted her from her earthly con-
cerns and carried her into the realm of uncharted heav-
ens. As if she were poised at the threshold to the uni-
verse, Arbour's music gave her power to spread her
arms, to soar into the darkness unafraid; it gave her the
courage to face the unknown with ardor, with a confi-

dence that the music would return her to safety, without diminishing the glow of the journey.

She was proud of her performance; it had transcended anything she had previously rehearsed. As powerful as his influence had been on her before, on recordings or over the radio, now, in person, as he stood beside her in the same room, each note expanded with an emotion she hadn't known before.

The pathos in his eyes remarked on the overall success of her performance. He had heard discipline and skill in the classical piece, a vulnerability in the Grieg; tenderness in the Debussy piece, but in the last—magic. He had seen in her rendition of his "Nocturne Sonata" another view of the picture he had painted. The eyes were fresher, keener, more astute than his own had been; even, he knew, when he had first imagined the piece.

She was the best pianist he had heard since—no, she was even better than Elise had been. His memory was not jaded by the bitterness he still felt for her: Elise had been merely skillful; this girl's playing was inspired.

He looked down at Melissa's uncertain smile, and again he was moved by her shy beauty. By the time she was his age she would play better than he; that is, if nothing stood in her way. He could help her, and maybe, he dared to imagine, she would help him. Perhaps it would be she who would inspire him to compose again. He had feared . . . hadn't dared to hope . . . could *she* have that kind of power over him? It was what he had hoped for when he had taken the appointment at Juilliard.

"Will you teach me?" Melissa asked. She had waited

for him to speak, but she couldn't stand the suspense another minute. He looked so pensive. She wondered what he was thinking. "I know I have a lot to learn," she started, "but—"

"No," he interrupted, shaking his head. He had started to tell her that she mustn't apologize for her playing, but his single-syllable utterance had darkened her hopeful face. "I will teach you, yes," he clarified. "But you must promise never to apologize for your playing. That is the first lesson."

"You will teach me?" she repeated, overjoyed with the news. She leaped to her feet, and in her excitement overturned the bench. Her attempt to right it sent the heavy stool crashing to the floor. "I am such a klutz!" she cried despairingly.

He took the bench from her hands and replaced it calmly. Then he took her shaking hands into his again and made her look at him. "When you play the piano you are Grace itself."

She swallowed. She didn't know what to say. His words were meant to calm her, she knew, but standing so close to him she felt shaky, as if all the strength had left her. "Thank you," she managed at last, and her voice was pitched so high she sounded to herself like a mouse.

"Thank you for making 'Nocturne' sound new to my ears," he said graciously. "Now I want you home, *mon amie,* for a full night's sleep. It shall be your last, I promise you, for the rest of the semester."

"But it's only five o'clock," she declared. Actually, it could have been any hour, she was so dazed by his presence, but she had heard the chimes just minutes before; they'd totaled five. "And I'm so wide awake I couldn't sleep, even if *you* insisted!" she said innocently.

Jean-Pierre laughed. He liked this girl enormously. "Perhaps a glass of sherry will help you sleep?"

"Now?" Melissa asked dumbly.

"If you have no other plans," he invited, sensing her hesitation.

"No—it's not that. I just wondered if this kind of thing would be frowned upon by the school."

"I should think not," Jean-Pierre answered. "It is your Dean Evans himself who has given me the beverage. Not to mention the glasses."

"Then who am I to question his generosity?" Melissa returned, sounding much more confident than she felt. Without the music between them, she felt very young and unpracticed. Jean-Pierre was a man of the world. She knew of nothing except her music.

"Good," he said easily. "The day has been long and, until you, very tedious. A glass of sherry will help me sleep, too." He didn't tell her how drained he had felt when she walked into the room, or what a disappointment the other students had been. He'd had little hope that Juilliard's "best" would inspire him, until he heard her play. Now his mind ran rampant with possibility. He seated her next to him on the sofa, absorbing her presence so that he might hold it, long after they had parted. She was as fresh and exquisite as her playing had been.

The sherry relaxed her. He was easy to talk to. He probed with interest into her life, and she answered him with surprising candor. She told him about her need to be first, and how painful that could sometimes be; how cruel the resentment had always been.

She spoke of feelings he himself understood all too well, but she couldn't have known that she spoke a universal truth: the struggle for artistry was a lonely one. She touched his heart with her words.

He watched her grow excited as she spoke about her friendship with Patrice, and the quick reversal to sadness when she mentioned her mother's early death and her father's resulting indifference to family life. Her face changed with each new emotion, but always it was lovely. Lovely.

He had felt something for her from the minute he had seen her. Those first instinctual feelings, which had sent him looking for her that morning, were microscopic compared to the ones presently developing. Her music promised real genius. Her youth promised great beauty. How could he love her and teach her, without damaging either? It would be difficult. Maybe impossible. But he had to try. Some instincts were sent from heaven, so loud and clear that they had to be followed. These were feelings that threatened to overwhelm him, even now, with Melissa so close to him. They were as powerful as those that had inspired his greatest works.

He knew at once that he would marry this girl, if she would have him. But the time had to be right. He had to be sure that his love didn't deprive them of their greater responsibility. For himself he could be sure; but for her, he must wait to speak. She mustn't be tempted. She was too young to distinguish between love and adoration. He wanted her heart, not her flattery. If she were to be his wife—his source of inspiration—she must undergo the trial of working with him. If she could withstand the demands of his criticism there was hope she could withstand the added strain of his love.

Without the music, love was a compromise that wouldn't satisfy either of them for long. He had made that mistake once, with Elise, courting talent without discipline. He shuddered to recall the tortured affair. As much as he had hated her for leaving, her absence had proved far less painful to him than her presence.

He would wait until the end of the semester before professing his love. It would take all his discipline. He would have to lean over backward to avoid the temptation of her charm and beauty. But he could. He would. And then he would ask her to be his. He smiled back at the soft glow of her pretty face.

"I'm sorry," he said apologetically. He realized she had been waiting for an answer. "My mind has been elsewhere."

"I'm afraid I've bored you with too much talk," she said meekly, standing to leave.

"No—please stay," he said, rising to stop her from going. "I have been rude once again," he said, wondering if he would spend the rest of his life apologizing to her. "I have been thinking about your tutorial. Please sit."

She perched on the edge of the chair, listening intently. "What is it?" she asked shyly.

"I like you very much," he began. Melissa's eyes widened. He was wondering how to phrase his plan without upsetting her. "Tomorrow morning," he stated, "when you arrive at school, do not expect to find your friend Jean-Pierre."

"Not find you here?" Melissa's face had filled with worry.

"You will find instead a mean old tutor named Monsieur Arbour."

"Oh." Melissa sighed with relief. "I thought you had changed your mind about teaching me," she explained. "I thought I had bored you with my chatter." She let out another breath of relief. "You did scare me!"

"I meant to. This is the last time I shall be nice to you." Melissa puzzled. Jean-Pierre continued. "Do not doubt my affection for you, Melissa. But my responsibility is to criticize your playing. The music suffers when friendship takes precedence. My criticism will be harsh, but only so you will excel. When you play 'Nocturne' with perfection, without a word of criticism from me, then we shall resume our friendship. Do you understand, my Lissa?"

She nodded happily. "I shall play for our friendship," she said, lifting her glass in a toast to their future.

She swallowed the last golden drops in her glass. She would miss his easy manner, but she could hardly complain. As long as she would have his attention in the studio, she was willing to relinquish everything else. "I can't imagine a better motivation to improve my playing," she said softly, and then blushed violently. She had been thinking of him in a secret, romantic way. Of how he had changed her name into an endearment: *My Lissa.*

Jean-Pierre smiled smugly. He had been right about her spirit. When they finished the semester they would meet as equals, in love and in art.

Melissa yawned sleepily. The sherry was taking its effect.

"Now it is I who have bored you," Jean-Pierre exclaimed.

Melissa grinned. If he only knew! "I'd hardly say that," she corrected. "But I'd better get home to prepare for Monsieur Arbour tomorrow. I hear he's ruthless."

Jean-Pierre shared her joke, wishing it needn't be so true. "Then home with you," he said, walking her to the door. "And sleep, mademoiselle."

"I will," she promised. If only to dream all night of you, she thought happily, walking down the empty corridor out into the cool night air.

CHAPTER TWO

The months that followed surpassed anything Melissa had ever dreamed possible. Her respect for Monsieur Arbour deepened. Her playing improved. She enjoyed the time they worked together immensely, for although he was admittedly never as warm and compassionate as he had been on that first day, his professionalism never faltered; his criticisms, however harsh, were always justified. He demanded a great deal from her, and only she demanded more of herself.

Her schedule was rigid. Except for weekends, when she practiced at home, she stayed in the studio to rehearse, returning home for a few hours of sleep each day and a hasty change of clothing. While Arbour tutored his other pupils, Melissa practiced in an adjacent studio; at two o'clock each day, to fortify herself for her lesson at three, she stopped work and lunched at the corner deli.

She was just finishing her sandwich when she noticed Jean-Pierre seated with Sue-Ellen at the rear of the restaurant. She dared a closer look, and was sickened by the expression of adulation on Sue-Ellen's face. Jean-

Pierre was so handsome and charismatic that she understood why Sue-Ellen would adore him, but she couldn't understand why he would want to spend time with her!

Melissa burned with jealousy. How could men be so easily fooled? Couldn't he see that Sue-Ellen was an indiscriminate flirt? Poor Jean-Pierre. As brilliant as he was, he was only a man, subject to the charms of beautiful, flattering women. And Sue-Ellen was as beautiful as she was insincere. Why didn't he know it was Melissa who sincerely loved him?

But he would never know. She had been too careful to conceal her feelings for him. She hadn't wanted to embarrass him, or herself, with her schoolgirl sentiments. Besides, love was one game in which sincerity was rarely rewarded.

She hurried to the cashier, anxious to be away from them, but their laughter followed her; it rose above the noise of the room and filled Melissa with sadness. He had never once encouraged her to joke with him, nor had he ever invited her to socialize with him off campus. Why couldn't it be she, just once, who shared his laughter? Why was she always the one on the outside hungrily looking in?

"Hello, Melissa," Sue-Ellen's saccharine-sweet voice sang. She had come up from behind her while Melissa was waiting for her change.

"Oh, hello," she replied, trying to sound indifferent. She could see Jean-Pierre now, walking toward them, and she was conscious of the contrast he must be making: Sue-Ellen's sparkling vivacity and Melissa's dark severity. It was bad enough that Melissa was so tall, but beside tiny Sue-Ellen she felt like an uncoordinated giant. She turned her eyes to the cash register, damning the clerk's slowness.

"Jean-Pierre—I mean *Monsieur* Arbour"—Sue-Ellen giggled. Melissa wanted to strangle the laughter right out of her throat—"we decided to spend *my* tutorial having coffee instead of the usual playing."

Melissa hated to think what the "usual playing" was.

Jean-Pierre greeted Melissa formally, but she was unsure how to address him outside of school, so she just smiled vaguely. His face was drawn. The laughter in his eyes had darkened to the intensity Melissa usually favored, but today it commented on his displeasure at seeing her. She had wondered, when she saw Sue-Ellen leave his studio in laughter, if he preferred her company to Melissa's. The look on his face now confirmed her worst suspicions. He looked almost angry, as if she had intentionally disturbed his enjoyment.

Sue-Ellen, oblivious to their discomfort, bubbled on inanely. "I guess even bitter coffee is an improvement over my playing, right, Jean-Pierre?" she said happily.

Melissa was about to agree, but Jean-Pierre beat her to the punchline. "No," he said solemnly. "Nothing is worse than American coffee."

Melissa laughed and was relieved to see the light return to his eyes. In spite of her feelings of jealousy, she could understand why he liked Sue-Ellen's company. She was like meringue: sweet, airy, but insubstantial; ultimately not satisfying, but he'd be back in France before he noticed the disappointing aftertaste. For now she was a delicious reprieve from his weighty existence. Melissa was too dark to bring joy into his life the way Sue-Ellen did. No, she didn't begrudge him his enjoy-

ment. She only wished she could be the one to give it
to him instead.

"Are you walking back to school?" he asked Melissa.

"No," she lied, glancing at the wall clock. "I have an
errand to run before my tutorial." She would have
loved to be in his company, even if shared with Sue-
Ellen, but she couldn't deprive him of his last few minutes of pleasure.

"Do not be late," he prompted.

"I won't," she promised, dashing out the door.

"Bye!" Sue-Ellen called after her sweetly. There was
a ring of victory in her voice.

Having lied to avoid walking with them, Melissa now
had twenty minutes to kill out on the cold November
streets. Drawing her coat lapels closer to her breast, she
turned north, and staying close to the storefronts for
protection, she hurried down the windy avenue. The
memory of Sue-Ellen's laughter stung worse than the
bitter cold.

How could she pretend it didn't matter? She cared
desperately for Jean-Pierre, yet for all her love, he
would never care for her. Clearly he dreaded the time
he spent with her. No wonder his criticisms were so
harsh. She wondered how flakey Sue-Ellen withstood
his brutal criticisms when Mel—who was infinitely
more disciplined—was repeatedly in danger of tears
from his words. Or could it be he didn't criticize Sue-
Ellen, but only her?

It was no use. She was who she was, and she couldn't
change her darkness for Sue-Ellen's cheer, even if she
had wanted to. She would have to find her reward

where she always had. Her music would always be with her, as long as she was faithful to it. In a funny way, by giving her full devotion to her music, she was giving her love to Jean-Pierre.

At Seventy-third Street she had an idea. Turning east, she ran down the street until she reached a tiny shop on the corner of Sixty-fourth Street. Again she had to wait for change, but in minutes she had her purchase secured. Now she would really have to run to be to class on time.

Jean-Pierre was pacing the room when she arrived. The clock confirmed her tardiness, if only by a few minutes. Sue-Ellen wasn't there. Melissa wondered if they had made plans to meet outside of school again.

"Please do me the service of arriving on time," he said harshly. But always, even when he spoke sharply to her, there was softness in his eyes, as if he hated to reprimand her.

"I'm sorry," Melissa said softly. Any joy that Sue-Ellen had given him had disappeared at Melissa's late arrival. "I had an errand."

"So you said. I trust it was very important?"

In spite of her reverence she had to laugh. "Yes," she admitted. "You might say it was very important."

He studied her delight. "Then you must share it with me." Again there was that softness around his eyes. A faint smile curled his sensual lip.

Melissa opened the cream-colored bag and extracted two smaller containers, each folded and sealed at the top. "I didn't know which kind you'd prefer," she said shyly, handing him the present.

He opened the first bag tentatively and peered in. He looked back at Melissa, not knowing how to respond.

"The other one's a French roast," she explained. The proprietor of the shop had promised her that blend would most please a Frenchman.

He inhaled the dark rich aroma of the freshly ground coffee beans. "You are too kind, my Lissa."

She shuddered at the nickname. He hadn't called her that since the first interview. "It's nothing," she said. She had bought the coffee, hoping to make him happy, the way Sue-Ellen did, but his eyes showed no light, no joy. If possible they looked even sadder than usual in her presence. Obviously she didn't have the gift of joy within her.

Resignedly she took her seat at the piano, trying not to let the disappointment overshadow her sense of good fortune. She shouldn't complain. She couldn't have everything, and she did have his counsel: that would have to be enough. And if she couldn't give him joy and laughter, she would have to settle for giving him her best in concert. "Shall I play?" she asked respectfully.

Jean-Pierre was silent. He held the coffee in both hands, shaking his head sadly. "My Lissa, you will have to forgive me. I do not feel well—suddenly. I would like to be alone."

He stared at her for so long and so hard she thought her heart would burst through her breast. "Can I do anything?" she asked timidly. She would do anything in the world for him. If he'd only let her.

He smiled at the concerned look on her face. "It is nothing—" he assured her. "Perhaps too much American coffee." He grinned weakly. "I will be all right. I just need to be alone now," he repeated. "Forgive me?"

Melissa rushed to his side. "Of course," she said fer-

vently. "Just take care of yourself." She wanted to
touch her hand to his brow, to check for fever, but she
knew she couldn't; mustn't.

He took her hand into his and pressed it to his lips.
"Thank you for the gift," he said quietly. "I will see
you tomorrow."

There was nothing for her to do but leave him, the
last thing in the world she wanted to do.

She hadn't realized how tired she was until she had
time to think about how hard she'd been working. The
ride home from school seemed to take longer than
usual. The bus had arrived late, and when the doors
creaked open, there was hardly room for another body.
Too impatient to wait for another bus, she fought her
way in, standing between a short man reading a newspaper and a woman holding a sleeping infant.

Melissa's legs ached. The tears of jealousy she had
refused to shed earlier in the day now burned in her
eyes. She was being too sensitive. Maybe she needed a
night off more than practice. A good book and a long,
hot bath. She hadn't taken a break for weeks, not since
classes had begun; in fact, she hadn't had a day off in
ten weeks, she calculated quickly.

With sudden horror, Melissa realized that in another
two weeks classes would be over, and Jean-Pierre
would return to France, impressed, at best, by her per-
sistence, but certainly not impressed by her ability. Her
exhaustion could not be indulged! She would force herself awake, if necessary, but she would improve her
flawed playing that night. There was time for improvement, especially if she cut out everything else. She'd

skip dinner—a cup of coffee would suffice—and use the extra minutes to play the piano. She would practice nonstop for the next two weeks.

The bus moaned forward past the crowded, burgeoning streets, up Eighth Avenue. The subway would have been faster, she thought impatiently, and as much as she feared the underground she could save valuable minutes each day by taking the train.

At Central Park West the bus load lightened, picking up speed as it chattled up along the park. Melissa counted the stops. At Eighty-sixth Street she was the first one out. Her weariness had been replaced by determination. She raced across the treelined pavement up the sparsely peopled street to her apartment. She reached the third floor in seconds. Before her key fitted into the lock, Patrice had unlatched the door.

"Welcome home, stranger," Patrice teased. It had been weeks since they had seen each other in daylight. Her smile of welcome darkened to a frown of concern as she saw the dark circles under Melissa's eyes.

"Hi, Trice," Melissa said, rushing past her into the apartment. "What's the word?"

"That you look like hell," she answered, unsmiling. She knew her criticism wouldn't be welcome, but she had watched her roommate dissolve into rubble over the weeks under Arbour's constant pressure. The initial glow of dedication had dissolved into a pathetic obsession which Mel was unwilling to see.

Melissa ran her hand through her disheveled hair. "I guess I do look awful," she admitted. "But I can't spare the time."

"I think you must," Patrice stated simply.

Melissa stopped short. "Really, Pat," she began, not

wanting to take the time to argue. "Sometimes your concern with appearances is too much." She walked back into the kitchen, her thin arms locked across her chest, as if barricading herself against conflict.

"If you took the time to look in the mirror you'd see I'm not talking about appearances, but health. You look like sin. You've lost weight. You haven't a shred of color in your face. You—"

"Leave me alone, Pat," Melissa warned. Her nerves were taut from lack of sleep. She moved to the piano and began sorting through a pile of sheet music.

"And I suppose you are going to chain yourself to the keyboard again tonight?"

"I have to."

"Why?" Patrice challenged.

"Because I'm not going back to school until I have this piece perfect, that's why." Her voice had grown loud, her tone unfriendly.

"Honestly, honey, you've already got it down perfectly! I think you need sleep more than more practice. You haven't slept a full night all semester."

"There isn't time!"

"You want to crack up? Is that what you are trying for?"

Melissa turned brashly to stare at Patrice, daring her to continue.

"You need sleep. Food. Maybe even some fresh air."

"What I need, dear concerned roommate," Melissa began, her voice tight with malice, "is a little privacy so I can get to work. I have only two short weeks before Monsieur Arbour leaves, and I can't afford to waste a second of it."

Patrice, unwilling to give in, strode across the room

and took Melissa firmly by the arm, forcing her to listen. "Is your idol Arbour aware that you are killing yourself to please him? Is that the kind of genius you respect? Isn't there any room for humanity in art?"

"Stop it!" Melissa screamed, her voice shrill with hysteria. "He is demanding just one thing from me: my best. At this point my best isn't good enough. My playing is painful for him to listen to. I am *not* going to subject him to another day of disgraceful music. He is a genius! He has a right to expect perfection!"

"At how great an expense?" Patrice shouted back; then, hearing her tone, she saddened at the hostility between them. Melissa, too, turned sober.

"It's just two more weeks. After he's gone I can sleep all I want. Please—?" Melissa begged. "Please don't yell at me. I promise I will sleep—later. But now I have to work."

"All right," Patrice conceded. She didn't like to fight with Melissa. "But at least take time for a quick dinner."

Mel shook her head. "Thanks anyway. I just haven't time tonight."

Patrice broke into renewed anger. "Then work yourself into your grave, damn you. But I'm not going to watch—or pick up the pieces." She grabbed her coat and scarf off the hall tree. At the front door to the apartment she turned once more. "I think, my naive friend, that your beloved Arbour is a royal bastard."

Melissa tightened at the insult, as if it had been directed at her personally. She was glad when Patrice slammed the door behind her, before she felt obliged to defend Jean-Pierre. Tonight there wasn't time. Not even for that. She needed every minute. Every second. She bowed her head in concentration and began her preliminary scales.

It was after two A.M. when Patrice returned home. Melissa looked up from her playing.

"Can I come in?" Patrice asked sheepishly, hoping to erase the afternoon's disagreement.

"Please."

The exhaustion and frustration that had earlier haunted her young face had gone; replaced by—it was hard to tell—an inexplicable joy? But what had happened? Patrice snuggled into the overstuffed armchair. "Okay, contented cat. What little bird have you caught?"

"I think," Melissa began, unable to suppress the elation of her secret any longer, "I have perfected the "Nocturne Sonata.' " She almost laughed out loud. Just a few hours ago she had been tempted to quit, to throw it all in, to sleep like the rest of the world. Her frustration had nearly overwhelmed her, but then she had found what she was looking for. When she had been too tired to care, the wave of tranquility that Jean-Pierre had expected from her, had demanded from her, rushed over her; it had felt like a warm spring rain. She wanted to share her success with Patrice, as much to appease their quarrel as to convince her of Arbour's brilliant effect. And she wanted to be certain she could repeat the miracle in front of an audience.

"Will you play it for me?" Patrice asked excitedly. It was impossible to stay angry. They loved each other too much.

"I was hoping you'd ask."

The room was chill, and Patrice wanted to turn up the heat, but Melissa started playing and the chill disappeared, along with the rest of the world. The beautiful music filled her soul with gladness, erased all her reservations. There was no need to worry. Everything would be all right. She watched Melissa absorbed in each note; each chord transcended the last. The serious, stately refrain yielded to a pathos so deep it was hard to fathom the source of such suffering. The phrasing was even, the transitions flawless; each note distinct, precise.

Melissa looked strangely calm, as, refreshed by a long, uninterrupted sleep. Patrice didn't know whether to burst into applause or tears—or if she had a chance to restrain either. She wanted to take Mel by the hand, hug her, hold her, apologize for the nagging, all at once. She started to speak, but found there was nothing to say.

Melissa could tell by her friend's helpless look that she had been moved. She offered her hand, and Patrice took it, squeezing it gently, giving reassurance as well as receiving it.

"It *is* perfect," Patrice managed at last.

"Yes. I think it is."

"You've done it, darling."

Melissa nodded, but Patrice could tell she was far away—where? She stretched lazily, hoping her yawn would be contagious, but it only elicited a lazy, satisfied smile from Melissa. "Would you consider a little sleep now?" Patrice asked, her hope as faint as the moonlight outside the apartment window.

"In a minute," Melissa answered. "I want to run over the last section one more time."

"Thank you for playing for me."

For a moment Melissa returned to the present. "Thanks for listening."

"Good night, Mel," Patrice said, on her way to her bedroom, but Melissa had already returned to her music. The room filled with the kind of sweet passion he must have hoped to inspire; the music as pure as the artist who now performed it, for him, for the hope of his love requited. The soft melody floated into Patrice's room as she undressed for bed. She only hoped it would be good enough to please Jean-Pierre.

CHAPTER THREE

"Shall we begin now?" Jean-Pierre suggested.

Melissa rotated her shoulders one last time, an exercise he had taught her. Her heart beat loudly, but her hands were calm, steady.

Jean-Pierre stood beside the piano while she played. He had noticed from the minute she entered the room that she was somehow changed. He ran his eye down her gracefully poised back, straight and long beneath a forest-green sweater; the material stretched tight across her breast, each breath rising, falling . . . until he could feel each breath inside himself, as if they were two bodies sharing but one life-force. He could hardly stand the urgency inside him. Yesterday he'd had to send her away, or break his resolve; her simple gesture had so deeply affected him. But today it was something more. Her music stirred his emotion to a point where he couldn't control himself. Unable to fight the heightened passion she wrung from him, he slapped her knuckles to stop her playing.

"Enough! *Vous jouez comme un routier!*" The violence of his action surprised him, but he *had* to make her stop.

Melissa looked up in shock. She had erred again. She had lost the delicate, mournful quality of the second movement. Her playing, she realized, had been maudlin, sentimental, not passionate at all. His criticism had been no sterner than usual, but today she couldn't take it. She was tired, and she had done everything to please him, but she just wasn't good enough . . . not pretty enough to make him like her, or talented enough to win his respect.

It was this realization, more than Arbour's criticism, that saturated her with anguish. She must try again! She could not look at him now, or she knew the last threads of her strength would break. She sat up straighter at the keyboard, returned her trembling fingers to the ivory keys, and forced her attention back to the sonata. But his words continued to burn in her ears: *Truck driver! You play like a truck driver,* and before Melissa could contain herself, she collapsed into tears.

Before Jean-Pierre could stop himself, he was holding her in his arms, quieting her tears, apologizing for his tactless reproof. Each sob rendered her nearer to him, filling him with remorse for what he had said. He brushed back the thick hair from her reddened face and repeated his apology, mingling his words with new vows of love.

Melissa pulled out of his embrace, wiping dry the flood of tears with the back of her hand. She was embarrassed by her display of emotion, and ashamed, but mostly she was confused by Arbour's words of comfort.

"I'm sorry," she began, her lower lip quivering uncontrollably.

"Shhh—*ma chérie*—do not cry. I was wrong . . . too harsh . . . I have not been fair with you."

She pulled back even further to answer him. "But you're not unfair. You have a right to expect—"

"I expect you to be the best. Therefore a certain kind of instruction is necessary, but I was wrong to criticize you so harshly today. Your music has touched me, here," he said, pointing to his heart. "And it hurt too much just then. I was not ready for you to touch me so deeply."

"But I'm not improving," she insisted, not hearing his confession. "I'll never be—"

"You improve each day. There was no reason for my contrariness. Do you want to know something truthful?"

Melissa nodded uncertainly.

"You play like an angle."

She looked at him in utter surprise, then burst out laughing.

It took her a minute to quiet herself, and before she did Jean-Pierre was laughing, too, although he didn't quite know why. When her laughter had subsided enough to speak, she asked him, "Do you mean I play like *un ange*?"

Jean-Pierre nodded. "What did I say?"

"You said I played like *un angle*—an angle." Laughter danced mischievously in her damp green eyes.

He had never loved more deeply. She was so beautiful. So fresh, so alive. How could he have possibly hurt her? She was strong, yet vulnerable.

Now her eyes flashed with pure pleasure. Despite the almost uncontainable joy surging through him, he suffered the deepest pain of longing he had ever known. "Will you play for me again?" he asked humbly. It was important that he erase his faux pas immediately.

Her eyes clouded with doubt.

"Ma chérie, tu joues comme une nymphe du ciel! Is that an angel?" Melissa nodded shly, *"Alors, va-t-en."*

Again she began the "Nocturne Sonata." Her tears had washed clear any need to hurry. She lingered over each cord, maintained flawless distinction, transported each bar into completion. Emotion and control swept every breath, sustained each note, then lulled it gently into the past.

Jean-Pierre sat beside her on the bench, but only in some vague way did she feel his presence. Her music held her, like the lover it had always promised to be, bringing her to heights she had previously thought unreachable.

When she finished the sonata he took her hand, and without a word, pressed his lips to the soft skin in thanks.

Then he played for her.

They sat together, side by side, like two children, but the room was full of untasted adult desire. They both burned with passion. She renewed him by her very presence, returned him to his youth, and he brought out the woman in Melissa.

Yet she had given him something more, something more surprising than the love he felt, and when he finished playing, he expelled a deep, thorough sigh of relief. It had been months since he had been able to play like that! He had been right to hope for inspiration. She had affected him already.

He looked at her expectantly, his dark eyes questioning. He wanted to propose, to offer her more than a life of devotion, but he couldn't find the words. When her eyes met his, he understood in an instant, from the glow from her heart, that they had said it all already, in a language more profound than any words they might choose to speak.

Tentatively she touched her fingers to the side of his face. He turned his mouth to kiss her hand, then lowered his lips to meet hers. She laced her long and slender arms around his neck; her fingertips caressed the nape of his neck as she yielded to his embrace.

This was the first time a kiss had ever been as he had dreamed it could be.

For her it was the first kiss.

And it led to others.

The room grew dark. Lights from the city reflected off the ceiling of the studio. They would need to talk, but there was time . . . there was so much to consider. He would give the world for her to stay by his side always—always his source of inspiration. "Do you know what we must do?" he asked her.

She nestled back into the warmth of his arms. *"Rien que ça,"* she answered, sighing.

Just this, Jean-Pierre reflected. She wasn't helping him to restrain his passion. "And after this?" he asked.

She looked up, mildly surprised. She hadn't thought about "afterward." All she knew was the warmth of his arms, a security she had never known. "Do you mean about school?" she asked.

"To begin with, yes, school." They straightened out

of their embrace. "What did you think I was referring to?" he asked her suddenly, his eyes flickering dangerously.

She blushed abashedly. "I—I don't know any other 'afterward.'" She was admitting a lot, she knew, but he had to know. She studied his face for signs of disappointment, but all she saw was concern.

"My love," he said quietly. "I am flattered. But if you are, as they say, *sans expérience,* then we must take these steps very seriously. Tell me, what do you want?"

"You," she answered without hesitation.

"And what else?" he prodded. He was ready to embrace her fully, at once, but he had to know, for her sake, what she wanted for herself. She was very young. She might regret her impulsiveness. And innocence lost was impossible to regain.

"I want," she said with childlike glee, "to play 'Nocturne' as well as the great Jean-Pierre Arbour!"

"Then listen to me, *mon amour.* Carefully." He unlocked her arms from around his neck, and held her hands in his. "It is not going to be easy, but I think we must reinstate the distance between us . . . student to teacher . . . until the end of the term. It will be hard, but not nearly as hard as it has been, to keep secret my love for you."

Melissa nodded her agreement firmly.

"When the semester has finished, then we will talk, if we need to. All right?"

"If you can stand it, so can I," she said joyfully. "All I know is that I love you, Jean-Pierre. And for now that's enough."

He hugged her warmly. "Yes, our love is enough, for now." He kissed her gently, as if in parting. *"Je t'aime beaucoup."*

They sat side by side, barely touching, contemplating the commitment they had just made. It was greater than any previous commitment, and one, they both knew, well worth keeping. Disheveled and stiff with cold, they rose from the piano.

"Boy, I'm starved!" Melissa announced. All the fear was gone from her voice. His love had erased it forever.

Jean-Pierre took his watch from his pocket. "It is no wonder. We are past midnight."

Melissa was stunned to learn that so much time had passed. "Can I convince you to try a pastrami on rye at Carnegie Deli? I've wanted to go there with you all semester."

He caught the possessiveness in her eyes. All he wanted was to devour *her,* but he forced his thoughts to food.

"How unkind of me, my Lissa. You have nourished my heart with your love, as you have filled my soul with longing. For you I will consider pastrami at Carnegie's."

They embraced a final time, platonic by agreement. Already it was too late to turn back. They had confessed their love. Thank God there were only two weeks left in the term.

Patrice noticed the drastic shift in Melissa, but couldn't convince her to divulge the secret of her happiness.

"Just wait until school is over," Melissa insisted. "*Then* I can tell you."

"I hate to wait!" Patrice complained.

"Now you sound like me."

Could it be a recital, Patrice wondered? Or a scholarship abroad? Some kind of prize? Convinced that Mel's secret was a happy one, she stopped questioning. She was glad that something good had resulted from all her hard work. So he had been impressed with her work, after all, the old buzzard!

The second Friday in December, Patrice broached the subject again. Juilliard was adjourning until the new term began after the holidays. "All right, happy one. Time to 'fess up."

"What do you mean?" Melissa asked innocently.

"School is over, and I want to know your good news."

"School's not over," Melissa said stubbornly.

"Melissa!" Patrice cried impatiently. "I am dying! You have to tell me now!"

"Not until school is officially over."

"What do you want, your report card in hand? Stop being technical. Today is just a formality and you know it. *Instruction* is over."

"But I—" Melissa weakened.

"Tell me!"

"All right," she said at last. "But you have to promise not to tell anyone."

"Who on earth would I tell?"

"Just promise."

"I promise I won't tell anyone," she said, holding her hand up in pledge.

"Well," Melissa began, her voice quiet with confidence. "I—I am in love!"

"Melissa! This is wonderful news. God, you sure look like you are, but I had no idea." Patrice was bursting with happiness. Melissa had never even mentioned a boy. "But why the big secret, darling?"

"Because," she said proudly, "I am in love with Jean-Pierre Arbour."

Patrice's smile evaporated at the name, but she did her best to conceal her shock. "With Arbour? Does he know?"

"Of course he knows, silly."

"And how—what does he say?"

"That he loves me, too! That's what started it all. That's why it's such a big secret until school is over, you see? So that neither of us can be accused of breaking any rules. Not that there is anything anyone would do actually, but it must be against the rules, for a teacher to—"

"To what?"

"To love his student!" she bubbled. "In any event, it's frowned upon. Oh, aren't you happy? Isn't it great news?"

"Yes," Patrice answered, less than convincingly. "But are you sure? Do you know what you are going to do?"

"Do?"

"After you let the secret out that he loves you."

"I don't know . . . all I can think about is when school is over, when I'm not his pupil anymore, I can kiss him."

"You mean you haven't kissed him?"

"That's just it! Well, we did kiss on the day he told me he loved me, just to try it out, I guess. It happened before we knew it. But since then we haven't even held hands," she explained. "So after school is out, we can kiss all we want. I can hardly wait for today to be over!"

"Do you have any notion what you are going to do besides all this kissing?" Melissa suddenly blushed. Patrice laughed. "Honey, I'm not asking for sexual expletives. I just want to know what your plans are."

"Oh, the plans," Mel answered, relieved. It worried her that she didn't know what would happen afterward. "We'll get married, and I'll continue with school, I guess. What else is there to do?"

"And you've discussed this with Arbour?"

"Well, we haven't actually talked yet, but—"

"Didn't you say his home was Paris?"

"Yes."

"Isn't he planning to return there?"

"I—I just assumed—"

"And isn't he a lot older than you are?"

Melissa stared at Patrice. "That stuff doesn't matter. Can't you just be happy for me?" Her mood had fallen.

Patrice regretted the damper she had placed on Melissa's high spirits. "Of course I'm happy for you, Mel. It's just such *big* news, and I had no idea. I'll part with you as a roommate, if I have to, but I would like to know on which side of the Atlantic you'll be living. Promise me you'll clear up those little details? Have you made plans to talk?"

"Tonight," Melissa answered dreamily. "We're going to celebrate."

"Where are you going?"

"He said he'd cook me dinner at his house. He doesn't like going out too much—too many fans interrupting all the time. I've been placed in charge of bringing the wine." She looked unsure for a minute. "Patrice . . . can I ask you a question?"

"Of course you can," Patrice answered, hoping she knew the right thing to say.

"What kind of wine do you think I should buy?"

"Honey, I think we have more important things to talk about right now."

That night their mood was somber. Released from the hold of their agreement, neither of them was certain how to proceed. Jean-Pierre poured Melissa a glass of wine, and without waiting for any kind of toast, she swallowed more than half the contents; her throat needed quenching as much as her nerves. She avoided making eye contact. She wondered if she could have been wrong.

When they finally spoke, it was at the same time.

"Did you—?"

"Are we—?"

She smiled and invited him to go ahead. He urged her to speak. But when they tried again it was the same.

"Are you—?"

"Did we—?"

They laughed together.

"I've forgotten what I was going to say," Melissa confessed.

"I was only talking to have something to say."

"I guess I'm nervous that you've changed your mind."

"We share the same fear. I guess we do not know

each other as well as we thought. No, I have not
changed my mind. Have you?"

"No, of course not. I just—"

He stopped her mid-sentence, bringing her face to
meet his, his lips brushing hers softly, as if to inhale her
sweet breath; then harder, as intoxicated with her kiss,
he held his mouth fast to hers. His body pressed close,
closer than the first time they had kissed.

"Je t'aime beaucoup."

"Oh, Jean-Pierre. I love you so much."

He wanted her right then, but he tried to be sensible.
She did not make it easy. Her passion equaled his, and
she made no attempt to stop it.

"My love," he whispered in between kisses. "We must
talk."

"I just want to kiss you," she said breathlessly.

"I, too. I want to kiss you, to know you, to love you
deeply."

"We can skip dinner," she offered impetuously, hoping this would solve all their problems.

Jean-Pierre just laughed. "Yes, we can skip dinner. I
can devour you to feed my soul. But what about tomorrow? I do not want you to wake and hate me for believ-
ing in your impulsiveness."

"Jean-Pierre," she said seriously, "I love you. You
love me. Do you think I will regret anything resulting
from our love?" Her eyes shone earnestly.

"My darling," he said, bringing her close to him once
more.

"Only—"

"Yes?"

"Only I don't really know what I'm supposed to do."
Her admission was spoken into his shirt.

"Ahhhh—I will teach you. But you are not afraid of your reputation?"

"Do I mind being a 'fallen woman'?" She giggled. "This isn't New England in 1700."

"This is the modern world, indeed. But so you do not worry tomorrow, will you promise me tonight—"

"What?"

"That you will marry me?"

"Of course!" she laughed. "Did you think I was going to give you my love for only one night?"

Without another word he took her hand and led her into the bedroom.

It was a large room, full of dark handsome antiques and tall mirrors, but all Melissa saw was the huge four-postered bed that would bare witness to their vows and the weight of their passion.

She stood at the foot of the awesome bed, fingering its ornate carvings, tracing the intricate curlicues, wishing she knew more than she did.

"You look very young, my darling," Jean-Pierre said softly, thoughtfully, as if he, too, might be wondering how to proceed with this most delicate embrace. "So shy," he said, lifting her chin with his thumb. Their eyes caught, and held. Melissa recalled all the reasons that had led to this embrace, all the reasons she loved him. His eyes never left hers, and even when he slipped open the line of tiny buttons down the front of her dress, he held her gaze; even when he parted the gossamer veil to reveal her soft and firm breasts, he let his touch lead him, not his eyes. His fingers told him her response: nipples that rose to his fingertips and hardened in his palm.

Nor did he break his steady look when she reached up and fumbled loose the buttons to his shirt, or even at her embarrassment when she couldn't unlatch the belt to his trousers. All the while his eyes blazed brightly into hers, as if to light a path down to her heart and soul.

When her breasts were bare, and he himself had discarded his own shirt, he closed the distance between them, but not the light. It continued to radiate from eye to eye, their hearts pounding loud against each other's smooth skin.

Only when she was completely undressed, and he had stepped back to remove the last piece of his clothing, did his eyes leave hers to travel downward, pausing to memorize each line, each curve of his new bride.

Melissa watched intently as he beheld her. His response flattered her; it was the same look of wonder she had seen when his playing was most inspired, when he was in communion with a deeper part of himself. She shared that feeling now. The last of her shyness dissolved and she opened up the caverns of her heart for him to enter. She felt an inward glow where his eye studied the several parts of her unclothed body, a heat radiating directly from his passion.

Jean-Pierre enclosed her with his strong, bare arms and held her close to his chest. She pressed her ear against his wildly beating heart, and she could smell the warm, sweet scent of his fragrance as he lifted her into his bed.

His hand on her thigh brought a burning sensation, he was so hot. However, it wasn't the sharpest pain, or even the most intense: it was simply the touch she would always remember as the moment she became a woman: Jean-Pierre's bride . . . one heart . . . one flesh . . . one soul . . . a burning embrace . . . until the last flames of their desire flickered out, and they slept.

It was dawn when she awoke. "Jean?" She was suddenly unsure of where she was.

"What is it, my love?" He brought her close to him. "Have you dreamed?"

"No. I just wanted to make sure you were still here."

"That is one fear you need never have again. I am here, with you, forever. You are safe with me."

She snuggled against his warm body. "You know what I want right now?"

Could she be that insatiable? To want him again so soon? Perhaps he would have trouble with so young a wife. "What is it you want?"

"Dinner! I'm starved!"

"The sex has given you an appetite, no?"

"I'll say. Gosh, I'm going to weigh a ton if we keep this up." They chuckled at the image of two very fat, lustful lovers, each climax as fattening as ice-cream sundaes.

"What shall I cook? Eggs? A fillet?"

"I want Chinese food!" Melissa announced determinedly.

"But I cannot cook Chinese food."

"We can go to Wo Hop's. They're open to all hours."

"I do not think I could eat egg noodles at this hour."

"I'll settle for eggs Benedict at the Algonquin."

"I cannot convince you to let me cook for you here?"

"Nope," she said wilfully. "I want to go out into the day. I'm wide awake, and I want to show you to the world. Unless, Monsieur Arbour," she said strangely, leaning up onto one elbow, "you would rather not be seen in public with me."

He shook his head. He was so in love with her.

"Do you mind if I shout our love to all the world?" she asked, suddenly playful.

"Is there a way to stop you?"

"Come on, then. Let's get dressed." She was already out of bed, throwing his clothes at him. "Last one dressed is a rotten egg."

Jean-Pierre shook his head helplessly. He was in love with a child. "Before we run, *ma chérie,* I have a question."

"What is that?" She was hurrying to dress. The room was chill, but she hadn't noticed until now.

"We will marry today?"

She slipped her blouse over her bare shoulders, her mood suddenly as serious as his own. Without any of the teasing that had been in her voice she told him, "There is nothing in the world I would rather do."

"But today?"

"Today," she said complacently. "If they will let us. I think we have to have blood tests and a sobriety test."

"Really? I should have guessed it of Americans."

"Hey! You're going to have to watch your slurs from now on."

"I guess with wild American girls molesting unsuspecting foreigners such a law is useful."

"Now wait a minute . . ." she defended, throwing her shoe at him.

He caught the shoe up and held it behind his back. "How badly do you want this back?" Jean-Pierre asked slyly.

Melissa grabbed for the shoe. "I'll look pretty funny

hobbling into the Algonquin in only one shoe. You don't want me to embarrass you," she returned, her own eyes dancing with mischief.

"If you had other clothes here, you could simply select another pair to wear, right?" Melissa reached again unsuccessfully for her shoe, and left her arms around his waist.

"If I had other clothes here, that would be like I lived here, right?" she said playfully. "But since we don't live together—"

"Yet—" he interrupted.

Melissa paused before commenting. "Yet," she agreed solemnly, then continued her taunt. "And since the shoe you're holding is the only one that matches the one I'm wearing, I guess I need it pretty badly."

"I need you pretty badly, too," he said, the playfulness in his voice edged with urgency. He feared it was he who was insatiable. He kept the shoe in one hand and brought the other around Melissa's waist. Except for her sheer blouse, she was still naked, and he slid his hand down her back, pausing to touch the two dimples above her buttocks.

"How do you expect me to fight for my shoe?" Melissa asked breathlessly, her lips parted slightly as his hand slid down the inside of her thigh. She went limp in his arms.

"What, not fighting for your shoe?"

"No," she whispered, "I've lost all my desire for the shoe."

"As long as that's the only desire I've destroyed."

Her answer was a sigh as he touched her. She tightened her arms around him, and leaned her cheek against his chest, collapsing her weight against him. She could feel his passion surging, equal to her own. They lost their balance briefly when she undid his trousers. She had to stand on her toes to meet his height. They found each other's lips and exhaled their pleasure, bringing each other into closer embrace, but gently, not wanting to rush the moment.

Suddenly their urgency overtook them, and they found the bed, moving apart reluctantly, then together again, as if the seconds of separation had been too long. Their words were foreign to them, but each sound, each sigh communicated their feelings in a way no words could. Where Jean-Pierre had earlier loved a girl, now lay a woman, as greedy for him as he was for her. He brought her to him with a force that matched the desire in her eyes. He caressed her with his hands and arms; he felt her instep slide up his leg to his thigh before her foot locked behind him. He held her until his muscles ached, his passion strained to the breaking point. Her first contraction released his own, and he filled her with love as she swelled to receive him.

When she squeezed him again he shuddered in her arms, drenched in the aftermath of their ecstasy. They lay together silently for a time, their thoughts as intermingled as their bodies were intertwined. Then, gently, Jean-Pierre rose and went into the other room but returned minutes later with a drink for them both. He was nearly dressed. Melissa lay back lazily against the pillows, the crumpled sheet pulled around her. He handed her the shoe they had fought over earlier, but Melissa let it fall to the floor.

"My darling," Jean-Pierre said with laughter. "You are, by your own admission, a rotten egg."

Melissa bounded out of bed, and before Jean could knot his tie, she was dressed and ready. In less than fifteen minutes they were seated for breakfast at the Algonquin.

They had been greeted once at the door by a man who claimed to know Arbour. As they crossed the room, she saw people looking up from their meals. Even the waiter indiscreetly greeted him by name, and complimented him on his music. Melissa had no idea he was this well known. She had seen people approach him at Carnegie Deli, but she just assumed it was the proximity of the school and recital hall.

Jean-Pierre noticed her look. "It is why I do not like to go out into public," he explained.

"But isn't it all exciting?"

"Yes and no. It *is* nice to have people like your music enough to want to tell you. It is not nice to lose your privacy wherever you go."

"Can't you just tell them to leave you alone when you don't want to be bothered?"

"It is difficult. It is important not to offend the very people who are responsible for my popularity."

"But it's your music that makes you popular, not them," she said emphatically.

"You and I know that," he joked happily. "But what if people hadn't liked my music at the beginning, had refused me when I wanted to perform? You would have never known who I was. We would have never met. I think myself ungrateful to them if I do not smile and accept their flattery, especially now that they have given me my love."

They ordered eggs and fresh-squeezed orange juice, buttered muffins and link sausage. Jean-Pierre requested Chinese food for the young lady, but the waiter just smiled an uncomprehending smile that forgave them their silliness, and refilled their coffee cups. Melissa threatened to announce their passionate love to the room, but when he challenged her, she grew shy enough for him to tease her. He wouldn't have let her tell anyone just yet anyway, not until they were married. Their love would make headlines, and in the wrong context, it could damage the beginning of her career. As much as her ebullience flattered him, he was grateful when she settled for sharing her news with him alone.

"I'm going to have to tell Patrice about our plans—and you have to meet her. She thinks you're an angry old bear."

"But I am."

"And I'll have to call my father, I guess."

"What will *père* say about a marriage of this sort?"

"I suppose he'll respond like he does to everything, with a noncommittal smile and wishes of good luck."

"I take it you and he are not close?"

"No. Not since Mother died. I think he'll be glad when I'm married safely. It's less for him to worry about."

"He won't mind if you live in France?"

"In France?" She set down her fork.

"But where else?" he asked.

"I thought we could stay here. New York is really a swell place, once you get to know it."

"But I must return to my country, my Lissa." He watched her graceful fingers clench into a fist. "Does that change your mind, my precious?"

"No," she said quickly, but her voice faltered. "But what about my music? Oh, Jean-Pierre, I didn't realize I would have to quit school. I'm so close to graduation." All the joy from the previous hours had vanished from her voice.

"You do not think well after hours without sleep. Sex must numb your brain. Or is it the morning we are to blame?" She stared at him blankly. "Do you think I would sacrifice the most talented young pianist in all of America for my own love? Does it not occur to you that I will tutor you daily, until you cry for respite? That each new piece of music I create will be for you to play?"

"You mean you will teach me more?"

"Very much more," he promised her. "We are just beginning. Now that I have found you, I will retire from the concert halls, to give all my time to composing music for you to play."

"Oh, Jean," she said happily. "Marrying you is twice as good as marrying a regular man."

He laughed at what she said, but he was moved by what she meant. The love in their life was bursting with the beginning of expression.

"Patrice, you are going to have to stop crying, or Jean-Pierre will drown in our tears. I don't want him to see us like this!" Melissa insisted, her own eyes red from crying.

But he did. He arrived at the apartment at three o'clock to meet Patrice, leaving enough time for a quick drink with Melissa's father before their departure to Paris. By morning they would be home, and already Jean-Pierre was anxious for the old familiar streets.

He brought Melissa into his arms and kissed her
tearstained face, discreetly offering her his handkerchief. He extended his arms to include Patrice, to comfort his fiancée's best friend while Melissa blew her
nose. She returned the handkerchief wet and soggy.

"I know it is not polite to offer you a used handkerchief," he said to Patrice.

She grinned at the limp cloth. "Thanks anyway but I
think I'll stick with Kleenex."

"I hate to be the cause of all these tears," he admitted. To Melissa he asked, "Would it make you less miserable to have Patrice come with us?"

"Oh——" Patrice started joyfully. "I was hoping you'd
ask, but I didn't want to be in the way."

"Please come to the airport," Melissa urged.

"Of course," Jean-Pierre answered for her. "But I
meant that I would like Patrice to come with us to
Paris." Melissa gasped, but Arbour continued. "She will
need help to buy the wedding dress," he explained. "I
am afraid with her French she will buy a suit of
armor," he said to Patrice. Melissa hit him affectionately. "But I ask only one thing. . . ."

"What—anything—" both girls chimed.

"That we hurry. I do not like to keep Monsieur Dennison waiting. Even now he waits for us, while we talk."

"The Plaza is only ten minutes from here," Melissa
explained. "And Dad is used to waiting for me. Come
on, Patrice, I'll help you pack."

Jean-Pierre frowned, and Patrice hurried to intercept
a disagreement. "You two go ahead. I'll meet you at the
hotel. I'll pack faster if I don't have to worry about
keeping you from Mr. Dennison."

Jean-Pierre smiled his gratitude. "Don't pack too

much," he suggested. "You'll want an excuse to shop for clothes in Paris. If I may dare to make comparison in front of my darling patriot, Paris is several degrees superior to New York in fashion."

"I agree with you one hundred percent," Patrice said enthusiastically. Melissa was secretly delighted to find them in agreement, even if it was at her expense.

The meeting with Gerald Dennison was just as Melissa had predicted: pleasant, amiable, and superficial. On the eve of her entry into a new life, her father talked about their flight arrangements and questioned Jean-Pierre about his impressions of New York. Melissa was enormously relieved when Patrice appeared thirty minutes into the affair, and gave them the excuse to leave. Mr. Dennison's congratulations were as perfunctory as the hug he gave Melissa, and with casual indifference, he transferred his daughter into the care of her doting fiancé Melissa noticed but didn't really mind. Now that she had Jean-Pierre, her father's apathy couldn't perturb her. Now that Patrice was coming with her to attend the wedding, Melissa longed for nothing. All the family that really mattered were propelling her out of the taxi and onto the plane.

The wedding was as memorable as the flight to Paris had been spectacular, transporting Melissa across the sea of her youth into the charge of her adulthood. Jean-Pierre's devotees welcomed her with a reception that befitted the wife of their national hero, and as Jean-Pierre's fiancée, Melissa smiled confidently, grateful for the warm greeting. With Patrice by her side the hundreds of personal details for the wedding became fun, not threatening. As the layers of lace were draped over her slender shoulders, Melissa radiated a confidence born from her awareness of her extraordinary good fortune. She accepted her position in Jean-Pierre's life as graciously as she received his friends and admirers at the wedding ceremony. But when Jean-Pierre closed the doors to his fans on the night of their nuptial, she was as thankful for the privacy as he was.

CHAPTER FOUR

"Dearest Patrice—" Melissa wrote, before putting her pen down. What could she say next? It had been so easy to write at first, but two months had passed since Patrice's last letter had arrived, and Melissa still didn't know how to answer her questions.

The separation weighed heavily on Melissa. Patrice had stayed in Paris for a week after the wedding, but that had been over a year ago; the year ahead showed no promise of a reunion. Patrice had graduated into a prestigious law firm, and it was virtually impossible for her to leave New York. Melissa crumpled the pale blue notepaper and dropped it into the wastebasket with the rest of her aborted attempts at letter writing.

She couldn't tell Patrice of her disappointment without making Jean-Pierre out to be the villain. That was hardly the case! She loved him more than she ever had. Their problem just wasn't simple enough to explain in a letter.

"*Ma chérie*. I have been looking for you." Jean-Pierre walked through the room and stood behind her, his hands resting easily on her shoulders. "What are you doing?"

Melissa leaned her head back against his chest. "I'm trying to write Patrice," she said. "But I'm not making much progress." She waved the empty sheet of paper for him to see. "Guess I just don't have anything to tell her," she finished, but they both knew she was avoiding the subject. If anything, she had too much to say.

Jean-Pierre smoothed her hair with his hand. She loved his touch. What was wrong with her? Why couldn't she be content with what she had?

"Have you told her about the tour offer?" he asked discreetly.

"No," she said. "The last letter I wrote her was about my debut." She had clipped articles from every newspaper that published the story of her success and mailed them to Patrice to read. "I'm not sure she'd understand why I turned down the tour offer."

"Do you?" he asked carefully. "Do you understand?"

"I guess so," she said unconvincingly. "But I still say you're wrong to worry," she added stubbornly.

"I told you," he said emphatically. "I cannot compose unless you are with me."

"But that's silly—of course you can!" she insisted.

"My Lissa. Please. I do not enjoy denying you." He could see the impatience gnawing away at her love for him, but he knew he was right about her absence affecting his work. He remembered with horror the months before he had met Melissa when he hadn't been able to write a line. It was she who had brought the music back into his life. And he wasn't going to risk losing the source of his inspiration by letting her travel away from him. "I need you to stay with me," he said softly. "Perhaps after I've finished 'Souvenir' you will tour." He had started the new sonata last month. It promised to be his greatest achievement.

"How long will that be?" she asked, the frustration she felt came out sounding like impatience. "Won't there always be another piece to compose?"

"I cannot hurry 'Souvenir' without compromising its quality," he said defensively. "Are you so discontented with our life together?" he asked bitterly. "Are you bored with your musical training? Do I not give you enough time each day?"

"Of course," she said decisively.

"Do you regret your decision to leave America for me?"

Melissa wanted to reach for him, to reassure him when he had doubts, but this time she forced herself to stay in her chair. He was missing her point entirely. "I've never regretted my decision to marry you," she said plainly. Not only had Jean-Pierre given her all of his love but also most of his time. True to his promise he continued to tutor her, only now practicing was more important because she rehearsed Arbour's compositions as *he wrote them*! And after their long hours together each day, he would go into his studio to compose. She would practice in her studio at the opposite end of the house until it was time for dinner. In one way or another they were together all the time. Even when she wasn't with him, her spirit was, just as his was always present for her, even in his physical absence.

That was the point! she thought. How could he fear that his inspiration would disappear if she left his side for a few days when she was *always* with him in his music? She was in his heart. She had to make him see that it was safe for her to tour, for *his* own sake, if not for hers.

Jean-Pierre turned away from her beseeching silence to face the window. The sky was gray although it was only early afternoon. The weather had been like this for days: dreary, without a ray of sunshine; heavy, without the release of rain. "I think I'll go out," Jean-Pierre said mournfully.

"I would like to go with you," Melissa added quickly. "Wait while I get my coat."

She felt the distance between them expanding, and somehow she had to close the gap. There was too much love between them to waste time with a quarrel. Why couldn't he see that the more room they gave their love, the more it would grow? His fear was suffocating her, and it would consume them both if she yielded to it. If their music was to survive—to thrive—she had to convince him that his possessiveness was unwarranted.

They traversed the streets without talking. For once people left them alone. No one stopped them for Jean-Pierre's autograph, and Melissa successfully ignored the critical looks people gave her. The French were understandably possessive of their national hero and his music. From the very beginning Arbour's public had watched her with great interest, as a mother might examine a future daughter-in-law, curious to observe her effect on Arbour's genius.

She held his arm and leaned her head against his shoulder as they slowed their pace. To the unsuspecting observer, they looked like Parisian lovers, but Melissa could feel the tension in her husband's arm. The chilly air penetrated the layers of her clothing, and a mist settled on her eyelashes. Melissa shivered in the cold, and Jean-Pierre instinctively pressed her to his side.

"Let's go home," Jean-Pierre said, brushing the mist from her hair.

"Oh, Jean—let's go away!" she urged suddenly. She dreaded going back to their house. "Somewhere where we can breathe again. Just the two of us." Their home had turned into a prison for both of them. "You can work on 'Souvenir' and I can—"

"What would you do, my love?" he asked tentatively. He relished the enthusiasm he saw mounting in her face, and it rekindled the joy in his own heart. He had felt responsible for her unhappiness, but he hadn't known how, without risking his music, to give in to her desire to tour. Now she was asking for something he could give her. "Tell me what you plan to do while I work on 'Souvenir'?"

"I—" She laughed hesitantly. "I'll be there to bother you—with kisses and caresses—in between refrains. And when you finish—"

"How could I finish anything with such promised interruptions?" he asked happily.

"You'd just have to work faster than ever," she teased. "Please say we can go away," she implored. "We never had a real honeymoon, and we've both been working too hard."

"You are right," he admitted. Often they fell into bed at night too exhausted to make love. They needed time to play, to touch the chords of their passion, to retune the essence of their love. "Yes, we shall go away." Jean-Pierre said matter-of-factly.

"Hurray!" Melissa sang.

"I know just where we can go," Jean continued excitedly. He lifted her into his arms and hugged her happily. "We can leave at the weekend."

They quickened their pace going home. Their talk was full of the details of their trip, but their thoughts lingered on the honeymoon they would begin, as soon as they were inside their house, out of their damp clothes, and warm in each other's embrace.

At the weekend they drove to Jean-Pierre's family's château in Vence. They had sent two of the servants ahead of them to prepare the house, but after Melissa and Jean arrived, they decided to send the help home, preferring solitude.

The château was large enough to accommodate a party of two hundred, but Melissa and Jean-Pierre were only interested in entertaining each other. In the soft glow from the stone fireplace, Melissa's pale skin lay against Jean's dark body, like moonlight glistening on the river Seine.

When the flames died into ash, Melissa lit candles to light their love.

When the wax melted and drowned the light, they lay in the dark until daybreak.

When they gave their love a rest, they were like children tired from a carnival: full of sweets, adventure, and joy.

They didn't bother to unpack until the second evening; instead, they spent the day in bed: talking, dozing, waking to renewed excitement, they reacquainted themselves with the love of their lives.

Melissa saw that they had been right to come away. Their love was renewed. Nothing could hurt it now. Jean-Pierre relaxed and so did she. He worked better in the country than he did in Paris. Soon he'd understand that the inspiration came from inside himself, and that her love was with him always. What did it matter if she was puttering around the kitchen, or practicing his latest sonata, or on the beach, for that matter? Her love didn't alter with location. It was strong enough to bridge any distance.

When they had finished work for the day, they'd walk down to the sea. It was too cold to swim, but they lay in the sand, wrapped tightly in blankets, and shared their dreams. She lay with her head against his chest, as content to hear his even breathing as she was to hear his easy reminiscences of childhood at the château. When the sun sank low, or the mistral carried their voices out to sea, they gathered their blankets around them, happy and tired, to trudge back up the hill for their evening meal; and later they feasted again, on food that always satisfied, but never satiated their appetites for one another.

When it was time to return to Paris, they did, but only long enough to settle their business and to make arrangements to move permanently to the château in Vence. The beautiful house overlooking the Mediterranean, with a view of Nice in the distance, became their home. They saw no reason to return to the pressures of the city when their happiness and privacy were guaranteed in Vence.

* * *

On their second anniversary, Jean-Pierre completed
"Souvenir" for Melissa. For her twenty-fifth birthday he
gave her "Etude" and the compliment that her playing
had bypassed his own. He created music for her alone,
and considered it an infidelity to let anyone but Melissa
perform it. Each year of marriage yielded a new song to
celebrate their love; each year Melissa surprised Jean-
Pierre by refining her ability to interpret the music he
wrote for her. She played Arbour's work exclusively
now, no longer interested in the definitive scores of
Beethoven or Mozart.

Together, they passed each morning working. They
saved the afternoons to nurture their love. In the evening Melissa stayed with Jean-Pierre while he composed his music. Sometimes he would ask her opinion
of a piece, or verbalize a dilemma, but she knew his
questions were rhetorical, and she never interfered
with his creative thinking, though she had come to know
his music so well she could often predict the choices he
would make.

His work taught *her* the patience and trust she was so
anxious for *him* to learn. She was so content at Jean-
Pierre's side that she didn't care anymore about tour-
ing. She had enough exposure when she performed in
Paris. Her musical ability, for all the time Arbour
coached her, was greater than she had ever hoped it
would be. There would be time for a tour when the
last of his fears had disappeared, if she was still interested. With all they had together, she was content to
stay by his side, talking, working or simply
playing. . . .

CHAPTER FIVE

His head was bent in concentration. He rested one elbow on the edge of the piano, and kept time to an internal yet unwritten melody with the tip of his pencil, varying tempos against his knee until one suited him. Then he straightened up at the keyboard, pencil clenched between his teeth, like a Spanish knife dancer, and played a few chords. Frowning, he scribbled changes onto the paper, and played again. When he reached the bottom of the page, he bit his lip in satisfaction, tucked the pencil behind his ear, and played it straight through.

He paused at the end, listening to the sound dissolve through the walls. It was good, but not perfect. He paced the large room, an idea stirring into clarity. All at once he had it. He grabbed his pencil and wrote as quickly as he could, tapping his foot against the marble floor. Excitement colored his face. He was never so happy as when he was working—except when Melissa was with him.

The phone rang from the other room, startling him

out of concentration. "Melissa!" he called twice as the ringing persisted, before he remembered she had gone into town. He ran down the vast arched hallway, his bare feet leaving faint impressions on the cool stone floor. It was April and already the days were warm with spring humidity.

He hated to answer it—a minute's distraction could destroy a train of thought—but it might be Melissa; it might be important. He grabbed the phone off the cradle, draping his long, agile frame over the arm of the chair.

"Hello? Jean-Pierre?"

"Patrice? *Allô, mon amie!*" As much as he hated the interruption, he was glad it was she. His affection for her was based on all Melissa had told him, and it had grown as deep as her own. "Are you in Paris?" he asked hopefully. She had been planning a visit, but the date wasn't set. Even as he asked, the crackling on the line told him the call was long distance.

"I wish I were. New York is underwater! It's been raining for a week," she said excitedly. "And I'll bet you're already sleeping with the windows open." She laughed, but her voice sounded hollow, like prerecorded applause. "Is Mel there?"

"You just missed her. She left for Nice at noon. She won't be back until late afternoon. Are you all right?" he asked, concerned about the tension in her voice.

"Jean—" All the pretense of gaiety disappeared from her voice.

"Tell me," he urged. "What is it?"

"Mel's dad—he had a heart attack last night."

"Is he all right?" he asked apprehensively. Melissa's

father had suffered from a weak heart ever since his wife had died, but his doctor kept him stable with pills and a strict diet. "Is he in the hospital?"

"No, Jean—he's dead." She caught her breath. She hated to bear bad news. "I've been trying to reach you for hours!" Her voice conveyed the frustration of the ordeal.

"I am so sorry for the news, Patrice," he said genuinely. He had only met the man once, but had liked him. "May he find greater joy in his next life."

Patrice hoped so, too, but she spoke to her frustration. "I had to bribe Lucille with morels to give me this phone number in Vence."

Jean-Pierre nodded silently into the phone. The orders to their housekeeper in Paris were strictly enforced: no one was to interrupt their work.

"Honestly, Jean-Pierre, sometimes I wish you weren't so famous!"

He smiled ruefully. "Melissa has the same complaint," he confided. "I am sorry we were so hard to reach."

"Do you want to tell Melissa?" she asked. "I could call back later. It's seven o'clock here now. What time did you say she'd be back?"

Jean-Pierre could tell from her hesitation that telling Melissa the news wasn't a job she cherished. "I will tell her," he promised. "Can you tell me what happened? She will have questions."

Patrice told him the little she knew. A heart attack had put him in the hospital at midnight; a massive stroke killed him two hours later. "I can make the arrangements," Patrice offered, "but I'll need Mel's help to settle the estate."

"Can she settle it from here?" he asked hopefully.

"Maybe." Patrice considered. "But she might as well take care of it when she comes back for the funeral. It won't take more than a week. He's left his affairs in order, I expect."

"You think it's essential that she be there?" he asked. "She wasn't close to him."

His question reminded Patrice of the possessiveness she had seen in Arbour during her last visit. Whenever Melissa left the room, Jean-Pierre would follow her with his eyes, sitting restlessly, half-attentive to conversation, until she returned. Patrice had been surprised—pleased—to hear that Melissa was away for the day. Maybe he had changed. People did. She had feared Mel might mistakenly encourage his possessiveness.

"I wasn't close to my father," Patrice told him honestly. "I've always regretted that I missed his funeral. It's important to say a final farewell. It helps to settle the loss, somehow."

"This is the worst time for me to leave work," Jean-Pierre confessed. He had four pieces in progress, and a new sonata nagged for his attention. A few months from now he could leave his work without risk—he had promised Melissa they would spend June in Greece—but there would be no way to keep that promise if he left work now.

"Don't worry about her," she advised. "I'll take the week off from work. I won't let her out of my sight."

"It's not that I don't trust her," he hastened to explain.

"Of course not," Patrice rejoined at once. "If I loved

someone as much as you love Mel, I wouldn't let him out of my sight."

Jean-Pierre laughed. "Thank you," he said softly. She was a friend to both of them. It would be fine for Melissa to go alone. He couldn't keep her from going to her father's funeral. There was no reason to. The fear that had kept her tethered to him had dissolved. Melissa had convinced him, with her love and patience, that her love was with him always. Their house was full of her love: he'd be sure to work in her absence. When she returned—if he worked as he planned to—he would consent to a tour next fall. By then she'd have five new pieces to add to her repertoire. "She would be back in a week?" Jean-Pierre asked.

"I couldn't keep her away from you any longer," Patrice assured him. "Not with her devotion!"

"I can drive her to Paris tonight. There's a flight from Orly at ten o'clock. She'll be in Manhattan tomorrow afternoon."

"Call me when her reservations are confirmed."

"Of course. And Patrice," he said quickly, "thank you for all your help. You are very special to both of us."

"You just compose another sonata for Melissa to play. That's thanks enough for anybody."

"*Au revoir,* Patrice."

"*Adieu,* Jean-Pierre."

After the quiet of Château Lupine, New York City was like heavy cream after skim milk. The crowds of people in the airport terminal, even the traffic jam, felt like a burst of sunshine to Melissa. Like a listless flower, she soaked up the rays of excitement that shine only in a bustling metropolis. This was her home! For all its flaws—the littered streets, the poverty and the crime, the lines and the waiting—New York pulsated with a life-force like no other city.

She hailed a cab and rode into the city in awe, enjoying the crystal-clear view of the skyline and the sunshine after the week of rain. She had convinced Patrice not to meet her; a trip from Wall Street to Kennedy Airport at rush hour was senseless. Melissa wasn't a child. She knew the city better than Patrice did. She felt proud to be able to maneuver her way into the city. It meant, despite her long absence, that she was still a New Yorker.

But there was another reason for wanting to enter New York City alone. In the four years she had been married she had come to rely on Jean-Pierre more than she had ever relied on Patrice. She wanted to test her independence, to make sure she hadn't lost her ability to handle a city the size of New York. If a tour did materialize—as Jean-Pierre's acceptance of her absence might suggest—she wanted to be sure it was what she *really* wanted. Too often she fought wilfully for something because it was denied her. She didn't want to disgrace them both by signing a contract to tour before knowing she could stand to be away from him. So far, even with the last-minute departure and the weight of her father's death, she was thrilled with the adventure of traveling.

Seeing Patrice was like erasing the years that had separated them. Her friend was as thin and as graceful as

she had been at twenty. The responsibility of her career
had added a look of substantiality, the way glasses can
turn a pretty face dignified. But Patrice wore no glasses.
Her brilliant blue eyes were as bright and dazzling as
ever.

"If it weren't for Dad's funeral, this would feel just
like old times," Melissa said as they climbed the stairs
to her former apartment.

"Does that mean you are going to play the piano the
whole time you are here?"

"You still have my old piano?" Melissa asked
incredulously.

"I couldn't pay anyone to take it," Patrice complained playfully. In truth, she had kept the old piano
as a reminder of her former roommate. She unlocked
the door to her apartment, and Melissa raced past her
to the piano. "Yep, just like old times," Patrice
quipped. Melissa lifted the cover and ran her hand over
the keys. "I dusted it, just for your arrival."

Melissa was delighted. "I thought you couldn't wait
to be rid of this old thing." It wasn't valuable to anyone
but Melissa; she had spent so many hours at its keyboard, that it felt like a friend.

"Will you play?"

"Maybe later," she said shyly.

"If you don't, I will," Patrice threatened.

"You learned how to play the piano?" Melissa asked
in astonishment.

"I couldn't let 'Ben' sit unused. He felt bad enough
when you deserted him for Jean-Pierre."

"Ben! You named my old piano Ben?"

Patrice wrapped her arm around the dark mahogany top, and pressed her face against the highly polished veneer. "If you call Ben *old* once more I'll—"

"Sorry!" Melissa said, backing off. "What can you play?"

Patrice sat stiffly on the bench and threw back her hair dramatically. She lifted her hands, in imitation of Melissa, and began to play. "Like it?" she asked seriously. "Don't you think I've improved?"

"But you could play 'Heart and Soul' when I left," Melissa declared, laughing.

"But only one handed," she said. "Watch!" She added a second hand and burst into improvisation.

"I'm sure glad you've kept Ben busy," she said, when Patrice had finished.

"Let's see if you can top that!" Patrice challenged.

"Later. Give me a minute to look around."

"I was wondering when you would."

Except for the piano, the apartment was completely changed. All the furniture which they had acquired over the years from their parents' discards had been replaced by antiques. The wall-to-wall carpet had been removed, and on top of the polished hardwood floors lay expensive Oriental rugs.

Melissa's bedroom had been converted into the study. Books lined three of the four walls.

Patrice had transformed her own bedroom from warm and girlish, as Melissa remembered it, to slickly modern, with low-to-the-floor Danish furnishings. A single abstract painting hung on the silver-papered wall over her bed. "It's stark, but I like it," Patrice acknowledged.

"That's all that matters," Melissa assured her, but

she was relieved to see that the kitchen remained the same. It had been too perfect to change, Patrice explained. It contained the memory of their endless dreams just as it was.

"Everything's set for tomorrow," Patrice told Melissa, when they had settled in the kitchen with tea and biscuits. Melissa nodded solemnly. She knew she should be sad, but the joy of her homecoming overshadowed her feelings of grief. "I've arranged for a quick service," Patrice continued. "His friends will be there. You'll say hello to them afterward, but you won't have to stay long. The following afternoon we have an appointment about the will." Melissa raised her eyebrows in question. "Nothing to worry about," Patrice assured her. "I know the attorney. Everything will go smoothly."

"He didn't have a lot, I think."

"No, I suspect not. I'd advise you to keep whatever stocks he had where they are. There's no use playing with them—you don't need the money now, and it might come in handy later."

Melissa nodded. Actually, now that Jean-Pierre was devoting all his time to composing music instead of performing his standard repertoire, and Melissa's performances were limited to two a year in Paris, they could use additional income. It would be a while before Arbour's new compositions produced dividends. "What have you scheduled for after the meeting with the lawyer?"

"I thought we'd have dinner at Carnegie Deli, just for old times' sake."

Melissa groaned. "I don't think I could stand it!"

"You lived on that food for years."

"I know. Don't remind me!"

"I'm glad French cuisine has influenced you at last. Now, about your week . . . I've left it entirely free. Whatever you want to do, I will find tickets. Even if it's Bernstein conducting Mahler's Ninth Symphony at Carnegie Hall."

Melissa gasped. "Now that's one I'd like to hear! Quickly she remembered the solemn occasion. She lowered her voice. "Just give me a couple of days, all right? I need some time to get used to Dad's death."

Patrice nodded thoughtfully. "You have all the family you could ever want between Jean-Pierre and me."

"Thank God for the two of you."

Patrice beamed. "Anytime you are ready, just let me know. I can't wait to show you *my* city."

"Mine, too!" Melissa interjected. "New York is my home, no matter where I live." She mused on the news of the Mahler concert. "Paris is a fabulous city, but the music is pretty mediocre."

"Wait a minute—my best friend performs *exclusively* in Paris."

Melissa blushed. She hadn't meant to criticize her own playing. "What I meant to say is that in New York City we could find theater, ballet, and opera any night of the week, and it would all be top quality."

"Just how I plan to fill your time!"

Melissa sighed. "If I could move you, and all of New York City to France, *then* I'd have everything. I guess I'll always want more than I have."

"Still hard on yourself, aren't you? There's nothing wrong with loving what you have *and* wanting more besides. It moves life forward."

"Why can't I think of stuff like that?"

"And put me out of a job? I've been bored to tears without you to mother!" Her eyes glistened. "But listen, I have a friend coming over tonight. I want you to meet him."

"Who is he?"

"The man of my dreams," Patrice sang.

"You're in love?"

"Well, he is good company, and I hated to break our date. We only see each other on Tuesday nights."

"Why so infrequently?" Melissa inquired. She had never seen Patrice so visibly interested in a man.

"Well—he spends his weekends with his eight-year-old son, and I'm so busy with work and all . . ." She seemed to consider this arrangement for a moment, then moved on. "He's dying to meet you. I've told him everything about you."

"Everything?" Melissa gasped in feigned horror.

"All except what a sloppy roommate you were. That's our secret."

"I've changed!"

"I noticed. You hung up your coat as usual."

Melissa reddened. She had dropped her coat over the back of the kitchen chair, just as she had always done in the old days. "Well, I *have* changed," she insisted. "I've even learned how to cook."

"Good God, no!"

"Thanks a lot. . . . But seriously, Trice, who's this friend of yours?"

"His name is Arthur Connell. I've had a crush on him for years, but he's as hooked on his career as I am on mine. There's not a lot of time to be together."

"You could make time."

"It's not that easy. Once you start the professional ball rolling, it picks up speed pretty fast. My calendar's packed. Besides," she added, her face darkening. "I'd make a lousy mother."

"I doubt that!" Melissa countered. She paused, thinking. "Are you working too hard?"

"Not at all. Remember the girl who used to say, 'If you love what you do, why take time off from it?'"

Melissa grinned in remembrance. "When you love someone enough, it's easy to take the whole day off from work, just to stay in bed!"

"Sounds good to me!" Patrice mused, "but I think Arthur would die if he couldn't go to work in the morning."

"What's he like?"

"Tall. Dark. Bearded. He's the director of Lincoln Center."

"That's a good person to date."

"It makes for good tickets," she admitted. "Anyway, he's crazy to meet you. Will you play for me before he gets here?"

She played "Nocturne" first. It sent chills down Patrice's back to hear the improvement in Melissa's playing.

"You've gotten so good!"

Melissa beamed proudly. "Jean-Pierre says I play as well as he does. That's because he hardly plays anymore—only when he's composing."

"You certainly sound good. I wish you'd give a concert in New York. You'd be a sensation, Mel."

"Maybe I will."

"Does Jean hate for you to travel?" Patrice guessed. "Is that why you don't tour?"

"I'm content to perform in Paris," she lied.

"Do you play often?"

"Twice a year."

"Is that enough? From the notices you get, you could perform in any concert hall in the world."

Melissa liked the idea. She would broach the subject again when she returned home. "Maybe Arthur would book me at Lincoln Center."

"Just say the word! Will you play something new for me?"

Arthur arrived in the middle, but Melissa didn't hear him enter. "God, she is brilliant," he whispered to Patrice.

"Shhh—" she mouthed. "I'll introduce you when she's finished."

When she finished he leaped to his feet in applause. The sincerity of his response compensated for any embarrassment. He took her by the hand and thanked her profusely.

"I'm so glad to meet you," he told her effervescently. "Will you play again? Please?"

"Are you sure you can stand more?"

He rolled his eyes to heaven. Patrice urged her to continue. She started "Sirens" but halted midway. "I just remembered," she said in embarrassment. "Jean-Pierre hasn't finished this one yet."

"But you play it already?"

"I practice a piece from the day he starts writing it.

He says he can hear it better if he doesn't have to think about playing it, too."

"Do you know how it will end?" Arthur asked.

"I have a suspicion," she admitted. "Something like this." She played a few bars—hesitated—then played a few more. "Maybe slower," she said.

"That's incredible," he told her.

"You'd know his music as well as I do if you lived with it day and night."

"Will you play another one? What else has he written lately?"

"Aren't you bored, Patrice?"

"Are you kidding? I suffered through years of scales for this day. The least you can do is play the good stuff."

So she did. After each piece, they convinced her to play another. At midnight she begged exhaustion.

"Poor girl," Arthur comforted. "I forgot you just arrived from Paris. I'm sorry to hear the news of your father."

"Thank you," she said. "I'm not too upset, really. Dad and I were never close. I guess I'm just one of those people who can accept death as a part of life."

"That's the spirit," he prompted. "Do you think you will feel up to a party Friday night? Or is that too soon?"

"Patrice said something about a concert," she said warily.

"The Mahler?" Patrice nodded. "Good. I'll be there, too. Afterward some friends are coming to my place. I'd be happy if you'd join us."

"I'd like to go," Patrice contributed. "If you feel up to it."

"Sounds like fun."

"If I asked you to play a piece or two, would you consider it singing for your supper?"

"Are you inviting us to dinner, too?" Melissa asked, slightly distracted—her thoughts were focused on her father—but she liked the idea of Arthur and Patrice spending more than one night a week together.

He laughed, sensing a scheme. "There will be food at the party."

"I know you're dying for a chance to show off!" Patrice said, nudging her.

"I'll play if Patrice will, too."

"It's a deal!"

Arthur had his arm around Patrice's waist. They were a good-looking couple. Melissa could see why they liked each other.

"I'll say good night now," she said. "Trice, will you be sure to wake me in the morning? And make sure I'm getting up."

"Just like the good ol' days," she said, walking with her to the study. The sofa bed was open and sheeted. "There're more blankets in the closet, if you need them."

"He's nice," Mel said approvingly.

"Hmmmm. I think so. We thought we'd go out for a bit. Do you mind being here alone?"

"Of course not," she said bravely. She had watched their attraction heighten throughout the evening, aided perhaps, by the romantic lull of Jean-Pierre's music. It had been clear for hours that they would want to lie together that night. "I'm fine alone," she said quietly, accepting Patrice's good-night embrace. "Have fun," she called out after them. It might not be love, the way she and Jean-Pierre knew it, but the affection was enviable. She stripped off her clothes, and for the first time in four years she climbed into bed alone, desiring Jean-Pierre's embrace.

CHAPTER SIX

The funeral on Wednesday was dignified and the visit to the lawyer's office on Thursday went smoothly, but Melissa felt relieved that they were over. Except for a second meeting to discuss the will at the beginning of the following week, her business was complete. She had spent the two days alone, walking the familiar streets, enjoying the stores and the crowds. Without Jean-Pierre beside her, she regained her anonymity, and was surprised by the sense of freedom it brought. Repeatedly, she was amused by the bold looks she received from men on the streets. Without Jean-Pierre to distinguish her, she was just another city girl.

"Are you ready to paint the town red?" Patrice asked Melissa on Friday morning.

"I'm ready and willing," she answered. The night before she had taken flowers out to the cemetery, strewing the single bouquet of red roses over both her mother and father's grave. In a peculiar way, she felt happier for her father than she had since her mother's death. At last they were together. The cab ride back into town served to purge the final feelings of loss.

Now she was anxious to enjoy the remainder of her trip. It would take three months to see and do everything that interested her in town. This trip couldn't do more than whet her appetite, but maybe she could convince Jean-Pierre to take holiday in Manhattan next fall. If not, perhaps she could come back for a week herself. "Where do we begin?" she asked Patrice excitedly.

"For starters, Bernstein tonight at Carnegie Hall."

"Are we going with Arthur?" Melissa asked.

"That's right. Try to dress sexy, will you? There's no need to wear black. He told me he wanted to be surrounded by beautiful women. It's a favorite fantasy of his."

"I'll do what I can." It would give her a chance to buy a new dress.

When Arthur picked them up that night, both Patrice and Melissa looked their best. Patrice looked stunning as usual in a backless silk dress, but it was Melissa who surprised them all. With Patrice's encouragement, she'd had her hair styled at Yves Claude's salon. Melissa had bought a simple black gown, suitable to her state, yet every move she made belied the dignity of the dress. The fabric clung to her curves, and her dark curls fell onto her bare shoulders. Arthur verbalized his regret about her happy marriage. Understandably, Patrice couldn't have been more grateful for Melissa's marital status.

They stopped briefly for drinks, and arrived at the concert hall just in time to hear the orchestra tuning their instruments. After all her years with solo piano, the size of the orchestra impressed her, but not nearly as much as did Leonard Bernstein. Jean-Pierre would have criticized him for stealing the show, but Melissa enjoyed him: his strong back and arms, his energy. His antics didn't detract from the music; in fact, his enthusiasm inspired the musicians. He understood the Mahler crescendo . . . and the conclusion . . . like angels ascending into heaven. The room was aglow with an inexplicable calm. Then, like heralds at heaven's gate, the audience responded to the inner peace, rising in appreciation, beckoning the maestro for a third and fourth curtain call. Melissa applauded to the very end.

"He's magnificent!" she exclaimed, on the way to Arthur's apartment. "I'd like to meet that man someday."

"I think he'll be at the party," Arthur answered. "But probably not till later. Remember, you promised to play for me."

Melissa withdrew into herself.

"I didn't know Bernstein would be present."

"He only promised to come after I told him you'd be there."

"He knew who *I* was?" she asked incredulously.

Arthur laughed heartily. "You're the seventh wonder of the music world! You're the only person permitted to perform Arbour's works. Exclusively in Paris. Now, that's the way to build a reputation!"

"We didn't plan it that way," she said truthfully.

"Planned or not, you've piqued people's interest. They're just waiting to have you satisfy it. Wherever you go, you'll play to packed houses."

Melissa debated the probability of his prediction. She would love the world to applaude Jean-Pierre's newest creations. She had worried that they might be too esoteric for general appreciation.

"Will you play 'Sirens'?" Patrice implored.

"I would like to," she admitted, "but it isn't finished. I improvised an ending when I played it for you, but I'm not sure it's anything like what Jean-Pierre intends."

"Sounded damn good to me," Arthur countered. "But play what you like best. You can play 'Heart and Soul' and I'd feel as though I'd heard a symphony."

"What kind of piano do you have?" she asked, to draw the attention away from her.

"I'll show you," he said, as the cab pulled up in front of a fashionable Park Avenue apartment building.

Inside, the party was already in progress. They had to squeeze through the crowd of people. The air was sprinkled with thimbles of laughter and debate. Conversations stopped as Arthur passed with his two guests. People were used to seeing Arthur with Patrice; tonight their eyes were on Melissa. He waved off the greetings with promises to share her with them later, and she smiled shyly at the people they passed, keeping a tight hold on her host's hand until they were standing in front of a handsome Baldwin.

"I thought when you said 'friends' you meant four or five. . . ." She laughed nervously, looking back at the room full of people.

"Can I help it if I'm popular?"

"Arthur never has small parties," Patrice confirmed.

"You knew?"

"Please don't change your mind, Melissa. Most of them came tonight to hear you."

She hated to disappoint Patrice when it would be so

easy to give in. She fingered the keys tentatively. The room quieted instantly. "I guess I'll have to play," Melissa said coyly to Arthur. "You'd look too funny with egg on your face."

Arthur looked enormously relieved. He said a few words to introduce her. He admitted he'd tricked her into playing for "friends" and everyone laughed. They stood around in small clusters, with their drinks in hand, or leaned against the plush modern furnishings. Melissa was grateful for the informality. In truth, she didn't mind playing for the crowd. It was easier to play for people than to mingle among them.

After the first piece she felt relaxed enough to enjoy the audience as well as the music. It was fun to play for Arthur's friends. They seemed to understand the music, and they knew Arbour's pieces enough to request their favorites. She could hear them responding at the right moments, and she marveled at their intelligence. She played "Nocturne" and "Etude" for them. She was midway through "Souvenir" when Bernstein and his entourage arrived at the party.

"What's Arbour working on these days?" he asked her later, after Arthur had introduced them. "Haven't heard much from him lately. You say he's working, eh?"

"Day and night."

"And you like the new work as well as the old?"

"I prefer it," she asserted.

"But then you're prejudiced," he bantered.

Melissa grinned broadly. "You might say I'm his biggest fan."

Bernstein shrugged, as if to dismiss her testimony.

"Play 'Sirens' for him, Mel," Patrice urged.

Arthur joined in. "Give him an earful!"

She wondered at the wisdom of playing an unfinished piece. "I guess it couldn't hurt," Melissa conceded. "It's not entirely complete, you see," she explained to Bernstein. "I'll have to improvise the ending."

"I'm sure it will sound fine," he granted, his eyes fixed on her pretty young face.

Everyone agreed that "Sirens" was Arbour's greatest achievement to date. They begged for an encore. Even Bernstein admitted "Sirens" surpassed all previous accomplishments. Melissa played one additional piece—also a new composition—before closing the lid to the keyboard for the evening.

Even mingling among the guests proved easier than Melissa had anticipated. For one thing, she didn't have to search for things to say. Arthur's friends supplied her with questions as steadily as Bernstein filled her glass with champagne. They listened with interest. They even laughed at her jokes, urging her on after she protested that she talked too much.

Between Patrice and Arthur's introductions Melissa figured she had met a hundred people, but it was clear, as they were leaving the party, that many guests had gone unintroduced. There were just too many people. As it was, she could not remember most of the names of those she had met. All she remembered was the quality of the evening, and now, as the noise and excitement faded into memory, she was struck by how kind everyone had been to her. It was the first time in her life that she felt equal to a roomful of people. She didn't have to apologize for her love of music as she had felt compelled to do during her Juilliard School days, nor did she feel compelled to hide other parts of herself. They liked her, and she liked the way they made her feel about herself. She had been Melissa Dennison Arbour, and they had applauded her, on and off keyboard. Never before had she felt so confident. She went home in triumph. The evening had been a smashing success.

The ringing telephone awoke her early the next morning. Patrice had left for the office, promising by note to be back by noon.

"My darling!" Melissa cried happily.

"Were you asleep?" Jean-Pierre asked.

"Yes. We were out late last night. At a party," she told him excitedly, stretching her long, bare legs beneath the covers. "I had *such* a good time!"

"Yes. I heard," he said curtly. "Your 'American debut' made the headlines this morning in France. You were naive to think I wouldn't find out."

"But I wanted you to know," she said emphatically.

"Why? To cut into my heart?"

"What's wrong with you?" she asked suddenly. He had never sounded like this before. Anger had darkened his usually pleasant voice. Even when they quarreled, as they sometimes did, he was always as anxious as she to be done with the fight. Now his voice sounded uncaring. Cold. Hostile.

"WIFE TO ARBOUR PREMIERS 'SIRENS' IN AMERICAN DEBUT." He was reading her the headlines.

"But that's not what happened!" Melissa exclaimed, sitting up in bed.

"Played to New York's musical elite . . ." he continued to read, despite her protests. "In attendance . . . Bernstein, Mehta, Eschenbach." He stopped. "Bernstein," he repeated angrily. "Of all people! Have you gone mad?"

His anger ignited her own. "Jean—you talk as if I'd stolen your music and sold it to the enemy. I've done nothing of the sort!"

"But the papers—"

"I don't give a damn what the papers report. You read a bad translation."

"Would you care to explain what happened?" he invited, but his politeness was falsified by underlying cynicism.

Melissa recreated the events of the previous evening. "I can see how the papers might have made a mistake," she conceded, "but that's what they've made—a mistake."

"I made a mistake letting you go to New York."

"You are being silly now," she chided. "I told you the truth of the matter."

"I don't see what 'truth' has to do with what's happened. All of France feels betrayed."

"What about you, Jean-Pierre? Do you feel betrayed?" She was suddenly very angry. This was all so silly. "Do you think I'd ever do anything intentionally to hurt you? Is that what our years together have taught you? Mistrust?"

"I think you had better come home right away," he said sternly.

"Why—so you can yell at me in person? No, thanks! I haven't done anything wrong. You won't convince me I have. I'm sorry if there is a misunderstanding in the newspaper, but I can't see how that should anger you. You are being childish—"

The line went dead, but the wire still reverberated with his anger. She dialed for the operator, but he had no luck in reconnecting her call. Swallowing her pride, she called Château Lupine, but got no answer. Finally she phoned Paris, but Lucille said he'd gone to Vence. Why hadn't she thought to ask where he was calling from? She'd just have to wait for him to call back.

Patrice arrived home at noon, but Jean-Pierre hadn't called again. "He hung up on me," Melissa explained unhappily. "I should be furious, but I can't stay angry at him. Even when he's so clearly wrong!"

When he hadn't called by that evening, Patrice suggested they contact the town authorities. "They can check the house. If something's the matter, you'll know. If not, and Arbour is being a bastard, you should be angry. But this wondering will drive you mad." She picked up the phone. While she waited for the operator to place her call, she watched Melissa's anger turn to regret, then worry. "No matter what, Mel, you didn't do anything wrong last night. No matter what the papers say, no matter what Jean-Pierre says. He's just upset. Understandably." She babbled in French when the call went through, covering the receiver in her hand at intervals. "If you start to believe his side, you're doing yourself, and him, a grave injustice. You played the piano at a party. Period. Understand?"

Melissa nodded blankly.

"Come on. They said they'd call back when they learned something. Get dressed and let's have lunch."

"Do you think I should go home?"

"Do you want to?"

"I don't want Jean-Pierre angry with me."

"Will he be less angry if you go back?"

"Probably, yes. But then I'll be mad!"

"There's no winning, Mel."

The police reported that Château Lupine was empty. They had found evidence of his recent presence—the morning newspapers askew in the living room—and would look out for his return.

So he had been at home! How could a grown man behave so childishly? She'd give him the rest of the day to apologize. Then she'd agree to come home. She wouldn't be able to enjoy the rest of her stay in New York with their quarrel unresolved. She called the airport and booked a flight for that evening. That would give them both time to cool off, but reunite them before bedtime.

"Patrice!" Melissa screamed from the study.

"What's happened?" she called, running into the room at once. Melissa stood by the phone, her face drained of color, her green eyes glazed. "Is it Jean-Pierre?" Patrice asked, prying loose the phone from Melissa's clenched white fist.

"He's hurt," Melissa said, stunned.

"Where is he?"

Suddenly, as though slapped twice across the face,

Melissa broke from the shock. "God! Patrice. He's been in an accident!"

"Is he . . . ?" She couldn't utter the word.

"He's unconscious." There was fear all over her face. "He has a chance, they said. A *chance*, Patrice?" It was the paradox of existence. "I've got to go to him."

"Go where?" a deep male voice asked. Patrice turned to find Arthur at the doorway. Patrice explained quickly. He kept his eyes on Melissa. He was aghast at the change in her since last night. "Get her to the airport," he said, taking charge. "I'll phone ahead for her reservation."

Melissa made a blind attempt to thank him, but she saw nothing, except the vivid image of her husband lying alone, unconscious. Because of her. Because of her.

"Make a reservation for me, too," Patrice told him. "I'm going with her."

"No!" Melissa cried, then tempered her response. "I need to go alone," she said simply.

"This is no time for—"

"If she wants to go alone, let her," Arthur instructed. "She's been pushed around enough already."

"You'll call me if you need help?" Patrice asked, when they reached the airport.

Melissa nodded numbly.

"Promise?"

"Yeah . . ."

Patrice delivered Melissa to the steward on board the plane, who promised to keep an eye on her. But there was no need. She sat immobile all the way to Paris.

* * *

Whoever had telephoned Melissa about the accident had also notified the press, and they were as anxious for more information as Melissa was. They slung their questions at her from all directions—some she understood, but most of what she heard was the *tone* of accusation beneath the unintelligible foreign onslaught. She managed to organize her thoughts enough to speak to the press in French, but they weren't listening. They seemed not to care about her answers. They seemed more interested in bombarding her with their questions. Had Jean-Pierre given her permission for the American debut? Was a quarrel the reason for her trip to New York, and was she ending the "separation" only because of his accident? Was she certain that it had been an accident?

Melissa crossed her arms over her chest as if to barricade herself from their insinuating questions, and slammed the door to the limousine on the reporter who tried to follow her inside the car. They were as relentless in their curiosity as they were unsympathetic to her plight.

She was thankful for the darkened windows, and the speed with which the chauffeur removed her from the crowds and questions. She appreciated the driver's tactful silence. He kept his eyes on the road, glancing into the rearview mirror only to count the cars that pursued them to the hospital. Melissa was left alone with her thoughts, which were little enough comfort, for the press had only asked the questions Melissa had been asking herself. The steady hum of the tires on the pavement drove the questions deep into the groves of Melissa's fears. Had she been indiscreet to perform without his permission? Had she been responsible? Had she betrayed him?

The questions plagued her, but what really mattered was Jean-Pierre's well-being. The doctor said he had a *chance*. *What did that mean?* Did that mean he would live, but in some way be physically paralyzed? Or worse, that he'd damaged his mind? They could cope with a physical handicap, but a mental impairment would be worse almost than death.

She cringed at the thought. Nothing could be worse. She would rather he be alive and silent than to lose him completely. No, she thought, at whatever cost she wanted him alive. But Jean-Pierre would be miserable without his health. He would consider life useless if he couldn't compose. He would hate her for reminding him of the life they had had together.

Melissa smoothed the tips of her fingers against her brow. Such thoughts were pointless, she knew, but it was impossible to quiet them. The man she loved was hurt in a hospital somewhere in the middle of France, and she felt responsible.

The limousine cut its speed as it neared the outskirts of the tiny town. The driver had covered the four hundred miles in less than five hours; even so, Melissa's thoughts were no more settled now than they had been when he had rescued her at the airport; if possible, her emotions were more askew. The feelings of responsibility—and guilt—were settling over the truth like a layer of dust.

The chauffeur fielded the questions from the press at the entrance of the hospital while Melissa ran inside to find her husband. At first none of the nurses under-

stood what she was asking, and when they did, they refused to help. No, they couldn't take her directly to her
husband; they first had to notify the doctor of her arrival. No, they couldn't tell her Jean-Pierre's condition.
She would have to wait for the doctor.

Melissa couldn't believe what was happening. They
weren't going to let her see him until some country doctor was with her? Bewilderment gave way to hysteria,
and Melissa only quieted herself when she saw she was
frightening the nurses. She couldn't risk hysterics now.
They might try to sedate her, and Melissa needed every
ounce of energy she had to get her through this quan-
dary.

But neither could she sit patiently until the doctor
arrived. What if Jean-Pierre were calling for her?
Couldn't they understand how important it was for her
to see him now? As she realized they weren't going to
help her, a cry broke from her throat. Her weak legs
gave way, and she sank into the chair by the nurses'
station. She clutched hold of the chair's armrests for
support and conquered her fears before they turned to
tears.

"Would Mademoiselle care for a tablet? For her
nerves?" a young nurse offered in broken English.

Melissa refused politely. "What I would appreciate is
the washroom," she replied. The young nurse looked
relieved that Melissa had requested something reasonable.

"Come with me," she said, leading her down the corridor to the water closet, a little awed in the presence of
the great composer's young wife. "Here we are," she
said politely, turning to address Melissa, but finding her
nowhere in sight.

"Mademoiselle?" she called, retracing her steps back to the nurses' station.

Melissa hurriedly peered into each room on the ground floor as she fled her escort. At the end of the corridor she opened a set of closed doors and in the solitary hospital bed at the far side of the immaculate white room, Melissa found Jean-Pierre.

"Darling!" she cried, closing the door noiselessly behind her. Her heartbeat quickened: Jean-Pierre looked as healthy as ever. His head was propped against a high pile of pillows and his hands were folded on top of the neatly folded sheet. His eyes were open, and he was staring in her direction, but when she reached him she saw that his stare was blank, as if he were looking through her, as if he didn't see her at all.

"Jean-Pierre?" she asked tentatively, lifting his graceful white hand into hers. She squeezed his hand again, but he didn't respond. Even the light in his eyes was dim. Her own eyes glistened. "Can you hear me?" she asked, bringing her face very close to his, and looking directly into his eyes, watching for the slightest sign of recognition. It was as if he was physically present, but otherwise absent. "Jean-Pierre, do you know me?"

"Most likely not," a man answered. Melissa swung around. A slight man with sorrowful brown eyes addressed her.

"Is he—?" She didn't know what to ask first. "Is he going to be all right?" she asked nervously.

The doctor shrugged his shoulders, his palms turned upward. "We do not know. At first we didn't think he would live. Now he gives us hope."

"Does he know I'm here with him?" Melissa asked.

"We cannot tell. He should be in a bigger hospital. We have no equipment to treat him properly."

"By all means, transfer him!" Melissa instructed.

"Unfortunately, it is not yet safe to move him. We will just have to wait."

"We can't just *wait*!" she protested. Why were they all insisting she wait? There must be something they could do!

"All we can do is make sure he is comfortable. God will do the rest."

Melissa groaned. "May I please be alone with my husband?" she asked resignedly. If they were just going to wait for Jean-Pierre to heal himself, she might as well be alone with him.

The doctor nodded and closed the door behind him. He would be in the nurses' station, if she needed him.

A half hour later a nurse interrupted Melissa's vigil and found her standing close beside the bed, not touching Jean-Pierre, except to hold his hand. "*S'il vous plaît,* will you sit?" the girl urged. "Please be comfortable," she added, dragging a folding chair over to the bedside.

"Do you think I would hurt him if I sat on the edge of his bed?" Melissa asked quietly. She needed to be closer to him and had been wondering whether she dared to try.

The young nurse nodded sympathetically. "I think he would understand," she said.

"Thank you," she remembered to add before the nurse left her alone with her husband. It was the first gesture of kindness shown to Melissa since she'd reached France, and frankly she needed it. Why were some people so thoughtless, and others so helpful, in a moment of crisis?

Carefully she lifted herself onto the bed beside Jean-Pierre. She touched his dark, silky hair with a trembling hand. His lips were warm, and she could have sworn he had returned her kiss, raising his lips to hers, if only slightly. She lowered her ear to his mouth, and listened to his shallow breathing. Why wasn't there something they could do? How could they just sit and wait?

"Jean-Pierre!" she called out helplessly. She couldn't hold back the tears anymore. She needed him now, and he wouldn't help her. She needed his strong arms securely around her, but he just lay there inert.

A light flickered in his eyes. Melissa pulled back to look at him. It was as if he had spoken to her. He had made a sign! He was with her after all. Relief flooded over her.

The light flashed again, but to Melissa's horror she saw it was the flash from a camera. Another bulb exploded light through the window, and Melissa saw that a crowd of reporters were watching her and Jean-Pierre from the courtyard.

Melissa swung to face them directly. Her anger, frustration, and feelings of abuse shot through her like an electrical current. She broke the barrier between her and the press as her fist shattered the window, showering her enemy with glass. They fled en masse, as much from the glass as from her anger but they stopped at a safe distance to photograph Melissa with her bloody fist clenched and raised in accusation.

The commotion brought the entire staff into Jean-Pierre's room. Quickly, the doctor attended Arbour and two nurses tried to placate Melissa.

"You are upset," the elder said to her, trying to remove her from the room.

"Let me go!" Melissa cried, wrestling free of her two captors. "I will not leave my husband!"

"You cannot be of help to him in your condition," the head nurse protested.

Melissa felt like collapsing into tears, but her fury held her together. "He is my husband! Why shouldn't I be upset? Would you be calm if he were your husband, if you weren't allowed to do anything but *sit* and watch him die?" she demanded, her eyes blazing. "You *couldn't,* not if you loved your husband the way I love mine," she said defiantly, tears gleaming through her anger. She no longer cared what they thought of her. All that mattered now was that she be allowed to stay with Jean-Pierre.

"Doctor, please?" She turned to him. "I'll be quiet," she promised. "Just keep the press away."

"Let me see your hand," he answered. She had cut it badly on the window. She could hardly uncurl it halfway. "It must be stitched at once," he said. "Stay here, with your husband." He turned to the consort of nurses. "Leave her alone. Come only if she calls. Suzanne, bathe her hand for stitches. I will return in a minute."

The room emptied except for the one nurse. Melissa returned her attention to Jean-Pierre. His eyes seemed brighter, but it was hard to tell.

She had hardly noticed the cuts on her hand until Suzanne, the nurse who had been kind to her earlier, began to wash off the blood. The girl worked diligently, trying not to disturb Melissa's silence, but the cuts were bad, and the silence was tense with unasked, and unanswerable questions.

"Do you know what happened to him?" Melissa asked her, never taking her eyes from Jean-Pierre.

"They found him unconscious at the foot of the embankment. Outside our town. The car was destroyed, but he was hardly scratched."

"Why doesn't he move? Do you know?" Melissa asked, facing the girl.

"We think—" She hesitated. She wasn't supposed to know, but she had overheard the doctor talking. For God's sake, his wife had a right to know. If she had been French instead of American the nurses and press wouldn't have dared to treat her this way. "The doctor thinks his spine is nearly severed."

"Does that mean he won't ever walk again?" Melissa started, but Jean-Pierre's abrupt movement grabbed her attention. She ripped her hand away from Suzanne to give her full attention to Jean-Pierre.

"*Mon Dieu!*" Suzanne cried hoarsely. Jean-Pierre made a sound in his throat. His eyes widened.

"Get the doctor!" Melissa dumbly ordered.

"I'm here," the slight man answered, crossing the room. He listened to Jean-Pierre's heart. He took the limp hand from Melissa and checked the pulse.

Melissa stood by, her lips parted expectantly, waiting for a further sound.

But Jean-Pierre was silent. The doctor released Jean-Pierre's hand and laid it across the other. "I'm sorry," he whispered solemnly, avoiding Melissa's questioning eyes.

"You're sorry?" Melissa repeated, not understanding. Suzanne crossed herself. "Do you mean—?"

"He is dead," the doctor said simply.

"No," she argued, shaking her head in disbelief. "He was just alive!"

The doctor shrugged, unable to explain what had happened. He looked almost as blank as Jean-Pierre.

"But he can't be dead!" she reasoned. She had never witnessed a death before, but she was sure it didn't look like this. Life didn't just disappear. It had to depart . . . the soul ascended into heaven . . . some big production. It had to be! A person didn't make a sound, as if he were clearing his throat, widen his eyes as if for one last look at the world around him, and die.

Suzanne was crying now. She knew what death looked like. So did the doctor. But not Melissa.

"It can't be!" She stared at Jean-Pierre, as if to challenge the doctor's lie, but he lay motionless. Even through the blur of tears, she saw that his spirit no longer occupied his body. She bent to kiss his lips, but it was too late. They were already cold.

The doctor assured her his death had been painless, but that didn't begin to alleviate Melissa's pain. He gave her a jar of pills, and told her how often she should take them. She could find accommodations for the night in town. The nurse at the desk would help to make the necessary arrangements the following day. He recommended sleep—she had come a long way and had suffered a terrible shock—and that she let him mend her hand before leaving the hospital. Melissa didn't want her hand repaired. She hoped it *wouldn't* heal. She never wanted to play the piano again.

* * *

Later, Melissa couldn't recall how she had held herself together, or how she had managed to have Jean-Pierre's remains cremated and the ashes released in her care *that same night,* but she had done it. That night she had returned to the château to collect Jean-Pierre's music, and before the press knew what had happened, she was out of the country, on a plane bound for New York City.

The press's outrage spoke for the nation. They had expected a stately burial for their national hero, and by scattering Jean-Pierre's ashes privately at Château Lupine, Melissa had denied them their right to mourn officially.

She refused to feel guilty about mourning her husband's death in private. By the time she learned of their anger, she felt nothing but scorn for the French sense of propriety. She was glad to leave France. It had been her home only because Jean-Pierre had chosen to live there. She was glad to return home to New York . . . if only Jean-Pierre had been with her.

Manhattan proved to be no better than France. The press met the plane at Kennedy Airport and chased her with their questions. This time they were louder and more insistent. Spoken in English, every word they shouted stung Melissa. They, too, wanted to know if she had quarreled with Jean-Pierre, if he had been angry about her debut. A woman journalist asked if he had resented her career.

Melissa refused to answer any of their questions, but she heard them all. Patrice worried, as she ushered Melissa into the car, that her friend would forget the truth of the situation. The press could be convincing—

we are taught to believe what we read—and Melissa, though holding up remarkably well considering the strain, was surely riddled with guilt.

"Thanks, Patrice," she said weakly, once they were clear of airport traffic.

"I hadn't expected such a crowd," Patrice admitted. "Were they this bad in France?"

"Oh, Trice. It's been awful. Why won't they just leave me alone?" she cried.

"They consider it their business," she said matter-of-factly, glancing sideways to study Melissa. The mask of strength she had worn at the airport was slipping.

As they drove past the cemetery outside Manhattan, a sight Melissa had seen countless times before, her facade crumpled. All the questions she had been asking herself silently now poured forth, in the company of relentless self-doubt and guilt.

Patrice made a split-second decision. Changing lanes abruptly, she turned north off the highway. The first sign to New England was in view before Melissa noticed they weren't entering Manhattan.

"Where are we going?" she asked nervously.

"Away from the madness. The press aren't going to let up for a couple of days. What you need is peace and quiet. A place where you can ask yourself the right questions, and hear the right answers."

Melissa didn't say anything. She was tired. She wanted to go to sleep. She wanted to quit being brave. She wanted . . . Jean-Pierre.

Melissa's shoulders lowered visibly as they drove away from the city. The roads emptied, and forests thickened. In just over two hours they crested the Berkshire Hills.

"Where are we?" Melissa asked.

"In Richmond," Patrice answered. "Last year I bought an old farmhouse for 'weekends away from it all.' It will suit you perfectly. You can stay here in absolute quiet until you are ready to come back into town."

They drove past the three buildings that comprised the center of town: a white, high-steepled church, the general store; a red, one-room schoolhouse no longer in use. The town's size suited perfectly its handful of residents who lived down the unpaved back roads, or high atop the steep hills. There was never any trouble finding a parking spot, never a line at the single gas pump in front of the general store. Richmond didn't even have a restaurant, or a pay phone, so the tourists stayed away, crowding the neighboring towns instead.

"The press will forget the whole incident in a couple of weeks—as soon as something more outlandish occurs, no doubt."

Melissa nodded numbly, not having heard Patrice's words. She was studying the house at the end of the driveway. Her sense of well-being was so overwhelming, it was almost as though Jean-Pierre were there to welcome her home.

PART
II

*Western wind, when wilt thou blow
That the small rain down can rain?
Christ, that my love were in my arms,
And I in my bed again!*

CHAPTER SEVEN

The screen door swung shut behind her as she ran down the steps to catch the mailman, but he was gone before she reached the yard. Just for the hell of it she continued running, enjoying the feeling of her bare feet on the lush green grass. It would be months yet before Melissa would have to dress in wool and down for each and every expedition out of doors. Richmond was like Eden for all its beauty and sanctuary, but the snake in the garden was the six-month winter. She loved the solitude, but the cold and the long winter nights did nothing to pacify her empty arms and bed.

Today's glory made the long wait worthwhile. During the slow, steady spring the trees had filled with leaves; now they hung dark and lush, obscuring her view of the barn. She could still spy a corner of the lake from her kitchen window, and the white birch trees that lined the far side of the cove were tall enough to stay visible all summer long.

Melissa filled the wheelbarrow with tools. As she left the barn a gentle breeze lifted the tendrils of hair off her neck. It was a perfect day for gardening. She could have the last of the corn planted by noon, she thought, unlatching the garden gate.

Melissa noted that the spinach had burgeoned from last night's rain, but so had the weeds. She could use the afternoon to rescue her precious greens from the flourishing weeds, but not until after she'd had a leisurely swim at noon. It didn't matter how hot and dirty she got working in the soil—not as long as she was guaranteed a swim in the pond.

She had just put on her gloves when Patrice pulled into the driveway sounding her horn. Even at a distance Melissa could see the smile on her face, but it was the bright yellow canvas life-raft on top of her silver BMW that stole Melissa's attention.

"Isn't it great!" Patrice beamed, stopping the car beside Melissa. "Your landlord was clearing out his barn for some kind of sale. I asked if I could buy it before anyone else saw it. Isn't it perfect for your pond?"

"It's wonderful," Melissa agreed enthusiastically. "It's big enough for five people."

"Or two and a picnic lunch."

"Which I'll bet you've already packed." Melissa smiled knowingly.

It took some skillful maneuvering to bring the boat to water, but soon Melissa and Patrice were ensconced in the new rubber boat, a hundred yards from the shore, lazily absorbing the midmorning sun. Melissa's pond was small but deep and clear and perfectly private. The southwest corner had overgrown, and the marsh yielded a variety of fish, none of which either woman could identify, but Melissa had grown adept at cooking them, and Patrice a bit less squeamish cleaning them.

"It's a tough life, isn't it, Mel?" Patrice lay back against the side of the boat, the top of her swimsuit untied. Her breasts were as evenly tanned as the rest of her dark skin.

"I don't know how you can stand going back to the city," Melissa remarked, dangling her hand in the water. "Especially in summer."

Patrice studied the setting, her eyes shaded with the back of one hand. "It *is* hard to leave Richmond. But I love my work, and the week goes so fast, when I have the weekend in the country. Besides," she added, reaching into the weighty hamper packed with fruit and sandwiches. "I like Manhattan."

Melissa nodded silently, accepting a handful of grapes.

"Don't you ever miss it?" Patrice asked.

"Sure, sometimes. But I can't go back."

"Sure you can."

"I can't," Melissa insisted. The finality of her tone closed the subject. Patrice knew she would change her mind eventually, but when? Already two years had passed, and Melissa showed no sign of returning to the city.

"Don't you ever get lonely up here?" Patrice tried again.

"How can I be lonely with all this?" she replied, casting her hand in a general gesture around the lake. "Besides, I have you each weekend."

"Don't you ever think about men? Richmond is a wonderful town, but it's hardly thriving with available men. Unless you count Mr. Swarthmore."

Melissa had to laugh. Mr. Swarthmore was ninety, hard of hearing, and barely five feet tall. "He's exactly the kind of male I like best," she said firmly.

"Honey, you're hiding. . . ."

"Patrice—please?" she begged. The pain had returned to her eyes. Patrice hated to make her friend unhappy, but she needed to make her point. She felt responsible for introducing Melissa to the country retreat. Her intention had been good, but she'd never imagined that Mel would choose to rent a house of her own. Now she had to find a way to pry her loose from her rock of reclusion.

"Do you still miss him?" Patrice asked, approaching the painful subject directly. Secretly she cursed the day Jean-Pierre had entered Melissa's life. For all the joy he had caused her initially, she now paid dearly with grief, and guilt.

Melissa hesitated before answering. "I guess I'll always miss him," she admitted. "I—I keep thinking he'll come home. I keep waiting for someone to tell me it was a mistake, that Jean-Pierre is not dead." She paused, steadying her voice. Patrice waited patiently. "But it doesn't happen that way, does it?" she said, smiling ruefully.

"It won't last forever."

"I know. Sometimes a whole day passes when I haven't thought about him once." She was admitting something new. "It makes me feel terribly guilty," she added. She didn't tell the whole truth. Lately, she had been surprised to find entire weeks could pass without a painful memory.

"There's no winning, is there?" Patrice grimaced.

"But you have to put it behind you. You have to think about marrying again—"

"No," Melissa interrupted definitely. "Jean-Pierre has my heart."

"But he—"

"And I'm not going to dig it up to have it broken again. I'll never love again," she finished sternly. The tears brimming in Melissa's eyes belied her severe tone; her thick lashes matted as they closed to blot them.

"I'm sorry, Mel," Patrice said quietly, rummaging through her handbag for a tissue. Melissa dried her eyes, and blew her nose discreetly. "Have you at least thought about when you'll perform again?"

She glanced down at her scarred hand. "I'll never perform again," Melissa said stonily.

"Does your hand still bother you?"

"It will never be the same."

"But I've heard you! You're every bit as good as you ever were, maybe better. Do you think if Jean-Pierre were alive he'd want his brilliant protégée locked away in a barn?" she prodded. "Why do you spend all your time practicing if you aren't ever going to perform again? Who are you playing for, night after night?" Patrice demanded.

"For myself."

"Why, honey," Patrice started. "That's about the most selfish thing you've ever said. How dare you keep all your talent to yourself? Jean-Pierre would smack your bottom."

"My selfishness was responsible for his—" she started. Patrice waited for Melissa to finish her sentence. She knew it must be awful living with such guilt, even if it were entirely unfounded. "He might still be alive if I hadn't performed at that party." Her mouth tightened into a thin line of self-admonishment.

"You still believe that, don't you?"

"I do," she said softly. "Once I had both love and music. I tried to have more. I wanted success. Affirmation. I wanted to play for the whole world. I should have been content . . . but I was so sure I could have it all."

"But you can!"

"No. I should have been satisfied with what I had. Now I have nothing." The sun disappeared behind a heavy mass of clouds. Melissa sat up straight in the boat. "Let's go home," she said quietly. "I'm tired."

"All right," Patrice conceded. She would have to be patient. She knew Melissa would come out of her shell eventually, but it was hard to sit by and watch a beautiful girl locked away when there were plenty of men who would love to meet her. Patrice watched the muscles tighten in Melissa's arms as she lifted the oars to the boat and rowed back to shore. Her eyes were dry now—there would be no more tears today—but her glassy stare off into the distance made Patrice's skin tingle with sadness.

Melissa expertly docked and tied the boat to the railing.

"What are you doing this afternoon?" Patrice asked.

"I thought I would attack the weeds in my garden. They are winning in competition with the vegetables. Do you want to have dinner with me?"

"I can't tonight. I have a friend coming from the city."

"Oh, yeah? Who is he?" she asked, her eyes flickering with curiosity.

"Just Kenneth," Patrice offered offhandedly. "I thought I'd broil shrimp. I can't ruin that."

"Do you want vegetables from the garden?"

"No, thanks. I'd overcook them, or something. I want to impress him, not show him what a klutz I am."

"You'll impress him, all right, even if you serve burnt water."

Patrice had more men after her than she knew what to do with. She treated them all well, but she never let them get very close. At twenty-nine, her primary interest was her work. It was going to take somebody very special and determined to refocus her attention.

"Want to stop by after dinner for coffee?" Patrice asked. Seeing Melissa's skepticism rising, she added, "He won't recognize you. He's entirely nonmusical . . . even though Leonard Bernstein was an actor."

Melissa rippled with laughter. "Nope, you're stuck with him alone. I'm working on 'Le Déclaration' tonight.

"Your constant love."

"My constant love."

Patrice shrugged. "Well, you're going to miss out on some really bitter coffee." They laughed.

"Help me lift this boat out of the water," Melissa bade. "We can eat lunch on the deck."

Melissa felt restless after Patrice left, and warning the weeds of her deadly intention, she unpacked the hoe and gloves from the wheelbarrow. Perspiration beaded on her upper lip as she bent to work in the sun, and glancing around the empty yard, she slipped her shirt over her head. Her shoulders were faintly red, but her back, which she turned toward the sun as she planted corn, was a deep brown.

When the last seeds had been covered and watered, Melissa shifted to weed the spinach and lettuce. As she deftly pulled the intruders from between the rows, the steady, unhurried rhythm relaxed her thoroughly. Her thoughts drifted from subject to subject as the clouds moved shadows across the vast lawn.

She was so far engrossed in her daydreams that the car from the road was halfway up her driveway before she heard it.

Embarrassed to be caught without her shirt, she turned her back to the driver, and retrieved her shirt from the wheelbarrow handle. Quickly, she pulled it over her disheveled hair, mildly amused to have been caught bare-chested.

"My God!" the driver said, as Melissa sauntered toward the shiny red sports car. "I stopped to ask the bare-backed 'boy' about the farm for sale," he explained to her. He ran his eyes over her figure. Even in faded blue jeans and a dirt-bespeckled T-shirt, her face void of makeup, she was far more beautiful than any of the sophisticated women he knew in New York. She was as exquisite and unspoiled as the land she worked on. "But now I'm far more interested in the owner," he admitted.

"I'm flattered," Melissa answered boldly, surprising herself. If he had known her, she thought, he would have seen that she was blushing, but the confidence in her voice disguised the color in her cheeks. "Are you in the habit of buying people's homes?"

His blue eyes dazzled in the sunlight. "Now I have to confess, I didn't really stop with the intention to buy your farm," he admitted. Her bemused, direct gaze deserved his candor. "I've passed this piece of property for years. . . . I've always been curious to see inside the cedar barn. Why are you selling it?"

"I'd never sell this farm," Melissa told him, digging her toe into the grass. "Even if I owned it," she added, laughing.

"You don't own the farm?" He looked confused. "Who does?"

"Mr. and Mrs. Delaney. I rent from them."

"And you say it's not for sale?" he inquired, clearly perplexed.

Melissa shook her head. "No."

"Then why the sign?" he asked.

"What sign?" Melissa quizzed.

"The sign at the edge of the property," he said. Melissa left his side. "Along by the road," he called after her, as she hurried in that direction.

He matched her long-legged stride through the orchard. "I hardly ever come to this edge of the property," she explained, "it's so big and this part's my least favorite, it's so near the road." The sight of a wooden sign staked into the ground stopped her nervous chatter. Her heartbeat quickened as she dashed the last hundred yards. "FOR SALE," it read. Underneath, in equally large print, was Mr. Delaney's phone number.

"I'm sure sorry to be the one to bear the bad news," the man said, standing between Melissa and the sign. The dazed look on her pretty face nearly broke his heart.

"I guess it's better to know . . . but he never even

told me!" she said, turning angry. She searched this man's eyes for some kind of solution to the dilemma, and saw that he shared her feeling of injustice. His compassion made her feel less wronged.

"Maybe there's some kind of mistake," he suggested. "Maybe he's selling another piece of land, and posted the sign here to attract attention. People do that sometimes."

Melissa shook her head. "I don't think he owns any other land. But maybe . . . I'll call him . . . come on. He must have known I could never afford to buy the place," Melissa admitted, dialing the four digits.

"Hello, Mrs. Delaney? Sorry to bother you but I just saw the sign. . . ."

Mrs. Delaney explained the reason for the sale at length . . . her husband's health . . . their return to England . . . the national health plan. . . . They had stopped by to tell her, but she hadn't been at home. They had intended to phone her later that evening.

Melissa listened halfheartedly, unconsciously studying the man standing opposite her. He was exceedingly handsome, but what impressed Melissa most was how at ease he looked in her home.

"She said I could have first option to buy," Melissa said, hanging up the phone, "but they require a ten-thousand-dollar down payment. And even if I could spare it from my savings, I couldn't manage the monthly payments." She leaned dejectedly against the high stool in the kitchen.

"Maybe the new owner will let you continue to rent?" he offered, straddling a chair.

"Maybe," Melissa said softly, as if contemplating the

possibility, yet she knew the unlikelihood of finding a new owner who wouldn't recognize her, or ask of her too many questions. With Melissa's luck, Leonard Bernstein would buy the farm. "Mrs. Delaney said she'd had three calls today already. The place will be sold in a week," she said, her exasperation fully exposed.

"I have a feeling whoever buys it is going to have his well-water poisoned," he said, hoping to bring a smile to her worried countenance.

Melissa laughed deviously. "That's sure how I feel right now!" she said vehemently. His horrified expression made her smile at herself. "But then I'm revealing the worst side of myself, aren't I?" she said apologetically. "You don't know me well enough to know I'm perfectly harmless."

"I'd agree with the 'perfect,' but you mean you aren't dangerous?"

"Hardly!" She laughed nervously, and caught his eye. In the sunlight she had noticed that his eyes were bright and vibrant, but in the soft indoor light, at such a closeness, the blue darkened to violet. He stared directly into her own eyes. His mouth twitched into a capricious smile.

"I haven't a clue why I thought you were a boy," he said. His words were ones of wonder.

Melissa feigned disappointment. "Not even a man?" she teased. He just shook his head, his thick hair falling onto his forehead. There was something powerful about this man. His good looks were undeniable, but it was more than that. She examined the lines of his face for a clue: strong yet sensitive, an aristocratic nose that led to a sculptured mouth; his full and senuous bottom lip curled into a smile as she studied him. He was strikingly tall, several inches past six feet, Melissa guessed, judging from the distance he surpassed her own height; the hair at his temples were silver, distinguishing an otherwise boyish appeal.

"What brings you through Richmond?" she asked. "It's clear you don't live around here," she remarked assuredly.

"How can you tell?" he asked.

"Your clothes give you away." He was dressed casually, but in a style that would admit him to the fashion-conscious circles in Manhattan. "You'd never dress like that if you lived around here." The weekend residents were so anxious to fit into the small-town atmosphere that they went to great expense to wear sweaters so tattered only the most frugal of blue-bloods could match.

"I was on my way to Tanglewood," he explained. "But may I change my mind to watch you garden?" The amusement in his eyes lit up his entire face. He liked this woman and the immediate affinity between them. It was easy to be with her; as with old friends meeting after a long separation who find that no time had lapsed, their rapport was instantaneous.

"I'm taking applications for weed pickers," she told him.

"I was thinking more along the lines of official overseer."

"The feudal system was abolished on this here farm years ago."

"Am I allowed to work with my shirt off, too?"

Melissa blushed. "Sure. I'll even lend you my

gloves." She had already noticed his strong, muscular back; imagined the deep tanned skin. Why was it so easy to joke with this man? And why was she inviting him into her garden?

He glanced at his watch. "Unfortunately, I'll have to take a rain check. This is one of those weekends where every minute is promised. But save me some weeds, okay? I'll be back."

"Sure you will," she said. "Hard work comes along, and all the barnyard animals disappear."

"I said I'll be back, my little red hen."

"In time for supper, no doubt!"

"Now that's an invitation I would love to accept," he said.

Melissa reddened. She hadn't meant to extend an invitation at all. Or had she? Did she care if he returned? She knew he wouldn't.

"Wish I didn't have plans," he said, interrupting her thoughts.

Had he sensed her ambivalence? Why was she feeling both relief and regret that he was leaving? It had been a long time since she had felt this stirring beneath her breast, not since—

Suddenly Melissa checked her emotions, bringing them back into control. How stupid of her to lose her head over a total stranger, to compare him to Jean-Pierre. This man was attractive, she was willing to admit, and there was something easy about his nature that precluded her reserve, but he was not Jean-Pierre. No one could ever be. In a minute he would leave. She would forget him. She'd return to her solitude and the solace of her music.

He watched the gleam disappear from her eyes, a

glaze replacing the familiarity. He wondered what he had done.

"I hope you find a farm to buy," she said, attempting indifference.

He listened to the quality of her voice as much as to her words. He hated to leave. He hated for her to finish speaking.

She dusted her hand free of dirt, then extended it. "Good-bye," she said softly.

He squeezed her delicate hand. "Sorry to bear the bad news."

There was nothing else to say.

At the end of the driveway he raised his hand and waved. She waved back, leaning nonchalantly against her hoe.

He was tempted to cancel his evening engagement, but he knew he couldn't. Too many people were counting on him. As always. When would he ever have time for himself again—time to include real beauty in his life? His thoughts were steeped in this woman when he reached the highway. God, she was radiant. He wondered what in the world kept such a beauty isolated so far from civilization?

"I'll be back," he spoke aloud, his voice caught in the wind and carried away. He shifted into fifth gear and sped out of sight down the highway.

Melissa toyed with the hoe in the middle of her yard for several minutes after he left, trying to compose her thoughts. Finally she shrugged her shoulders, returned to her garden for the rest of her tools, then trudged back up the hill to her house.

She cooked herself a simple dinner, wishing Patrice

hadn't been engaged that night. She straightened the house for a second time that day, then put herself to bed, checking a book from the shelves. At ten thirty she shut off the lights, not understanding the intense pang of loneliness surging inside her chest. She thought about the distressing news that the farm was for sale, but her thoughts didn't stay with the misery. Instead, they drifted back to the man who had brought her the news, and as little as she liked the news he had brought, she couldn't help but smile when she remembered his shining blue eyes and the trust she had felt from his first sympathetic smile.

CHAPTER EIGHT

No matter what Melissa did during the next two days, the emptiness never left entirely. She had talked again with Mr. Delaney, but there was no altering the fact that the farm was for sale, and that she wasn't the one who would buy it. It was just too expensive. True, she *might* not have to move. Still, it was hard to sit patiently when the future was unsettled, and unknown.

Saturday morning she conceded to have breakfast with Patrice and Kenneth, and though he didn't recognize her, she found that their company did little to erase her melancholy. She left them before noon to return home, to exhaust the weeds, and herself, in the garden.

At five o'clock, when she left the garden with a basket full of vegetables that would complement the pasta she was planning for dinner, she left somewhat less anxious.

She showered off the dirt and humidity and dressed in a white oxford cotton shirt and an ankle-length cornflower-blue skirt. Leaving her feet bare, she poured herself a glass of wine and stretched out across the sofa to listen to the afternoon news on the radio. But she was too restless to lie passive. She shut off the radio and turned to her piano, hoping the concentration required for a Beethoven sonata would settle her nerves. The "Appassionata," as always, did the trick, and soon she was absorbed in a difficult passage, her thoughts free of the man she had met days before. Even Jean-Pierre, who had been haunting her mind of late, disappeared. She was alone with her music and at peace with herself at last.

When she finished, she sat drenched in an exhausted calm. She nearly jumped out of her skin when the silent aftermath was interrupted by a timid knock on her door.

"Come in," she called. She hadn't expected to see Patrice again today, but maybe she needed to borrow something. The store in Richmond closed early Sunday evening. The door opened, and Melissa didn't quite know how to gauge the emotion that stirred in her at the sight of this already familiar man.

"Ready to pick weeds?" he asked, aware that this moment was awkward for them both. He had broken an important engagement to see her again. But he had had to, had been able to think of nothing but her all weekend. He'd spent the drive from Stockbridge to Richmond figuring out a good introductory line, but as he reached her house, parked his car on the hill, and heard the first chords from the piano, he couldn't even remember his name. He stood outside her house, and in the yard newly blossomed with poppies and day-lilies, he strained to hear the pathos behind every note. The more he listened, the more he recognized her expertise.

There was something vaguely familiar about her style, and he wondered with whom she had studied. One didn't become that good alone. But why was she hiding out here, in the middle of nowhere?

Melissa smiled as she left the piano bench to greet him. "Never thought I'd see you again."

"I never turn down an invitation to dinner," he lied. "And there is still an hour of daylight left, if you want help with those weeds."

Melissa noted his fine silk shirt, the cut of his French-tailored linen trousers. "Let's wait until it rains, until the garden is really muddy, so we can really ruin your clothes." Her eyes gleamed mischievously.

"Well, I tried. It's up to you," he said earnestly. He attempted to gauge her expression. "Should I go?" he asked tentatively. "I didn't mean to barge in on you."

"Sure you did, but it's all right. I wasn't busy. Would you like coffee?" He nodded gratefully. "I might even heat it up if you're nice."

He watched her disappear into the kitchen; then, for the first time, he took account of his surroundings.

It was a beautiful, carefully decorated house with the rustic quality of the old barn intact. The living room had a cathedral ceiling. The walls were decorated in turn-of-the-century watercolors and antique etchings, mostly French, he noted, but some Italian. The furniture was sparse but tastefully arranged, over the wide-planked, highly polished floorboards. The open areas were partially covered with quality rugs. The expansive room was divided by a couch in front of a massive stone fireplace; the far side of the room held Melissa's mahogany grand piano, as at home in this setting as its player obviously had been at its keyboard. Bernard approached the old Steinway shyly, and fingered the worn ivory keys. Melissa returned to the room after a half-dozen notes.

"Do you play?" she asked.

"A little. Do you?" he asked.

"A little bit," she lied, and handed him a mug full of steaming coffee.

"It's a beautiful piano," Bernard stated, as much for something to say as to compliment the grand old instrument.

"Thank you. It's precious to me." She seated herself carefully on the couch and invited him to join her.

"Can I entice you to have dinner with me tonight at Wheatleigh?" he asked.

"I thought you had plans all weekend."

"I changed them."

"Just like that?"

"Just like that," he answered. "What about dinner? And a concert?"

"Gosh, like a date," Melissa said, then wished she hadn't.

"Much more important than that."

"I don't even know your name," Melissa protested.

"That's easy enough to remedy. I'm Bernard Van Atman," he said formally.

She accepted his hand, recalling the first time.

"Melissa Dennison," she exchanged, using her maiden name, as she habitually did in the few introductions she made of late.

"Well, Miss Dennison—I assume it is Miss, or have you a husband hiding in the other room?"

"My husband died in a car accident, a few years

ago," Melissa answered, more easily than she would have thought possible.

"In that case, how about dinner and a concert? We have time if we hurry."

"That's a hard offer to turn down, but I think not. I don't go out much, really." She watched his face drop in disappointment. "But I was planning *linguini à la rustica* for supper, and you're welcome to join me, if you think you can stand gobs of garlic."

"I think I would *love* gobs of garlic, as long as I'm not alone in committing the offense."

"Good. Are you hungry now?"

Bernard wanted to prolong this evening for as long as possible. "I'm hungry, but not starved. Can I drive into town for a bottle of wine?"

Melissa chuckled. "Have you seen this town?" Bernard nodded. "The store *might* have a couple bottles of domestic beer, if it were open. But it's thirty miles round trip to the nearest store that sells wine. Besides, I have a bottle of Frascati that I was planning to open with dinner. And we can catch the concert tonight on the radio, if you like. I was planning to listen."

"Terrific. Dinner's settled," Bernard said. "Now, if I promise not to bid on the property, would you mind showing me around outside? I'm curious to see the estate."

Melissa glanced at the clock on the wall. "I'd be proud to show you around. I need parsley from the garden anyway."

"But no weeds?"

"Nope. They aren't ripe yet."

For the next half hour, while the sun took its leave

from the sky, Bernard followed her across the carefully manicured grounds surrounding her house, appreciating the gentle sway of her hips as much as the setting. He was relieved to find she didn't associate him with the unfortunate news of the farm sale. Melissa showed him inside the three-story cedar barn; the east wall of the old haybarn was pecked full of woodpecker holes, letting light into an otherwise dark room, like a thousand stars in a blackened sky. Melissa had poured them each a glass of cool white wine, which they sipped as they walked. She showed him the pond, the apple trees, the high-windowed, elongated sheds that had been designed originally for horses. He stood close beside her as she explained about the shed that housed goats. "Billy goats," she had called them, eliciting a deep round of laughter from him that turned contagious, and they both laughed for several minutes, finally wiping dry their eyes, as the laughter subsided. Two adults . . . such laughter . . . they giggled like school kids, and that started the rounds of side-aching laughter again. Melissa finally gave up trying to control her shaking, and they headed back to the house, exhausted.

She declined his offer to help cook dinner, and ordered him out of the kitchen.

"Do you mind if I play your piano?"

"No. Make yourself at home," she said. "There is sheet music in the bench."

While Melissa prepared dinner, Bernard sat at the piano. She would know soon enough that he knew something about music, that he knew how to play as well as listen, an unexpected advantage of his job.

"You play well," Melissa remarked, appearing at the doorway to the kitchen. "Do you play often?"

"I try to play with some regularity," he answered truthfully. His schedule these days was impossibly busy and there was little time for music, or for any other simple pleasure.

"What do you do for a living?" she asked.

"I'm in publishing," he said. "And you?"

"I'm an indolent farmer," she quipped, before disappearing back into the kitchen.

They carried their plates out of doors to sit under the darkening sky; an occasional star burned a million miles away; a pair of candles lit their faces in complementary hues.

"Delicious," Bernard proclaimed.

The pasta was rich in texture, the sauce perfectly seasoned; the wine distinct, yet not overpowering. In between bites Bernard told her about his work, the onus of an inherited business, the pressure to turn commercial and his struggle to retain integrity.

"What kind of books do you publish?"

"The ones other companies won't risk buying."

"What exactly do you mean?"

"Well," Bernard started, trying to find a way to explain. "Have you ever heard of a record company called Amazing Records?"

"No, why?"

"Their motto is: If it's a hit, it's Amazing!" Melissa giggled. "That's what I would have named the company, if it hadn't already been named to memorialize my great-great grandfather."

"Are any of the books you publish successful?"

"I think they are all successful. Are they well written? Yes. Do they make me a ton of money? No."

"I see."

"The premise of our company is to make sure a present-day Shakespeare can get published, *even if* the books will never make back the cost of printing."

"Why do you take the risk?"

"Because I want to make sure my children—or your children—have the opportunity to read the quality prose written during our lifetime."

"My kids will probably be illiterate."

"Undoubtedly." He grinned broadly. "Nevertheless I want them to have the *opportunity* to read something literary if they want to. I mean, what if Hemingway hadn't been able to find a publisher for his works? *You* know the poverty and humiliation Beethoven faced. Aren't you thankful someone preserved his music?"

Melissa nodded thoughtfully. "But how can you afford to publish a book if you know it won't pay for itself?"

"Ahhhh, that's where Great-grandfather's hard work and wise investments come in. The business is financially solvent in its own right."

"Does that mean you are independently wealthy?"

Bernard smiled at her direct question. "As president of the firm, I'm allotted a respectable salary. But the company can buy just about any book it likes, and will continue to be able, unless I make a huge error in judgment. Even then, the trust funds are pretty hard to deplete."

"You must read constantly. Do you love your work?"

"I do," he answered quickly. "When I've discovered a brilliant manuscript, I am proud that my company will publish it as a quality, cloth-bound book—"

"For my children to read?"

"Exactly. It is important to me that great literature be given a voice in a too-commercial literary world."

"I would call *you* a 'success,' " Melissa said. "Defining 'success' as doing something worthwhile and gratifying."

Bernard thought about what she had said. "By your definition I would consider myself successful, too. Of course, there are parts of the job I could do without, like the endless socializing; even the pressure to *find* the quality manuscripts. Once again, my predecessors did most of the work. They established the company's reputation along with its name. Serious writers know to contact us. For instance, I recently found a manuscript on folklore that changed my perspective on early American history. I was actually fascinated to read history! But since folklore, by tradition, is verbal, it risks extinction if people forget . . . or lose interest. This young writer, Matt Drybas, spent years gathering stories from old sea-captains and railroad engineers. It took him eight years to write his book, and then he couldn't find a publisher."

Melissa shook her head. "That's too true to believe."

"And," Bernard continued, "the book is not only historically accurate, but sensitively written. I would hate for that book to be lost."

Melissa nodded her head. She was impressed by what she'd heard from Bernard. "I wish the music world had a philanthropist."

"If you search, you may find one. Are you looking

for someone to publish your music?" Maybe she was a composer; that would explain her solitude.

"No, I don't write music," she said. She didn't count the work she did on Arbour's compositions as original. "I'm an indolent farmer, remember? But there are a lot of fine musicians who can't find an audience. A benefactor who cared about quality music, on the scale which you describe, would mean a great deal."

"Well . . . maybe those children of yours will strike it rich and establish a fund for serious musicians."

His words struck a deep chord in Melissa. "Wouldn't that be nice," she answered remotely. "Wouldn't that be nice."

They finished dessert before the air turned cold. Melissa had mixed fruit with brandy, and it warmed their insides as delicately as it heated their desire to know each other better. She had just suggested they move indoors— the wind was threatening to extinguish their candle light—when the phone rang. Melissa nearly jumped out of her chair, and she had to admit she was still nervous.

"Shall I wait out here until you've finished talking?" he asked politely.

"No. Come on in. I'll only be a minute."

She answered the phone by the third ring. "Hi, Mel. Did I wake you?" It was Patrice.

"No, I was up," Melissa answered enigmatically.

"Good, I hoped you would be. Kenneth just left. I burned dinner and gave him heartburn, surely." Patrice's voice sounded easy from a good deal of wine. Melissa could hear her settling in for a long conversation.

"Trice—"

"Yes?"

"Can I call you tomorrow?"

"Sure, honey. Are you all right?"

"I'm fine. But I have company."

"Really?" Melissa could hear the interest rise in Patrice's voice. "Who is it?"

"Just a friend. Can I call you in the morning?"

"If you don't, I'll never forgive you."

"Good night, Patrice."

"Good night!" she sang.

Bernard was pouring himself a second brandy when Melissa reentered the room. "Important?" he asked.

"No. Just a friend." She watched his eyebrows rise in interest.

"Must be a close friend to call you so late." He had checked his watch while she was on the phone. It was after eleven. Maybe he had been mistaken. Perhaps she wasn't alone after all. He didn't want to pry, but he had to know.

Melissa relieved his doubts easily, without even knowing how important it was to him. "My best friend, Patrice. I've known her for—gosh, nearly twelve years. We met our last year in high school."

"That must make you—thirty?" he guessed.

"Pretty close. Twenty-seven. Going on eighty."

"I know what you mean," he said. Bernard had just turned thirty-eight. Some days that felt like a hundred. But not today. Melissa got up to turn off the radio. They had listened from the terrace: Mozart live from Tanglewood delicately orchestrated the fireflies dotting the darkened meadow.

"Leave it on," he said.

The switch clicked. "I'll put on something else," she said. "I have little patience for Stravinsky's frenzy, especially after Mozart." She flipped through a high pile of records stocked beside the stereo. "Do you like any other kind of music, other than classical?" She leafed through another stack. "If I can find it, I've got all kinds."

Bernard studied her slender figure, her quick hands. He thought a minute before requesting. "Do you have any Ella Fitzgerald?"

She looked up in surprise. 'Uh-huh," she said, chewing her lower lip. She reached for another pile of albums, pausing at two or three before selecting one. "Gershwin?" she asked, holding up a record.

"Perfect. Just what I would have chosen."

She adjusted the volume and returned to Bernard, but chose to sit in the bentwood rocker opposite the couch. Ella's pure voice rang clear throughout the room as she sang of winter, then spring, happy one minute, sorrowful the next, in London, San Francisco, Paris.

"You seem awfully far away," Bernard said.

"I am," Melissa answered candidly. "Here, is this better?" she asked, stretching her long, slender legs beside him on the sofa.

"Thanks a lot!" he said indignantly. "And I thought you had manners."

"Nope. You had the wrong idea." They were relaxed from the wine, at ease with one another.

"I'd say." He looked at her bare feet. The nails were manicured; the arch gracefully high.

"Is there any chance of them being clean?" she asked, watching him observing her feet.

" 'Fraid not," he said, lifting both feet into one large, strong hand. "I'd say we are going to have to operate to get them clean."

She laughed, but didn't try to remove her feet. "If you think I am going to let an old publisher attempt surgery on my feet, you've got another think coming."

"An old publisher!"

"Well . . ." she shrugged.

He tickled the bottom of her foot.

"Stop it!" she cried.

"I think I'll brand you right about here," he teased, running his middle finger down her instep.

"Stop it!" she begged, managing to pull one foot away. He held on tightly to the other.

"I'll stop if you promise me one thing."

"No!" she laughed. "Stop it!" Her sides hurt from laughing.

"Come on, promise?"

"No!" she protested. He tickled again. "All right!" she cried. "Yes!" He stopped instantly. "Okay, mister. What's my promise got to be?" The room was quiet. Ella was warming up before beginning the next song.

"I want the next dance."

Melissa stared at him. Ella began to sing. "Guess you chose a good song," she said coyly.

"So good you might say I had planned the whole thing right to the minute." He held out his hand, which she accepted reticently, and rose to join him. She placed a hand shyly on his shoulder; his strong hand curled gently around her waist.

"Please, don't tickle me," she said quickly. "Promise?"

"I don't want to make you laugh." He pulled her a

little closer to him. They moved together slowly, a gentle sway to the music. Melissa sang along with Ella. "Gosh, it's so mushy," she said, her laughter starting to ripple.

"Shhh," he whispered. His mouth was very near her ear. "You can laugh during your song. This one's mine."

She didn't even try for a retort. She didn't even have to stifle the giggles that had threatened a minute earlier. She gave in, enjoyed his arms around her. She hadn't felt this safe in ages.

When the music finished, Bernard felt her slip away. He caught her at arm's length. "Don't run," he protested.

"I'm not," she assured him. "I'm just changing sides, for *my* song." His hands slid along her forearms as she moved, as if in slow motion, across the room to the stereo. The fine, large room held the music perfectly. She obviously knew what acoustics worked, and what music best filled the room.

She started the record and returned to his open arms. Without reservation she settled into his embrace; any thought given to holding herself back had dissolved. He clasped her hand down by his side; with his other arm he circled her small waist.

Melissa laced her fingers at the back of his neck, touching the hair at the top of his collar. Ella's slow, seductive voice embraced them both, as she sang about what Melissa was feeling.

Bernard couldn't have been more flattered if she had written the lyrics herself. He wanted her so badly he hurt. He knew he had to move cautiously or he'd scare this fragile beauty back into her shell. He would be patient . . . let her come to him. He only hoped it wouldn't be too long a wait.

He felt Melissa's body against him, and as if she had read his mind, she stopped dancing to study him. "You aren't so scary, are you."

"No," he said hoarsely. "You've spent a long time being scared, haven't you?"

"Yes."

"Too long?"

"Yes." Her chin quivered. "I'm not sure I can come out yet." Her voice was small, like a child's.

He held her close to him. "You know, I'm not going anywhere you won't like. If you want I'll let you lead entirely." They looked at each other, their faces only inches apart. He wanted desperately to kiss her, to envelop her pouting lower lip.

She looked up at him, searching his eyes for reassurance that loving him wouldn't hurt. "I'm frightened."

"I'll leave it up to you, madame," he said. "Whenever you're ready . . ." He could wait a long time for her, as long as he knew eventually she'd be his. He wouldn't risk rushing her. She was very important to him. He started to speak but it was unnecessary to say anything more. She knew what he was thinking. Already she knew him that well.

"Sounds safe enough to me," she said, taking his hand as the music started again. "But will you lead the dancing?"

"If you promise not to step on me with your dirty feet," he said. She punched him affectionately on the arm, and he pretended it hurt. When he held her close in his arms, his heart pounded so loudly he was sure she could hear it. She might have, except that her own heart pounded as loudly.

"Come," he said, leading her to the couch. The record had finished, and she had switched the radio back on. A Brahms symphony played softly in the background. She sat close beside him, her legs tucked beneath her. Bernard put his arm over the back of the sofa. "I feel like a damned kid in the movie theater, on my first date."

She giggled. "I feel funny, too. Because we are adults, things are supposed to be easy, but I feel adolescent inside. It's strange, but when I was a kid, I didn't think about what to do. It just happened. And now that I am adult, and have been through 'love,' I haven't a clue what to do."

Bernard let his hand rest on her shoulder. "I know what you mean."

"I'll bet you do. I know a man-around-town when I see one. You are as smooth as they come," she said, her hair falling in her face as she spoke.

"Now, wait a minute! I could say the same about you."

"Only about you it is true!"

He looked hurt. "What can I do to convince you I'm sincere? I can't erase my past, no matter how strongly I feel about you. Nor can you erase your past." She nodded, and frowned. "We just have to trust right now." They were sitting very close, face to face. He caressed her smooth skin with his fingers.

Melissa bit at her lower lip. "Can I forfeit the lead—momentarily?" Bernard looked puzzled. "Because," she explained, looking down at her lap, "I would like to kiss you. . . . If you leave it up to me, it might never happen."

"Ahhhh—" he said, lifting her face to meet his.

"But—" He stopped at her hesitation. "Can you do it when I am not expecting it?"

"Of course," he agreed, as if it were the most reasonable request he had ever heard, and lowered his hand to the couch.

"Whew!"

As she let out the breath, Bernard placed his mouth against hers. When she breathed again, it was from his mouth, and his kiss satisfied her more than any breath of fresh air. She languished in his arms, and he held her soft, supple body. He felt her melt, and he followed suit. There would have been no stopping his desire, even if he had tried. They gave in to their passion, exchanging kisses as if each new breath depended on fuel from the other. Instead of the passion outgrowing the kisses, it was patient, enjoying each new taste, texture; his tongue on her lips or exploring the inside of her mouth.

There was no need to hurry this love. It would ripen by degree. It might take weeks, even months, before she trusted him enough to let him stay the night, but they had time. And, on the other hand, it might not take so long. Neither of them had expected a kiss tonight. The kiss she gave him tonight was complete. No more empty nights with casual intimacies. No more waking up wishing he hadn't. They had taken the enviable first step in love. Already it was too late to turn back.

"Bernard?"

"Melissa?" They had ceased kissing minutes before,

but had held the embrace in silence. There was a lot to say, but neither knew how to say it, or what words to use. "What is it?" he asked again when she didn't speak. "Do you want me to leave?"

"Will you think me awful if I throw you out?"

"Of course." He smiled weakly. "But I'm afraid I understand. In fact, I think it's a good idea."

"Now, don't force your credibility."

"You're right!" On impulse they kissed again. "Will you invite me back?"

"No," she teased, but he looked miserable, as if he thought she meant to keep him away. "But you can invite yourself back, if you want. Let's make a date!" she said, sitting cross-legged now, like a school kid suggesting a cookout.

"Why don't you come to New York, and I'll show you a real night on the town."

Her smile faded as quickly as it had appeared. "No," she said simply.

He was sorry he had mentioned it. "Well, don't fade, my violet . . . it was just a suggestion. I'll make another one if you don't like that one."

"I'll never come to New York."

"Okay, that's all right, too. Now, how about a date up here? Can I take you out for dinner next weekend? I hear there is a great French restaurant in Hillsdale."

"No, I don't like to go out, even up here." Her old fear of recognition caused her to crawl back into her shell.

"Well, gosh, Miss Particular, what if I bring groceries and we'll cook it all right here? Or would you like to bite off my head and serve that on a platter?"

"Gosh—I wouldn't do that." Melissa giggled. "I'm a vegetarian."

"Yeah, I can tell. Not a cruel bone in your body. Tear a man's heart to shreds, but won't eat a dumb old fish."

"Oh, I eat fish, all right. And don't presume my motives are moral ones."

"All right. Fish it is. And what, may I ask, are your motives?"

"I'll tell you next week at dinner. I'm going to boot you out now. I have to get some sleep, or I'll be thick tomorrow."

"We wouldn't want that," he said, stretching his arms over his head as he stood. He was glad, as long as he had to leave, that her mood was revived. He had been afraid for a minute he had lost her.

He helped gather glasses from the table in the living room and followed her into the kitchen. He brushed his hand back through his hair and straightened his collar. "May I help you with these dishes?" he offered, very much at home in her kitchen.

"No, thanks. I'm going to let them sit tonight. I never wash a dish the same day I use it." He looked around the tidy kitchen. She had overstated her truancy. There were two or three glasses, aside from the ones they had used, and their dinner plates, but nothing else. Even the copper-bottomed cookware was polished and hanging attractively over the stove.

"Okay, then. I'm off."

She turned on the outside light. There was a big yellow moon hanging over the treetops. "May I call you tomorrow?" he asked, hating to leave.

She nodded. "If I don't answer, I'm in the garden."

"Just keep your shirt on, you hear? You never know who might drive by." He unfolded his cashmere sweater and fitted it over his head.

"Anything else?"

"Yes. I would like an affectionate, not to say a passionate, kiss good night. I have a very long ride before me."

"Poor Bernard! Let me kiss it all better." She lifted her face to meet his, and kissed his mouth, biting his lip playfully.

He didn't even try to lead this time, just enjoyed. "I'll call you tomorrow, Melissa," he said, releasing her from his arms. He stepped outdoors, the night air greeting him with a warm breeze.

"Are you awake enough to drive home?"

"I've never been so wide awake!" he answered regretfully.

"Good night!" she called. The interior light went on when he opened the car door. "Are you going to keep the top down? The radio said it might rain."

"I think I'll risk it, it's so nice out now." Together they looked up at the sky brilliant with stars. "Want to go for a quick ride?"

"I'm tempted, but I don't dare," she admitted. The next thing she knew she'd be inviting him to stay the night. She couldn't do that yet. Tonight it was important that he go. "*I'll* take a rain check." He closed the door to his car and fitted the key into the ignition. "Sorry I made you miss the concert at Tanglewood tonight," she called.

"I'm not. I didn't miss anything tonight."

He rolled down her steep gravel driveway. She had

waited until he was down the hill before switching off the porch light.

He could see the bedroom light switch on as he reached the paved road.

She was undressed and in bed by the time he reached the highway.

He was going to have to do a lot of explaining about where he had been tonight. He had skipped an important dinner with the wife of the late conductor Franz Ramoussevitsky, not to mention six or seven other "important" people. He had thought to call from Melissa's house when he found he could stay, but there was never a chance. He would have to explain the best he could. They would forgive him. They always did.

The sound of rain woke Melissa from a deep, peaceful sleep. The patter landed rhythmically on the slanted roof; she could hear the water's fall broken by the leaves on the maple tree. She glanced sleepily at her clock. It was four o'clock. Good, she thought, he'd be home by now. She didn't want him to get wet on her account.

She fell back into sleep, her arms wrapped around herself, dreaming of him. It had been a long time since she had dared to feel as deeply as she had tonight. It *hadn't* hurt. In fact, it had felt good, every delicious step of the way.

Her eyes dampened as she bade Jean-Pierre adieu. She knew she'd never stop loving him, but it was time for life to resume, and with it the passion Bernard had uncovered in her that night.

Bernard sat in his study, watching the rain. The ride home had given him time to think. He didn't have any answers yet, but the problems had become clear. He would find a way to have this woman in his life, always. . . . There were obstacles, yes, but they could master anything together. He fell asleep in his large leather chair, a stack of unopened mail in his lap. The rain pattered softly outside the window. The East River rose in swells to catch the drops, then carried them en masse down to the sea.

CHAPTER NINE

She had her car keys in one hand, and was halfway out the door when she remembered the grocery list on the kitchen counter. Normally she would have shopped from sight, picking up what looked good and then arranging it into meals as she thought appealing, but this week's shopping trip into town needed to be more precise. For one thing, Melissa had been so involved in her work this past week, inspired to complete "La Déclaration," that she had depleted her store of food. More importantly, Bernard was coming to dinner the following night, and would probably stay the weekend. This was a huge step, having known him for only one week, but from their numerous phone calls, she felt she knew him well. There was the question of where he'd sleep—she wasn't at all sure she was ready—but they'd face that problem together, as it arose. Right now her mind was on another basic need: food.

Melissa had carefully planned their meals so she wouldn't have to panic at the last minute if she wanted to make a soufflé and had run out of eggs. The list was long and required a dozen stops, but once she was finished, she could relax until he arrived, and get used to the idea of his company.

The sound of tires on the driveway interrupted her reverie.

Opening the door, she protested, "Hey! You're here a day early!"

"I have to admit you are right," he conceded, "but I just couldn't wait another day to see you. Do you mind too much?"

Melissa could only grin. She couldn't think of anyone she would rather have arrive a day early. "Fine with me, but you'll have to entertain yourself for a few hours. I'm off to shop for tomorrow's dinner. I have an important guest coming."

"Anyone I know?"

"Maybe. . . . Listen, I'm going to run ahead and get this shopping over with, so just make yourself at home. The coffee on the stove is fresh."

Bernard caught her by the waist. "Wait, I'd like to come with you, if you don't mind."

"Are you sure? Haven't you done enough driving for one day?"

"Not at all. I'd love to see where you shop." He could see her hesitate. "Worried that the neighbors might talk?" he teased.

"Hardly!" she retorted. "It's just—" She searched for the right words. "It's just that—It's that I'm—" She stopped, removed herself from his arms, and started again. "I'm a bit off balance by your early arrival."

"I hoped to catch you working outdoors without your shirt."

"Some plan! Once was enough!"

"I hope not!" he taunted. "Now, let's go. We've got shopping to do."

"If you can stand it, you're welcome to come along."

"I'm ready. We'll take my car."

"Only if you'll let me drive."

"I'd have my first tour of the Berkshires under no one else's care."

The trip gave Bernard a chance to see where Richmond lay in relationship to the other hill towns. The main road to Tanglewood was all he'd known previously. It would take months to know the roads intimately: the old cow paths hadn't been improved except to be paved, and they forked and curved without logic. One town was separated from another by stretches of farmland. They stopped at the dairy in Lenox for milk and cream and at a farm in Great Barrington for eggs, cheese, and two tubs of yogurt. The milk they bought had been in the cow *that* very morning; it clanked in quart bottles in the rear seat.

Melissa sped down a dirt road through the woods until they reached another white provincial town. A dozen buildings lined each side of Main Street; the fountain at the town rotary; the brick bank; the high-steepled church at one end of town and the post office at the other end repeated themselves town after town, until all the errands had been finished, and Bernard was restless to return home.

"I warned you," Melissa said, easing down into the seat of the car and lifting her foot from the gas pedal to reduce the speed. Cloud wisps floated overhead, and the intermittent heat from the sun felt good on her shoulders. There was no reason to hurry home. She felt relaxed, now that the shopping was finished. The number of houses decreased, and the cars on the narrowed roads vanished. They were still ten miles from home. "I really live in the sticks, don't I?" Melissa admitted.

"*We* live in the sticks. Don't forget you have a house-guest all weekend."

Melissa took her eyes off the road just long enough to catch his eye. She lifted her right hand from the gear shift and curled her fingers around his forearm. "What part of the tour did you like best," she said dreamily.

Bernard settled back into his seat, thinking over the sights they'd just seen. "I think it was seeing Officer Obie directing traffic in the middle of Main Street!"

Melissa laughed. "Quite a traffic jam, wasn't it?"

"I got a kick out of seeing Alice's Restaurant, even if it is defunct."

"With all the history and culture I included on the tour, you liked those two things the best?" She had stopped by The Mount so he could see where Edith Wharton had once lived. They had seen Melville's home and Hawthorne's, not to mention the Vanderbilts', and the Wildes'.

"Can I help it if I lack cul-ture?" Wait a minute—stop here."

Melissa halted on the brakes. "I thought you wanted to go home," she said.

"I do. But we forgot something." He jumped out of the car and disappeared inside a farm stand they had passed on the way into town. He was back in an instant, waving a bouquet of colorful spring flowers. "In case no one gave you flowers this week."

"I've never had so many flowers in one week!" Day after day the florist had had to drive from the neighboring town to deliver still another arrangement of flowers. Monday Bernard had sent her red roses, long stemmed and dark leafed. Tuesday the white roses arrived. By Wednesday, when the florist returned with an armful of purple and mauve iris, he had quite an interest in Melissa's mysterious admirer, and by Thursday, when he delivered the basket of violets, he had gathered the local gossip on the flowering romance. "You have all my neighbors wondering what's going on," she told Bernard.

"Good, they need something to rejoice about. There probably hasn't been a good love affair in Richmond in ten or twelve years."

"Oh, I don't know about that," Melissa challenged. He looked at her suspiciously. "I mean, Patrice has some pretty handsome men calling on her," she explained.

"But the townfolk have never had a chance to talk about you, have they?" His eyes twinkled. "You've always been private and discreet, right?"

"You give me too much credit! My life has been too dull for them to bother with."

"I'll bet they do wonder . . . a beautiful girl alone in the country. I'll bet as many wives hate you as husbands love you."

Melissa had to laugh. "You've got it all wrong. I don't even know the women in town. No one but Patrice has ever been inside my house, except for the Delaney's, that is."

"You're right. I had no idea."

Melissa grinned slyly. "That's why I was so perplexed when you showed up today. Even a planned guest is extremely unusual."

"Have there been no men in your life since your husband's death?"

"None. No one before or after. To be honest, I never expected to fall in love again. I thought that part of my life was over."

"How do you feel now?" he asked seriously, adding, "Now that we've known each other all of one week."

"That's my point. It's all happened so fast, and without my being able to stop it, really. I keep thinking something has gone wrong, but when I try to think of what it is, I can't find anything I'd like to change."

"I can think of several things I'd like to change," he said deviously.

"I dare you to try to shock me with your lurid imagination!"

"I was thinking . . . I'd like to change your last name to Van Atman," he said softly. "But now that I've heard evidence of *your* lurid wonderings . . . I think I'd rather change other things first."

"I don't even want to hear your ideas," Melissa protested loudly. "First you woo me with flowers and get the town talking about us, and now you're talking about changing my name! That's what I mean! It's all as crazy as it is wonderful."

"As long as you are enjoying yourself, that's all that matters. We can sort it out when we get bored. Honey, keep your eyes on the road or we won't live to startle the landlord."

"And to think all this goodness came out of such bad news."

"Strange how spring follows winter each year."

"But there is always fall after summer," she said, remembering the end of the warm days and balmy nights.

"True. Maybe winter won't be quite so long or cold in each other's company. And if it is, maybe we won't mind it so much for the warmth we can generate together. Who needs the sun when we rotate around each other?"

"Boy, are you nuts!"

He bowed his head, as if she had paid him a high compliment.

Melissa leaned over to inhale the flowers. "They smell wonderful. Where am I going to put them?"

"I'd suggest in your bedroom."

"Are these flowers a ploy to get into my bedroom?" she charged, trying to keep a straight face.

"Of course not!" he answered, looking wounded. "And if they were, would they work?"

"They are awfully pretty," she said vaguely, pulling the car into the driveway. "And they'll look beautiful on the bedstand. Thank you, Bernard, for all the flowers you sent."

"You're welcome," he said softly. "By the way, while we're on the subject of your bedroom . . ." His voice was serious, and when Melissa glanced over at him she saw his face had also turned serious.

"What about my bedroom?"

"You are not to worry about our sleeping arrangements," he said at the door to her house. It bothered him that she might feel invaded. The fact that they lived in different towns made overnight arrangements necessary, but he didn't want her to feel obliged to share her bed with him. He wanted *that* invitation to come from her heart, and not until she was ready. "I have the perfect solution for maintaining your respectability!"

"Pray tell!"

"I've got my camping equipment in the trunk of the car," he informed her. "No one can gossip about two kids camping out back of your house."

"What a terrific idea," Melissa said happily, setting a bag of groceries on the counter. She liked the idea enormously. It took care of an awkward decision that she wasn't prepared to make yet. "Is that an invitation to sleep out under the stars with you?"

"I have two sleeping bags. . . ."

"That sounds like adequate protection. Zipped up to our chins!"

"They zip together," he added dangerously.

"Promises, promises, promises. All I hear is talk!"

Bernard threw back his head and howled with laughter, till it echoed off the pond. Melissa never heard the echo. She was wrapped in Bernard's arms, engrossed in his kiss. All her senses turned to the quality of his mouth pressed against hers, and the passion churning inside her heart.

"What do you have planned for dinner tonight?"

"I don't know. Do you have any good ideas?"

"What if I catch us a fish or two from the pond?"

"Yummm. I could put these things away."

She finished in the kitchen, and in a few minutes she joined Bernard at the pond. "Catch anything?"

"Two bass. I'm trying for a third."

Melissa sat at the bank and watched him. He had stripped off his shirt and shoes and knelt against the middle seat in the boat, not far from shore. He gave all his concentration to catching their dinner. Melissa lay back and listened to the jay birds' siesta call. Clouds shifted overhead. The water rippled.

"I've got one!" Bernard leaped from his knees to his feet. The yellow boat wobbled beneath him. "I think he's a big one."

The line pulled straight out. As Bernard reeled it in, he lost his footing on the slippery bottom. The boat nearly tipped over, and Bernard fell into the pond, losing his rod and reel to the fish.

Melissa scrambled to her feet.

"Are you all right?" Melissa called. "Can I help?"

"Just don't laugh," he said, reaching the shore and climbing onto dry land. His trousers clung wet to his legs and Melissa could see the outline of his muscles. Water beaded on his chest, caught and glistened in his tangled hair.

Once Melissa saw that he was all right, it was hard not to laugh. "He got away," Melissa remarked.

"With my reel and your boat," he added, shaking his wet hair on Melissa. "Wouldn't you like a swim? The water's warm, once you get used to it."

"I don't have my suit." Melissa dipped her toe. "I'd have to go back to the house."

"Don't bother." Seeing she was merely shy, he offered her his T-shirt. "Wear this instead," he prompted. "I'll even avert my eyes while you change," he said, turning his back to her.

Melissa pulled her thin cotton shift over her head and replaced it with his T-shirt. She dropped her panties to the ground next to Bernard's clothes, and self-conscious of her bare exterior, she bolted into the water. She surfaced just in time to see Bernard dive in after her.

She felt him grab her ankle and put his other hand on her waist; she pulled away easily and swam across the small lake. Bernard followed.

When he caught her again she was in the middle of the pond where she couldn't reach the bottom and had to tread water. He wrapped his arms around her waist. She could tell that he had stripped off his wet trousers on shore, but for some reason the water engulfing them helped make respectable their near nakedness.

"I didn't know they stocked mermaids in this pond," Bernard said, sliding his hand down Melissa's hip.

"With kicking fins," Melissa warned.

"I understand," he said, staying his hand.

Melissa didn't struggle. She liked him to hold her this closely, and the setting was innocuous enough to keep their embrace innocent, like lights dimmed before love-making. He touched his lips to her eyelids. Melissa raised her mouth to meet his, and felt his skin cool against her cheek.

"What do you say we set up the tent before dinner?" Bernard suggested, emerging from their kiss as if his thoughts had raced ahead. "That way we won't have to hurry the rest of the evening."

"Good idea," Melissa said, floating on her back toward shore. "Now, remember, you promised not to look," she added, touching ground. Bernard let her go ahead, submerging himself one last time.

"Hey!" he called indignantly. "No fair staring!"

"*I* made no promises not to look," Melissa taunted.

"Just you wait, lady. . . . I was going to pretend not to notice the wet spots on your dress."

"I didn't have a towel," Melissa defended. She had dressed quickly and the thin cotton clung to her breasts and thighs. Her hair dripped water down the back of her dress, molding the material to her taut buttocks.

He changed in the bathroom while she used the bedroom. She felt a little ridiculous closing the door while she changed—they had just held each other practically naked beneath water—so she left it ajar. She could hear the water running as she dressed.

She met him emerging from the bathroom door. His hair was wet and newly combed. His skin was dry and reddened beneath the collar of his white polo shirt. He had changed into a pair of dry khaki shorts.

"I need to hang up my shift," she said, passing him at the door.

"I left my trousers to dry in the shower. Is that all right?"

"I'll put my dress there, too."

She fixed her hair, turning the damp curls into a tier of braids. The bathroom was a bit steamy. He had taken a shower and had returned everything to its place. Even his towel over the rack was folded. Discreetly placed on the counter was a leather toilet kit, open. Melissa peeked in, and the sight of his comb and shaving tools reminded Melissa just how unusual his presence was. A month ago she couldn't have imagined this day, and now she felt so much at ease with him in her house she could have removed each object from the travel case to stow it until his next trip. It was ridiculous, but nonetheless true: she wouldn't mind if he considered this his home.

Yet in a real sense he was a stranger in her house. No matter how at ease his toiletries looked in the bathroom, or how familiar he made himself in the kitchen, it was still *her* bedroom. She felt a deep stir of gratitude to Bernard for suggesting they camp. She saw that he understood her need to go slow, and instead of begrudging her the pace, or trying to convince her to hurry, he seemed to enjoy her, no matter what speed they traveled. Tonight they could lie together side by side, and enjoy the intimacies they had already established.

"I know the perfect place to pitch the tent."

"I thought up on top of the hill . . . ?"

"Just where I would suggest."

They emptied the trunk of the car and carted the equipment up the hill. "We can eat out here, too, if you like," Melissa offered. "We can cook everything indoors except the fish and the coffee."

"Camping with the conveniences of home."

"My style of camping," Melissa said, beaming.

"Hey, lower the screen. I'd rather not invite Richmond's mosquito population into my house tonight."

"How unsociable," she scolded playfully. She untied the net, but the zipper caught and she nearly pulled the tent down. She sat perplexed under the tumble of netting.

"Haven't you ever been camping?"

"Nope, just a city kid at heart."

"You surprise me! You appear so self-sufficient here, alone in the country."

"My self-reliance comes from necessity," she explained. "I learned how to cut wood, how to tend a stove for maximum heat, and how to shovel snow. I can even fix my car at times, but there's been no call for camping."

"That's where friends come in handy. To bring the pleasures of life into a mundane day. After tonight I bet you'll ask to borrow my camping gear. You'll never want to sleep indoors again."

"How come you're such a nature boy? I thought you grew up in Manhattan."

"Upper East Side, born and bred, but Mother has family in Maine, and I spent my childhood summers there. Wonderful times," he reminisced. "Twenty-seven cousins . . . we must have driven our parents mad all summer long. I can still see Mother running after us."

"Do you see her much? Are you close?"

"No much. We're all pretty formal when we do pass an evening together."

"You have brothers and sisters?"

"I'm the oldest of six. Two sisters, three brothers. All of us grown to adulthood. They've all married and settled. Both of my sisters have kids. I've disappointed my mother, I'm afraid. But nonetheless I inherited the business when father retired," he said with forced conviction. "Oldest son, you see."

"Your mother couldn't be all that disappointed in you."

"I'm afraid she is. She'll never forgive me for refusing to marry Susan Marie, her best friend's daughter. There was a sizable business merger involved, you see, but I couldn't marry for that reason alone."

"You didn't love her?"

Bernard nodded. "In fact, Miss Dennison, I've never loved anyone but you."

"Now, that news would disappoint any mother! Tell me more about your family."

Bernard returned to his description of his family life. "It's a life built on valuable traditions," he said, "but it's a pretty inflexible world. I value my mother highly and I respect her a great deal, but I can't live my life to please her."

"Favorite son rebels!" Melissa taunted.

"I honestly don't mean to sound rebellious. If I can bring some joy into her life while living my life freely, I'm happy to—for instance, though I know you'll please her very much, that's not my main goal in being here."

"I'm terrified to meet her."

"Me, too! We'll have to wait until either one or both of us have more nerve. Now, what about some supper?"

"Why don't I make the salad while you clean the fish."

"How long will it take you to get ready to eat?"

"Thirty minutes?"

"Perfect. I'll have the fish broiled at precisely eight fifteen," he said, checking his watch.

The sun set during supper. The day cooled off and the coals from their campfire took the chill off the air.

"Breeze feels good after the heat today."

"Manhattan was unbearably hot."

"I can imagine! I can't believe I used to spend all of July in the city. I even used to like it."

"Where did you live?"

"I grew up in an apartment on West End Avenue near Sixtieth—"

"We lived at opposite ends of practically the same street—"

Melissa took in this information. "Before I was married, I lived with Patrice on Eighty-sixth Street, near the park."

"Why won't you come into the city anymore, Mel?" His voice deepened with the sincerity of the question.

"Oh—I—" she didn't know what to say. She didn't want to lie to him, but she didn't feel she could adequately explain the truth. "It's just not a place I enjoy anymore."

"But why?" he pressed. "Did something unpleasant happen?"

"You might say that."

Bernard waited. Melissa hesitated. "I—When my husband died, I—I disagreed with his relatives about certain things. . . ."

"What things?"

"Oh, like the funeral, and what should be done with his work."

"What kind of work did he do?"

"He was a writer."

"And he left unfinished manuscripts?"

"Exactly. His relatives thought I should put the manuscripts into their care, but I refused. They were also mad because I wanted a private burial, and they wanted a national holiday."

"So why do you stay away from New York City? I don't understand the connection," he pursued.

"I stay away from the city now because it reminds me of all that—my late husband's relatives live there."

"I see." He paused to digest her meaning. "Did you always live in New York City?"

"No. For a few years my husband and I lived abroad."

"Where?"

"In France," she answered. "But that's enough. I don't want to talk about it. It's kind of like thinking about the disagreement with your mother. I can live with the difficulties, but I'd rather not dwell on them."

"Well said. How about some of that coffee you mentioned?"

"Fine. I'll put another log on the fire. We can make it out here."

When the fire burned low and amber, they agreed to let it die. "I'm tired," Melissa admitted. "Let's go to bed."

"Best idea you've had all evening."

"I'm not so sure about *that*," Melissa said, mostly to herself.

Bernard stopped her by the shoulders before she entered the tent. "You've nothing to worry about. You're in charge of this, remember? I only cook the fish," he said cheerfully. "The rest is up to you."

They sidled out of their clothes and into their individual sleeping bags, lying still, side by side, like two caterpillars transformed into cocoons about to metamorphose.

"I'm hot," Bernard complained after a few minutes. They had been lying silent listening to the katydids and the frogs by the pond. Melissa heard the deer drinking from the pond and some distant bird defending her territory. A breeze ruffled the tent sides, but the sleeping bags were stifling.

"Me, too," Melissa reluctantly admitted, hating to forfeit her protective covering.

"Let's spread the sleeping bags beneath us. We'll be warm enough without a blanket."

Melissa did as she was instructed, unzipping the sleeping bag completely and spreading it over the floor of the tent. It made a soft bed and when she lay down again beside Bernard, she sank into the down feathers.

The light from the moon shone through the netting over the door of the tent, laying shadows and light over both of their bodies. Melissa studied the strength of his build in the faint glow. Here they were lying together, without the cloak of water, clothes, or darkness, unashamed and unembarrassed, but not yet ready to further the embrace.

"Now roll over on your side and go to sleep," Bernard ordered, wrapping his arms and legs around her. "I have an early date tomorrow with a boat-stealing, rod-robbing bass."

"He sure did dump you!"

"Just wait. I'll outsmart him yet."

"We'll see."

"Shhh," he whispered into her ear, curling her against him for sleep.

When Melissa awoke she found Bernard dressed, crouched at the foot of the tent tying his sneakers. Her own clothes lay neatly folded at her side.

"I've got coffee started. If you want to sleep more . . ."

"I'm ready to get up." She had awakened refreshed and feeling inexplicably happy.

"Good, it's the beginning of a spectacular day."

"Are you still interested in getting revenge on your bass friend?"

"Most certainly. I never give up what's really important to me," he said, leaning over to kiss Melissa, as casually as if she were fully clothed, and he had been her mate for forty years.

"I'll make us breakfast."

"Just remember the main course is fish."

"That's what you said last night."

"Thanks for the encouragement."

"No trouble. But you should know that I've been trying to catch that particular fish for months, and I've had no luck."

"But I'm a man! I'm supposed to be good at conquering nature."

"Then get busy. She's more of a challenge than you can admit."

"Just don't cook an entrée!" Bernard said and left the tent to conquer nature.

Melissa cooked eggs, country-fried potatoes, and toast over the fire. In addition she halved grapefruit and brought them outside with a tray full of utensils and condiments.

Bernard returned with a white package in his hands.

"What's this?" Melissa asked.

"It's still another example of man's dominance over nature." He handed the parcel to Melissa. She looked from him to the offering with skepticism. "It's lox," he said, as she unwrapped the fish. "From my favorite deli."

"This is fabulous!" she said excitedly, lifting a paper-thin slice of smoked salmon to her mouth. "Great with eggs."

"Better than an old bass, right?"

"Absolutely."

"Good. Because I had *no* luck catching it. Mother Nature looks after her favorites."

"Gosh, this is the best lox I've ever had."

"Why not come down to the city next weekend, and I'll introduce you to the genius who imports this salmon? He's one of my best-kept secrets."

Melissa laughed. "Thanks for your generous offer but I told you—"

"Afraid of running into your 'relatives?' "

The way he stressed 'relatives' made Melissa look up from her plate. "Yes, I don't think I could stand to see them."

"You don't think they've forgotten—or at least forgiven—after all this time? How long has it been since you were last there?"

"Two years, but I doubt they've forgotten."

"There are plenty of ways you could visit New York without seeing them."

"You think so?"

"I could keep you locked in my apartment all day and all night."

"We can do that here."

Bernard raised his eyebrows. "True, but the unfortunate part of that plan is that I can't be here during the week and I'm not free next weekend."

Melissa's heart sank. "Why not?"

"Business. I have to take the president emeritus out to dinner Saturday night. It's his seventieth birthday."

"Your father?"

"That's right. Want to come along? You'd be doing me a big favor."

"I'm not ready to meet your mother and father yet."

"I don't blame you," he agreed.

Melissa didn't like the notion that he'd be away for two weeks, but neither was she prepared to visit Manhattan.

Melissa searched his eyes. She wondered if it was easy for him to stay away two weeks, or if he regretted the extended separation, too. "I'll miss you," she said shyly.

He grinned. "No, if you missed me, you'd come to New York. If you trusted me, you'd know you'd be safe, from any and all your lousy relatives."

It was harder to say good-bye Sunday evening because of the time together than it had been the last time he'd left. They knew each other better, and had added three full days and three dreamless nights together. Melissa regretted his departure in every way, except that she'd now be able to return to her piano work. It wasn't that she couldn't play—she did, from time to time, sit down and run through a Beethoven sonata— but she didn't dare play an Arbour composition in Bernard's presence. As worldly as Bernard was, he'd surely recognize the composer, and Melissa wasn't prepared to supply any more clues to her past.

And this was an important time in her work. She was close to completing the last measures of an untitled rhapsody. Jean-Pierre had started it in a burst of inspiration, but it had never been completed. Had the news of her "debut" not interrupted his work, he would have finished scoring the work in a day or two, but it had, and he hadn't. Melissa had traced his idea back to the source of inspiration, from the pages of music he left; then she'd speculated as to where he would have gone with his ideas. It had taken her a year, but she had finally calculated a plausible ending. She was anxious to hear how it sounded after three days away from it all. If she stayed with it and worked straight through the next weekend, maybe she wouldn't feel his absence so drastically.

For Bernard, his consolation for leaving was equally complicated. Quite simply, he couldn't be near Melissa any longer without consummating his love for her. He understood her reticence—in fact better than she suspected—but his passion for her was ardent, and he was straining his will to wait. The strength of his love for her warranted a full embrace, but she'd suffered in love, and this next embrace was undoubtedly a major step for her.

Something else bothered him. He felt uneasy, as he drove back into town, that in spite of their closeness— an intimacy far more important than a physical embrace—she was hiding something. Although he could understand why, it nonetheless angered him that she didn't trust him more. It was just a matter of patience.

"Patience is a virtue I *can't wait* to achieve!" Bernard said meanly, speaking only to himself as he drove into town. He'd have to do something about his urgency soon!

* * *

"Melissa? I have to go into town Friday for a meeting. Why don't you come along with me?" Patrice had spent a vacation week in Richmond. "I'll be back in the country Saturday afternoon. I could really use the company."

Melissa knitted her brows.

"We'll only be there twenty-four hours," Patrice went on. "No one will pay you any attention, unless you walk naked, or wear a sign, and either way, no one will link you to Jean-Pierre's widow."

Melissa debated. It was true, there was no better place for anonymity than the streets of New York . . . if only she dared. It would free her to see Bernard, when otherwise she'd have to spend the weekend without him, and that wasn't a happy prospect. "Bernard has been urging me to come down. He can't come up this weekend."

"Then let's go!"

"Are you sure?"

"Listen, Mel. If you don't like it, I'll never suggest you try it again. All right?"

"All right!" she said, the determination sounding deep in her voice.

"Bernard?" She set the phone on her lap and picked up her afternoon cup of coffee.

"Melissa! I was just thinking of you!" Pleasure rang in his voice. He had thought of little else but her all day.

"I was wondering . . ."

"Yes?"

"Would you like to have dinner with me on Friday night?" she asked shyly.

"Darling, of course I would, but I have to be here Saturday, remember? and I'm not free on Friday until after business hours. I really shouldn't come up for so short a time," he explained regretfully.

"What if I came into town?"

"Would you?" he asked excitedly. This is what he'd hoped for, but hadn't anticipated. "Would you really?"

Melissa laughed. She had been nervous when she called, but it was hard to stay frightened with such an enthusiastic reception. "Patrice has to come into town for a meeting Friday and is coming back up here Saturday. She wants company and I thought—"

"So do I! I want company, too!" he cheered. "I'm thrilled! What would you like to do while you're here?"

"Something very quiet."

"You're on. I know a fabulous little restaurant up high in the sky. Vastly private. In fact, I'm certain I've *never* seen a 'relative' there."

"You have the idea," she said appreciatively. "Where shall I meet you?"

"I'll pick you up."

"I'll be staying at Patrice's," she explained. "But I'd rather meet elsewhere." She wanted to wait awhile longer before she introduced them to each other.

"I'll send a car for you at seven o'clock. I'll arrange to meet the car at the restaurant."

She gave him the address of Patrice's apartment.

"I can't wait!" he exclaimed.

"Nor can I!"

She replaced the receiver thoughtfully. Had she done

the right thing? She'd just have to go to find out. If she'd made a mistake, she'd know better next time. If all went well, she'd be free . . . to return home when she wanted to . . . free to see Bernard . . . even if he was too busy to come to her in the country.

CHAPTER TEN

"Is it too late to change my mind?" Melissa asked, her voice stretched thin from taut nerves.

"Absolutely. Now, take a deep breath," Patrice instructed, "because just around the corner is our first view of the skyline."

She couldn't have predicted more accurately. The Palisades Parkway wasn't the most efficient way to drive into Manhattan, but it was the most spectacular.

Ahead of them at the edge of the water and sky loomed the ridge of towering buildings. Between the car and the buildings lay the Hudson and today it sparkled in the bright summer sunlight in a way that reminded Melissa of Bernard's eyes. How could she have gotten herself into such a position? How could she have left the security of the Berkshires, where her anonymity was guaranteed, for the chance of discovery in the city— and in mid-July? Where was her sanity?

"I have to admit it always does look more impressive than the last time."

The weather was on its best summer behavior. A

breeze stroked the river into currents and followed it downstream. Melissa shook her head in wonder, in spite of the smile on her face.

"Wait till you see what they're wearing on Madison Avenue this season." Patrice was speeding over the bridge now, her spirits charged. "Darling, you've been away a very long time!"

Melissa looked down at her outfit. It had taken her an hour that morning to select her dress, but now she regretted her choice. The simple cotton dress was perfect for the day, but now she thought it looked too countrified. She worried that she'd look like a tourist.

"Patrice, do you think we might shop this afternoon?" she asked shyly.

"I can't think of anything I'd rather do," Patrice assured her. "I have a couple of things I have to do in the office, but I'll head you in the right direction, and we can arrange to meet when I'm free. You'd look great in the new Christian Aujard collection at Bloomingdale's."

Melissa leaned back in the car seat. She was scared, but she was also excited. They were over the bridge and heading south into town. For the first time since she had agreed to this scheme, she began to think she might enjoy it. Bloomingdale's!

If the evening had been with anyone other than Bernard, Melissa would have predicted an anticlimax, the day had been so fine. Patrice had met Melissa in Midtown and together they had ridden the elevators in three different department stores. She knew it was silly to spend so much money on clothes for just one evening, but she gave over her reservations to Patrice's insistence that Melissa deserved a splurge.

By five o'clock they had found shoes, handbag, ear-rings, stockings, and perfume, but still hadn't found the perfect gown. "It's all right, Patrice, I can always wear the blue dress I brought with me. It's attractive enough."

"Tonight you must be more than attractive," Patrice argued. "Tonight you must outshine the moon!"

"That's going to be hard. It's full tonight."

"That's how you must be. Here!" she said, pulling a gown from the rack. "*This* is perfect."

"I think you're right!" Melissa agreed at once.

The dress was as light as a handkerchief, and easily as transparent, but made modest by yards and yards of material. "What about headlights?" Melissa worried as she stood in front of the three-tiered mirror.

"We'll just have to stop at the lingerie department on our way out," Patrice counseled.

"Now, let's hurry," Patrice said, finally taking the wrapped parcels from the lingerie saleswoman. "We've less than two hours to transform you before your dinner with Bernard."

Alone with Bernard in the elevator up to the restau-rant, Melissa studied their reflection in the mirror oppo-site them. She admired their similarities: their height, their dark hair, their formal attire. She was pleased with the gown she wore beneath Patrice's sable coat. The soft apricot voile fell gracefully around her slender fig-ure; the color accentuated the peach glow of her com-plexion. She wore her hair loose and curled softly, around her face.

She caught Bernard watching her. "Not bad looking for a country girl," he joked.

"Thanks a lot," she retorted, but she could see he was pleased with her effort. His eyes shone with approval.

"By the way," he said. "I told the maître d' it was our anniversary so we'd receive special care. I hope you don't mind."

"On the contrary." Melissa laughed. "It's been a lovely marriage."

The elevator doors opened onto a vast circular room and an expansive view of the city. The entire room was furnished in a train motif. Their table across the floor was the actual first-class travel compartment of an old Pacific railroad car. The train compartment offered them all the intimacy required of a honeymoon train trip.

"What a perfect view," Melissa exclaimed. "I had forgotten how spectacular Manhattan looked at night. This must be the best view in town."

"No, that's for after dinner," he said. Melissa looked puzzled. "The Rainbow Room for dancing. Or is that too corny?" he asked, suddenly unsure of his choice. Mostly tourists went there, but the view was spectacular and the big band music was good to dance to.

"Sounds wonderful to me," Melissa said dreamily, leaning back in her chair. The evening was turning into the kind of night she had always imagined. She reached her hand across the table to hold his and her heart tripped lightly from its usual regular course.

He ordered for them both without bothering to consult the menu. When the waiter returned with the bad news that the chef was out of shrimps Provençal Bernard reordered. They were at the best restaurant in town; whatever was served would be excellent. Besides, food didn't seem to matter much to him tonight. He had more important things on his mind.

He deliberated a minute over the wine list, but finally Bernard insisted they order champagne. It was their anniversary, after all. And when the champagne was delivered and the cork popped, he stood up to deliver his anniversary toast before leaning over to touch his glass to hers. The ring of fragile crystal reverberated in the air as he brushed his lips against hers.

"I love you, Melissa," Bernard said simply, as if reading her thoughts. "I know this is sudden—God, we've hardly known each other two weeks—but I know it's real." He looked shy, Melissa thought. "Can you stand it? Have I sent you running by confessing my love too soon? I'd hate to lose you just when I've found you."

Melissa had to steady her nerves. For an instant she felt panicked. It was much too soon! Where was her sense? Why was she responding like a nervous child to each gesture he made?

But she wasn't a child. The woman in her was claiming expression. When she met Bernard's eyes she was relieved to see that he felt as strongly as she. Good, she wasn't being silly. She respected him and his perception of things. She herself, having been locked in the woods since Jean-Pierre's death, might have gone a bit crazy. She had worried that her intense feelings, occurring so quickly and uncontrollably, might have burst from some unhealthy need. It was Bernard sitting across from her who convinced her she hadn't gone mad. She had met a fine man. She was right to listen to her heart and not her fear. He wasn't going to hurt her. From the look in his eye she was certain his plan was to care for her as much as she'd let him. Right now she was willing to give him all of herself.

Melissa stared at him silently. It *was* too soon. This was crazy! But she had to agree with him. He was right. "I love you, too, Bernard," she said, speaking matter-of-factly, her arms resting on the table. "It's as though I've known you for years. And at the same time there are so many things I don't know about you. Basic things. Like if you sleep in pajamas?"

Bernard grinned. "I admit that's an important thing for you to know about me." The waiter delivered their first course. "After all these years of marriage, there is still mystery," he said rather loudly, for the waiters' benefit.

The uniformed man took the cue as an opportunity to pay compliment to their well-being. "You certainly have a beau-ti-ful wife," he said to Bernard, but never taking his eyes from Melissa.

"She looks as beautiful as the day I married her," Bernard added. Melissa blushed. "See, still blushing like a bride."

"He's grown more handsome over the years," Melissa contributed, taking the waiter into her confidence. "He was skinny as a rail when I first met him. And so bold!"

"Love has mellowed me," Bernard said, shaking his head. "And fattened me in my prime." He lifted one of the glasses the waiter had refilled with champagne and handed it to Melissa. He lifted his own and toasted her again. "To the most beautiful woman in New York.

May the coming years be as perfect as the first five have been."

They giggled between themselves after the waiter left.

"Just wait until they bring dessert!" Bernard predicted. "We're bound to be put on display as the happiest married couple in Manhattan." When they had finished the last of the champagne, and the dishes had all been removed from the table, their waiter appeared at the head of a procession. In his arms, baked Alaska flambé. When the waiter extinguished the flames, the others dining in the restaurant applauded spontaneously. They applauded again when Bernard kissed Melissa from across the table.

"Happy anniversary, Melissa," he said, handing her a black rectangular box.

"For me?" She reached out to accept the present.

"Open it, darling."

Inside the box, against a bed of burgundy velvet, lay a cluster of gray Mallorcan pearls, a single strand with a diamond clasp.

"Bernard, they're beautiful!"

"Like the woman who will wear them."

The restaurant emptied while they lingered over their brandy. The lights flickered on and off across the city, the patterns changing as the hour grew late.

"Shouldn't we be going?" Melissa asked. The waiters were busy with the next day's preparations.

"Hmmm. Maybe we should. Are you interested in dancing?" he asked, returning his napkin to the table.

Melissa shrugged her shoulders. "We could."

Bernard studied her expression with a smile. "But you have a better idea, don't you?"

She smiled shyly. "My favorite New York pastime is to walk the streets at night."

"A veteran streetwalker?"

Melissa took his bait and ran with it. "What would that make you?" she chided. "There's a name for men like you."

"What kind of talk is this on our anniversary?"

"You started it."

"Come on, we're going to walk up Fifth Avenue," he said, helping her into the luxuriant sable coat.

Just as the elevator reached them another couple joined Melissa and Bernard. "Oh, go ahead," Bernard said, gesturing the other couple in.

"Aren't you going down?" they asked, puzzled.

"Yes, but . . ." Melissa began. They'd had the same impulse.

"We're waiting to ride down by ourselves. It's our anniversary," he explained.

The other couple held the elevator door open for them. "By all means, you go first."

"How long have you been married?" the woman asked Melissa.

"Ten years," she said proudly.

"My, how the years fly by," Bernard exclaimed.

"Don't they look *happy*," the woman said to her husband, keeping the doors open, so struck was she by their happiness.

"How refreshing to see a marriage look like yours after ten years!" her husband agreed. "I'm impressed."

Bernard smiled and squeezed Melissa's shoulder affectionately.

"Do you have children?" She wanted to know the secret of their success.

"One," Bernard said proudly.

"Darling," Melissa corrected, "we have two. Don't forget Watson."

"Sorry," he said off-handedly. "He's so quiet and well-behaved I sometimes forget him."

The other couple were still ogling them for their happiness when the elevator doors closed. Melissa pressed the bottom button, but Bernard stepped between and pressed a number in the middle.

When the doors opened on the twenty-first floor, he pulled her out, and wrapped her tightly into his arms. He brought his mouth near to her ear. "I couldn't wait any longer," he whispered urgently, and Melissa could feel the intensity surging through the rest of his body. Her own passion had been building all night; each moment increased her desire for him. Even his kidding had kindled her affection for him. Their conversation during dinner—even the unexpected admission of love— had barely touched the depth of their feelings for each other. He kissed her now, slowly, carefully, as if, should he hold her too tightly, she might vanish. He didn't need to bruise her to convey the power of his feelings.

When he signaled the elevator to retrieve them, the urgency had been checked into an anticipation too delicious to be hurried. Their kiss promised a future far greater than physical satisfaction. They walked out of the building, and finding the night air warm and clear, walked the fourteen blocks to his apartment, as leisurely as if they had been married for years.

She could hear the East River as they reached the corner of his street. In all the years she had lived in Manhattan, Melissa had never been on this block. It was perhaps the shortest street in the city, and undoubtedly the most exclusive: in total, six well-kept townhouses comprised the neighborhood.

Inside the house, Melissa stood speechless at her surroundings, focusing her attention through the double glass doors to a courtyard, pretending to study the garden by moonlight.

Bernard pressed against her. "Come on," he said, sliding open the door with one hand. In the other hand he carried a bottle of Napoleon brandy and two snifters. "There's a bench under the apple tree," he said, leading Melissa toward it. "I thought you might like to see another view of Manhattan."

They snuggled close together on the bench and watched the moonlight leap off the river's currents. The brandy warmed Melissa inside, and Bernard's strong arms around her deterred the slight breeze. It felt as though the rest of the world had disappeared.

"Hard to believe we're in the middle of Manhattan," Melissa exclaimed. "But you must be used to this."

"Funny, but it's not like this most of the time. My life is rushed and hectic. Hardly ever quiet."

"Even out here in the moonlight?"

"I'm ashamed to admit the last time I came out to enjoy the river by moonlight."

"Well, I'm kind of glad to hear it," Melissa confessed softly. "I'd hate to be the only one of us feeling special."

"Too special for words," he said, and turned Melissa's face to meet his. "Now that I've known you, I can't imagine being without you."

"But—" Melissa started to protest. She felt as deeply for him as he was confessing he felt for her, but there were problems. Logistics. She couldn't live in Manhattan, and he could hardly retire to the country yet. Already the weekly separation was tearing at her.

"Now, now," he persuaded, seeing the questions in her eyes. "Nothing to spoil the evening. We'll work past every one of those old obstacles." She started to speak again, but he stopped her with another kiss, this time more insistent. "This is too good to forfeit. We'll just have to find a way to have what we want. I love you. Nothing more."

And without another word he led her back into the house and upstairs to the bedroom.

The moonlight on the river reflected into the handsome bedroom and Melissa could see the simple but strong line of the modern furnishings. The west wall, made entirely of glass, faced the river; against the north wall was a formidable brass bed.

He undressed her slowly, stopping after he unbuttoned her blouse to kiss her. He slipped the flimsy material off her shoulders. His lips touched her warm skin so softly that she shivered in excitement. Then his mouth was on hers again, and Melissa was no longer patient. She fumbled loose his tie and slid her fingers under the buttons to undo them. His dinner jacket fell to the floor. They were hurrying now. Her gown slipped to her feet.

"God, you are beautiful," he said, stepping back to study her. He had seen her undressed before, but he hadn't dared more than a hasty glance at her body. "I almost can't believe it." For all his imagining—and it had been extensive, at night when they were apart—he had never imagined such perfect breasts, such smooth skin, or the gentle sloping curve of her hips. The silky camisole added mystery to her beauty. The sight of her took his breath away, yet as much as his eyes marveled, the rest of him insisted he embrace her. He lifted her into the enormous bed, untied the fragile undergarment, and lowered himself beside her.

"Darling," he whispered, pressing kisses onto her neck. He felt her swallow hard, and he lifted himself to look at her.

"Are you all right?" he asked gently.

She released a breath of air. "Just a bit nervous," she explained, embarrassed by her behavior. Everything had been going so smoothly. It felt perfectly natural for her to be in bed with Bernard. In an important way it *was* their anniversary. She did feel married to him. But she hadn't been in bed with a man in a long time and she wasn't a student anymore with a tutor. "Remember when I told you I felt adolescent kissing you," she said. Bernard nodded quickly. "Well, now I feel *infantile!* It's like I don't know what to do!" she said, more embarrassed than before.

"Then do nothing," he said lovingly, laying her back into the bed. "Just enjoy."

She lay back with her eyes closed, feeling the sensation of his gentle hands exploring her body. He touched each part as if he didn't want to go on; as if the night were not enough time to know her well. He touched her all over, but not only with his hands. He fingered her tangled hair while his arms spread against her skin in even strokes. His lips explored the hollow of her neck, her arms, her breasts. His mouth covered her erect nipple, and he sucked as if to bring forth nourishment.

Melissa found it impossible to lie still. Bernard's caress taught her what to do. It wasn't that she suddenly remembered how to make love, or that she remembered a technique that might please him. Rather, she felt things anew and responded as the occasion demanded. Her body had a mind of its own. As if they had been lovers for years, she followed his moves: he beckoned forth a woman and Melissa rewarded him with passion. Her body met his; in his arms Melissa forgot all her fears. She forgot the doubts she'd had, or the problems they must face.

Their voices carried the song of ecstasy into the breaking daylight like the first lark. They lay together exhausted, breathless but clinging to one another, unwilling to release their hold. Melissa rested her head against Bernard's damp chest, tasting the salt from his chest when she moved to kiss him. She didn't know whether to laugh or cry. All she knew was that she was full of an emotion that she had identified as love, and she hoped it would last forever.

"Can it go on?" she asked in wonder.

"For you, it can go on all day," he answered, bringing her on top of him.

It wasn't what she had meant when she asked, but she was just as happy with the answer as if he had understood her.

*   *   *

When Melissa awoke the room was flooded with sunlight and she was alone in bed. The wall opposite the bed was mirrored, and Melissa had to laugh at the tousled bed, the pile of clothes on the floor, and herself, as mussed as the rest of the room. But she was too happy to care. Downstairs she heard noises in the kitchen, and she was just about to search for Bernard's bathrobe so that she could join him, when he appeared at the door with a tray full of food.

"A feast for my love," he said. He looked happy and proud of himself, and nearly as disheveled as she did. Pointlessly she smoothed back her hair, and pulled the sheet up to cover her breasts.

"No fair," he said, lowering the sheet. "You can't keep them a secret from me anymore. I think we should move to Haiti where you could go bare-chested all the time. Honestly, Mel, I've never seen a more glorious sight." He leaned over and kissed one of her breasts appreciatively. Melissa laughed. She was embarrassed, but also moved by his praise.

"What's for breakfast?" she asked happily, propping up pillows for him to lean against.

"Scrambled eggs with Nova Scotia salmon, potatoes, and toast. We begin with grapefruit," he said, placing a tray over Melissa's lap and serving the sectioned fruit.

"But that's what I fixed for you!" she said, surprised. He had told her he didn't know how to cook anything but steak.

"I know. I've been practicing all week."

"You've achieved immediate success," she said, taking a bite of the eggs. "Delicious."

"Only the best for my love," he said, joining her in bed. He had brought the *Times* with him, but that would be for later. He poured her a glass of champagne. There were sliced strawberries floating over the surface.

The telephone rang and interrupted her second bite. Bernard made no attempt to move. "Aren't you going to answer?" Melissa asked. She'd been surprised to hear the phone ring, as if they really had dismissed the rest of the world, but more surprised when he didn't answer it.

"Someone will answer it," he said, reaching over and kissing her.

Melissa frowned. "What do you mean 'someone' will answer?" Suddenly she was afraid that there was something to interfere with their privacy. "Are we alone in the house?"

"I have to confess we're not. In fact, I have to confess I didn't cook breakfast. Tommy's been practicing this menu all week, until I was convinced he'd matched your meal."

"Tommy?"

"My houseboy."

"Gosh, how rich are you?" she asked, relieved to learn they weren't about to be barged in upon by some estranged wife or ex-girl friend who still had a key.

"Exceptionally," he said modestly. "So rich that I'll buy you anything you want—as long as it's a sufficient bribe to keep you with me always."

"You couldn't be that rich," Melissa answered defiantly, returning to her eggs. But she feared he might be. When she studied the room more carefully, she could see the expense with which it had been designed. The picture on the wall above the bed was an original

Matisse. The throw rug over the thick carpeting was Oriental, and very old. Even the drapes were silk.

"Well if you're that rich you can afford to quit your job and move to the country," she said lightly. "The weeds are getting out of hand."

"Don't tempt me unless you're serious," he said. "I might quit my job tomorrow."

Melissa caught her breath. She hadn't expected to have her invitation realistically considered, but when he did, she was even more baffled by her own desire for him. Where was her sense? Where was her sanity? How could she even kid with so serious a subject as long as she kept her identity concealed from him.

"Don't quit your job just yet," she said softly. "But could you take off for a few days toward the end of next week, so we can play?"

"Nothing I'd rather do."

"We might as well enjoy the farm while I still live there."

Bernard laid his arm over her shoulder. "I wish you would let me help you," he said sympathetically. "Won't you let me lend you the money?"

"No," she said automatically. "I appreciate your offer, really I do, Bernard. But I don't have any way to ever pay you back, and I can't let you buy it for me. That would make me feel worse than losing the land altogether."

"Lousy independence!" he said.

"Independence isn't lousy," she said insistently, but without anger.

Bernard nodded. "I know. I didn't mean that. I think

your independence is admirable. But sometimes it does block good ideas. What if I bought the land myself, and continued to let you rent?"

Melissa shrugged. "The answer is no. Thank you, but no." Her head spun. Could she continue to admit him into her life when she had begun the relationship falsely? How could she tell him who she was? He wouldn't understand why she hadn't told him earlier. He'd take her mistrust personally. The world had taught her to keep a distance from intimacy. Bernard had taught her that it didn't hurt to love, and she wasn't willing to lose his arms around her by confessing her identity. It wasn't as if she had lied about her age a couple of years. The issue was important. She didn't know if he'd understand. No, she'd just have to keep the secret to herself. She could give herself to him completely in the present, but not in the past. As long as the past stayed out of her future, she would be able to give Bernard all the love she had.

"I'd love to take a few days off next week. What do you say we camp overnight on the Green River?"

"Oh, Bernard, that sounds perfect."

He lowered the empty trays onto the floor and turned his attention to Melissa's pretty mouth. "Just the thought of making love to your naked body surrounded by wildlife brings out the animal in me," he said, sliding his leg in between hers.

Melissa squeezed him boldly. She didn't care to worry about the future when she was so perfectly content with the present.

* * *

"Hey, I've got to call Patrice!" Melissa announced suddenly.

"Why?" Bernard asked lazily, dreading anything that would hurry their last hours of daylight.

"Because I was supposed to stay there last night. She'll be worried."

"Won't she just assume—I mean, you said she knew we were spending the evening together."

"Patrice *knows* how often I spend the night with a man in his apartment."

"How often?" he interrupted.

"Never!"

"Here's the phone. If she wants a note from me, I'll be happy to draft one." He stroked her thigh while she talked with Patrice, doing his best to distract her.

"She wasn't even worried!" Melissa complained, hanging up the phone.

"She must trust your taste in men," Bernard asserted.

"Are you sure you two aren't in this campaign together to get me off the farm?"

"Honey," Bernard admitted, pulling Melissa into his arms. "A farm is just where you belong. In the pigsty!" She had jam all over her fingers. One by one he sucked them clean.

Melissa had read about women coming home from parties in broad daylight, dressed in elaborate gowns and furs, but she'd never imagined it happening to herself. She turned down Bernard's offer to escort her home to Patrice's apartment, choosing instead to take a taxi.

"I'll see you next weekend, my love," he said. "I had a perfect time last night . . . the finest anniversary I've ever had."

Melissa smiled shyly. "I just wish the time hadn't passed so quickly."

"There will be more."

"That's the only reason I can bear to leave you," she confided. "Good-bye, Bernard." He tried to delay her departure a minute longer, but the taxi driver's impatience piqued her own need to hurry. "I've got to run. Patrice is going to be waiting, and she wants to hear all the details."

"When am I going to meet the infamous Patrice?" he asked.

"Maybe next weekend," Melissa promised. "If you promise not to fall madly in love with her and run off."

"I'd never do that."

"She's very pretty."

"Well, if I *do* run off with her, I won't be gone long."

"Oh, you!"

Bernard closed the door to the taxi. "Wait at the door until she's inside," he told the driver, handing him a folded bill.

The cab driver nodded indifferently. If he had noticed her clothes, he didn't bat an eyelash. It was all part of a day's work. Richmond would have filled their gossip quota on a detail like the hour in which Melissa was found dressed in a floor-length gown, but in New York no one bothered to comment. It was one of the qualities Melissa missed most about the city. Here one could do exactly as one pleased, and no one flinched. Someone might smile discreetly, but it was harder to elicit a dramatic response from a New Yorker than it was to elicit real warmth from a Frenchman.

* * *

As much as Melissa enjoyed being with Bernard in his apartment she never fully admitted to herself, until she was back in Patrice's car en route to the Berkshires, how successful the trip had actually been. Unfortunately, along with the success came the unanswered questions, and Melissa tried to lose herself in Patrice's cheerful interrogation. In spite of herself she had loved the twenty-four hours she'd spent in Manhattan. She couldn't wait to visit Bernard again, and yet . . . and yet . . . there were issues to face before she made a second journey.

CHAPTER ELEVEN

"Before you raise any objection, I have something to propose."

"Hey! Where do you get off talking to me that way?"

"We're in love, aren't we? Doesn't that call for some tender abuse?"

"You're impossible!"

"Agreed. Now listen to me," he said, holding her at arm's length. "I have to spend next weekend on Nantucket."

"Why?"

"Remember I told you about that folklore writer? He and I have to meet for business and he's invited me to his house on the Island. I have to agree with his claim that Nantucket is preferable to Manhattan in August— but if I go, I'll miss seeing you, and that prospect is worse than any heat New York could host."

"You want me to come with you, right?"

"Smart girl I've come to love," Bernard sang. "You can read my mind as if we'd been married for years. Say you'll come?"

Melissa had already considered the possibility. Matt Drybas would never know her. She wouldn't have to mention her interest in music. The thought of Nantucket, and a weekend on the beach with Bernard, was too good to pass up. "I would like to know more about this writer," she said. "And I'd get a kick out of seeing you at work."

"It will hardly be work," he said. "We'd just spend time with him. That's the best way for me to know how to promote his book. Are you saying you'll come with me, Melissa?"

"I'd love to."

He picked her up, in spite of her protests that it was out of the way for him; he insisted that the scenery was far better traveling across the interior of New England than up through the Eastern Seaboard towns, and Melissa was helpless to argue.

It had taken Melissa hours to select the clothes she would bring, but once she had, they all fit into one roomy overnight bag. Her bathing suit, which she regarded for the first time since she had bought it years before, was dropped into the wastebasket, it was so dated. She'd phoned Patrice to buy a stylish suit for her to wear in Nantucket, and Patrice had agreed to look during her lunch hour. Once that problem was solved, the rest seemed negligible. She packed shorts and cotton shirts for daytime, and a cotton dress for night. She wore espadrilles, and packed ankle-strapped heels in the bag.

When Bernard opened the trunk to his car, and Melissa saw that his suitcase was precisely the same size as her own, her labors were repaid in confidence. She knew it didn't matter to Bernard—he was so blind with love he couldn't see what she wore—but it mattered to her. She wasn't going to fret about her appearance—she simply wasn't vain enough—now that her wardrobe was decided.

"Can you read a map?" he asked, as they left the familiar Berkshire hills for the Housatonic Valley.

"What a silly question," Melissa answered, taking the map from the dashboard, and opening it upside down. "There's nothing to reading a map, once you can figure out how to open it." She struggled with the folds until it was open completely, and she was blinding Bernard's view.

"Hey! I'm going to crash, if you're not careful."

Melissa jerked back the road map. "I'm sorry," she said solemnly, folding the map into a square. She studied it briefly to locate their position.

"We want to take Route Forty-four—it's slower than Ninety, but I hear it's through spectacular-looking country. "Turn east in Canaan," Melissa dictated. "Looks like we have a long drive ahead of us."

"It will be over before you know it. We can count out-of-state license plates, unless you can think of a better game. . . ."

"Just keep your eyes on the road," she threatened.

The tired old car-games they had played in their respective youths were transformed into combats of intellect and wit. Bernard was faster to invent puns, but Melissa knew all the show tunes from the thirties and forties. Sometimes they sang—Bernard surprised her with his rich, deep baritone—and sometimes they talked. When they ran out of things to say they drove along in silence, holding hands on top of the gearshift.

They stopped once for gas, and again briefly for coffee, but both of them were anxious to get there. The last ferry left at five o'clock, and if they missed it, they'd have to spend the night in Hyannis Port and that wasn't nearly as picturesque as Nantucket.

They reached the Hyannis dock just as the long line of cars was filling the ship's hold. "What if there isn't enough room for us?" Melissa worried.

"We have reservations," he explained, and Melissa sat back to watch the activity.

"Go on the top deck," he suggested.

"You don't want me to wait for you?"

"I'd rather you save us an aisle seat."

She boarded the ferry and went directly on the top deck where she found two seats facing each other along the railing and put her feet up on the seat saved for Bernard.

"I was right to send you ahead," Bernard acknowledged when he joined her a few minutes later. "I'd forgotten how crowded the Island would be midsummer. You should see this place in the winter."

"I'll bet no one stands outside!" Melissa imagined.

"There's always one or two fools, but I've never seen anything like this!"

The boat was filled from stern to bow, and everyone was in a holiday mood. When the ferry passed a pilot whale, the passengers cheered loudly. Some folks drank beer. Many had brought picnics to share with their families. Lots of people snacked on the food sold below.

"I can see land," Melissa cried. "Look."

It was the first peak of land in two and a half hours. They had been studying the sea and listening to the

gulls, each one watching the other on the sly. Bernard
had never noticed the threads of silver in Melissa's hair.
"Your age is showing," he provoked, pulling free an
aberrant hair.

"Not age," Melissa countered. She had discovered
her first gray hairs in the mirror on the night after
Jean-Pierre's death. "Worry."

"I'll bet," he bantered. "I've never seen anyone so
burdened by worry. Deprivation all over your face."

"Egg all over your face, mister!"

"Sand sandwich in your mouth!" he rebutted, but he
stopped when he saw Melissa's face darken. "Don't
turn sensitive! You started it!"

"I know. I'm sorry," she said pensively.

"What's wrong?"

"It's nothing. . . . I just had a thought."

A voice over the loudspeaker boomed the instructions for passengers with vehicles to disembark.

"That's us," Bernard said, springing to his feet, and
grabbing Melissa's elbow he steered her below to their
car.

"Oh! can we walk for a minute?" Melissa coaxed.
"I'd love to look inside some of these stores."

"There's no such thing as a minute inside a Nantucket store, but go ahead," he said, pulling the car to
the side of the cobblestone street. "I'll phone Matt to
tell him we're here. Then we can take our time."

All of Nantucket was beautiful, as Melissa was soon
to discover, but it was the first impression that struck
her: a postcard-perfect shop-lined cobblestoned main
street. She peered into the candy store, heavenly with
sweet smells and sights, and glanced at the fashion de-

sign in the Paula Jaq'lyn Boutique, but it was the window display of handknit sweaters in Nantucket Looms that took her indoors, and the texture of the wool fisherman pullovers that made her want to own one. She had discovered the scrimshaw in the Main Street Gallery—elaborate carvings in ivory—and was just about to ask the salesperson for the price when Bernard found her.

"Matt told us to take our time. Friends of his dropped by, so there's no hurry."

"Great," Melissa remarked. "I think I could spend a fortune in here."

"Anything you want," Bernard said hopefully.

Melissa just smiled. She knew he was telling the truth. His generosity knew no limits, and as much as she wanted to own one of the beautiful sweaters or the scrimshaw she couldn't let him buy her expensive gifts. She was careful not to show too much enthusiasm for any one thing.

"Finished already?" he asked, surprised at her sudden disinterest.

"I'll have time to look later," she said.

"True."

They drove away from town to Siasconset, the writer's community eight miles from the harbor side of the island. The smell of the ocean carried in the wind from all sides of the island. There were marshes of grass, and lots of water, but no trees anywhere. An occasional house dotted the lunar landscape.

They pulled the car into the driveway behind a Volkswagen van, and started toward the modest cottage, leaving their belongings in the car. Music poured from the house out onto the driveway.

"Is that Drybas?" Melissa asked. "You didn't say he was musical." Suddenly she was worried. The music that assaulted them was hardly the strummings of a beginner. Whoever was playing the guitar had expertise in the field.

"Matt never told me," Bernard said. "It might be the friends he mentioned. There he is!"

They were greeted at the door by a long-haired young man. He was dressed in frayed cutoffs, and his slight build was tanned. He smiled at them from beneath a trimmed reddish beard.

He welcomed them inside, and as he sped through introductions—four of his neighbors reclined informally on the well-worn furniture—all of Melissa's uneasiness disappeared. She liked Matt at once. He and his friends were so relaxed she had no choice but to be. They would never know her past. She was Bernard's friend. Nothing more, nothing less. She felt enormously relieved.

They sat around for an hour while the chat continued. Two of the men had brought their banjos and were entertaining the rest. The prettiest of the two girls brought out a mandolin and played along. Bernard asked for a harmonica, was supplied with one, and won instant acclaim for his playing. Not to be outdone, Melissa picked up the other banjo from the floor and picked along with them. They played songs she didn't know, but the basic key was always one she could follow, and their playing was so relaxed, it didn't matter if she erred.

They stopped after a lengthy improvisation, and Mark's neighbors left for dinner at home. Melissa felt as if they were old friends, even if she couldn't remember all their names. That's what music could do: at its best, it brought people together who would otherwise remain strangers. "Where did you learn to play banjo?" Matt off-handedly asked her as he put their dinner together.

"I don't really know how to play," Melissa said. She had offered to help him, and he put her in charge of baking the biscuits. She stirred the dough with a fork. "I used to play as a kid, but I haven't picked one up in years."

"You're kidding? You play like a pro. Do you have any musical training?"

Melissa stirred the dough. "I play the piano a little," she said shyly.

"Tell him the truth," Bernard chimed in from the other room. He was supposed to be reading Mark's revisions. "She plays like an absolute angel."

Melissa felt a chill down her back. "I play like a two-footed mortal," she said. "Bernard's just prejudiced." She cast him an appreciative look.

"You may play piano like a mortal," Matt interjected, "but the music you draw from the banjo is heavenly."

There was nothing she could do but accept the compliment. "Thank you," she said, and spooned batter onto a baking sheet.

There were a few words about business during dinner, but most of the talk was about the Island. Matt filled the hours with folklore, which, he carefully explained to Melissa, was the polite name for stories with only a partial basis in truth. "It's more important to have the sense of what happened than the actual dates and facts. I've learned more about human nature—what makes men go to sea for *years* on end. Can you imagine how those women must have felt, waiting for their husbands to come home, never knowing if they would or not?"

"I think I can," Melissa mused. The flat landscape had disappeared in the night. Melissa could hear the sound of birds on the water. In the distance a bell tolled. "What's that?" she asked.

"Town bells," Matt told her. "They used to ring the bells every time a man was lost at sea, but that doesn't happen much anymore. Now they ring the bell in memory of those who were lost . . . it is one of the few ways the whaling tradition is kept alive on Nantucket. Tonight, however, the bells ring for a more practical reason."

"Why?" Bernard asked.

"Karen and John are giving a concert down near the pier. I told them we'd try to come. Are you up for more music?"

"I'd love to hear more," Melissa said at once.

"There's my vote, too," Bernard agreed. He was glad they were going. He had never seen Melissa so vivacious as she'd been when she was playing the banjo, and he was suddenly determined to bring music back into her public life. Damn her 'relatives'! He refused to let them haunt her any longer.

"Would you mind if we jammed back at the house?" Matt asked them when the concert was over. "Nantucket has a lame midnight curfew for street music, but I doubt anyone wants to stop playing for the night."

"Are you tired, darling?" Bernard quizzed. He had seen the light in her eyes at Matt's question, but he wanted to hear her ask for the music to continue.

"I'm far too awake to sleep," she explained. "I'd love to hear more. Those old sea chanteys are really special."

"Will you play, too?" Matt asked.

She hesitated for just a minute. A sickle of moon lit their path home. "If Bernard will play the harmonica."

They reached the house at the same time John and Karen did. Janie, the striking blonde who had been with them earlier, returned with her husband, Peter, and their five-year-old son. All brought their fiddles. They crowded into the living room of Matt's beach bungalow, more densely for the additional friends who had joined their party.

One quick look around the room assured her she knew no one. Melissa grabbed up the banjo and played continuously until the party broke up five hours later. The first island birds had begun to sing. The sky had lightened, but the sun hadn't rounded the earth enough to show.

She was on the beach in time to see the first rim of gold, Bernard's bulky red sweater thrown hastily over the shift she had worn the night before. Her long legs shivered in the cold morning air as she dug her toes into the wet sand.

Bernard wrapped her in his arms and brought her face to his warm chest. Absently he traced her arm with the back of his middle finger. "We should think about sleep," he said.

"I'm too happy to think," Melissa declared. "I never want to go to sleep. . . . I want to stay awake forever, playing music with overnight friends, hearing those songs until I know them by heart. Oh, Bernard, thank you . . . this has all been perfect."

"I did nothing but bring you along. You are responsible for your good time. You and that banjo, that is."

"Well," she compromised, musing over what he'd just said. "Thank you, anyway. I wouldn't have had such a good time, no matter what you say, had it not been for you."

"Only because you wouldn't have known where to come. That's all the credit I'm willing to take. No," he protested, taking her by the shoulders and turning her to face him. "I won't hear anything more. If anyone gave joy last night, it was you! Everyone in the room was smiling brighter because of the way you played banjo, and I, for one, felt happiness far deeper than that."

Melissa broke into laughter. "You sound like *you* could use some sleep, mister. We'd better get you to bed."

His eyes flashed wickedly. "You've identified the location of my need, but not the activity."

Melissa wasn't going to be outdone. "With all these sand dunes, you want a bed?"

Bernard reached for a final answer. "I've made my bed," he said determinedly. "Now lie in it with me." His victory was Melissa's unequivocal submission.

The dunes had retained the heat from the previous day. Melissa felt the particles of sand shift beneath her as Bernard's weight shifted against hers. Sand got in her hair. Without thinking she poured handfuls over his bare back: it slid down his sides and landed on Melissa's belly. He kissed her face, her ear. She wanted him badly and told him, whispering the words of her desire into his ear. Her hands showed him the path of her longing, but he held her immobile beneath him. He

pulled at her earlobe with his teeth. Melissa released
the breath of anticipation she had been holding and
dropped her arms back over her head: her palms together, her fingers interlinked. *He* was in no hurry, she
thought to herself, there was no reason for *her* to hurry.
She closed her eyes and lifted her head to kiss him. She
submitted to his leisurely lovemaking. With one hand
he pressed her arms back hard against the sand and
held her there as his intent grew ardent. Melissa cried
out in surprise as he moved to explore her body more
intimately. She needn't have worried for the sound she
made; his mouth on hers muffled her cry of exaltation.
"Come inside," she beckoned feverishly.
"Exactly what I had in mind all along," he said, lifting her in his arms from the sand, and carrying her indoors to their bedroom. "Our love is coarse enough
without adding *sand* to the menu."

They spent most of the morning in bed, dozing from
time to time, but mostly lying together, as closely as two
people could within earshot of their host. It was some-
time after noon—Melissa had seen the sun reach the
top of the sky from the bedroom window—when they
heard Matt stumbling around the kitchen.
"Do you want to sleep some?" Bernard asked softly.
Melissa nodded her head. She lay curled in Bernard's
arms. "I'm going to check with Matt about his plans
for the day."
"Hurry back," Melissa said sleepily.
She must have fallen fast asleep, because when she
woke it was late. She was hot. She could only guess how
long she had slept.
Bernard's voice carried in from the deck. She could

hear Matt talking, too. They sounded awake and alert. She would have to make an effort to rise.

Bernard heard the shower water. "Sounds like your musician friend is awake at last."

"She sure is something on that banjo."

"You should hear her on the piano, Matt."

"Where did you find her?" Matt asked in amazement.

"Do you think I share such secrets?"

"Well, does she have any friends?"

"Here she is. Ask her yourself."

Melissa slid open the heavy glass door; it was crusted white with salt from the ocean. "I'm going to make every effort to pretend I'm awake," she said cheerfully.

"I don't understand why you're tired," Matt prodded. "*I* slept perfectly well, except for those damned rabbits outside the house. Did you hear them?" he asked innocently.

"No," Bernard answered for her. "She was too busy munching carrots."

"I think I'd better not start this day," Melissa contended. "How did I lose you to his side, Matt?"

"You haven't lost him," Bernard interjected. "In fact, he's been trying to turn my head so he can turn yours."

Melissa pressed her face against the dark skin on Bernard's arms. "You're adorable when you're jealous," Melissa whispered. "But it's entirely unnecessary." She said it more seriously than she intended. Matt cocked his head to one side, interested in her words. Bernard cleared his throat and started to protest.

"I'm—I'm not jealous," he insisted, but his voice broke too high.

"Voice tells all!" Matt punctuated, and broke into a song about true Nantucket lovers.

"Are you still sponsoring the Regal Competition?" Matt asked, clearing the table of dishes. Having surrendered to an off-schedule day, they ate breakfast on the deck as the sun set. Matt had sautéed sea scallops in butter and baked them in a vintage white wine before enclosing them inside a paper-thin crêpe.

Bernard thought for a minute. "It is about that time of year again, isn't it?"

"Are *you* associated with the Regal Competition?" Melissa asked, her voice full of curiosity.

"It was one of my father's pet projects," he explained, "to launch worthy musicians into their careers. I've continued to support it as part of the tradition." He sipped coffee from his cup. "It's not Tanglewood— we've intentionally kept it small and highly selective," he added, trying to underplay the importance of the ritual.

"Yes, but for those who *know,* it is eminently respected," Melissa defended. She studied him closely.

"I don't have much to do with it, really. I only sign the checks, but I've always enjoyed the music. Are you interested in entering?" She shook her head abruptly. "Don't be so quick to dismiss it. I've heard you play. You're good enough."

"Besides," Matt broke in, "the prize money is considerable."

"The very idea of competing sends chills down my back," she confessed.

"Well, it was just an idea."

* * *

That night Bernard took Melissa and Matt to dinner at the Harbor House. They lingered over their dessert, savoring the native blueberries buried in rich scones and cream. Matt introduced Melissa and Bernard to the restaurant's chef, and he was so taken by Melissa's enthusiasm for the dessert that he offered to show her the carefully guarded bush in 'Sconset where the berries grew.

"Does she do this to everyone she meets?" Matt stammered.

Melissa tried to disguise her delight. "I didn't do anything!"

Matt ignored her, pressing Bernard for confirmation. "She has us all under her spell, doesn't she?"

" 'Fraid so . . . I no longer try to fight it. I knew from the instant I saw her that it was useless to struggle."

"Now, stop it!" Melissa protested. "You talk as if I'd cast a magic spell."

"Didn't you?" Matt and Bernard asked simultaneously.

"I give up! That's what I get for being so nice."

"Nice?" they chorused.

Melissa stared at them, speechless. "Forget it. I'm going out for a walk before I'm further humiliated."

"Can I come along if I promise to behave?" Matt asked. "I need to work off some of this food." He rose to join her.

Melissa looked to Bernard, waiting for him to join them. "You two go ahead. I'd rather sit with my coffee and look at Matt's manuscript."

"Now?"

"I might never have another chance, but take your walk." He was speaking to Melissa's uncertainty. "I'm fine where I am."

"Should I stay to answer any questions?" Matt asked.

"No, go with her," he said, watching Melissa glide through the dining room. "And keep track of the things she admires. Whenever I'm around, she feigns disinterest," he explained.

"Gosh, you never take me shopping!" Matt complained, punctuating his sulk with a flick to his wrist.

"Just find out what she likes," Bernard answered, glowering.

Most of the stores were already closed, but Melissa didn't mind. It was fun to stroll along the sparsely peopled streets, dreaming of the first Nantucketers, and not having to deal with twentieth century prices helped to maintain the illusion.

Matt caught up with her, and told her stories about the changes that had occurred over the recent years. They passed a street musician, and Matt stopped to introduce him to Melissa. "A year ago musicians weren't allowed to play on the streets," he explained. "There was a big court case: the town officials against one musician. He took the town to court and won his rights. Now there is music on the streets every day in summer, just like in the first days of Nantucket."

Melissa stopped him with a hand to his sleeve. "You make me understand why I need music in my life."

Matt nodded briskly. "It's our tradition," he affirmed, then frowned. "Why don't you share your music, Melissa?"

"How do you know—" she started, her thoughts speeding ahead to what Bernard must have told him.

"I could tell the instant you picked up the banjo that you were used to playing alone," he confessed. "Your whole face changed. You looked to me like a woman starved to share her music. Why *don't* you perform?"

"It's a long story. . . ." She exhaled a long breath before beginning. "My husband died two years ago. . . . He was a musician. . . . I've had to reexamine how I feel about music without him." She studied his concerned expression. "I used to think I wouldn't ever play again, but I must play if only for myself."

"He wrote music?"

Melissa hadn't noticed her admission. For a moment she didn't know how to respond. "Yes. He composed and played piano. No one you'd know," she hastened to add.

"Bernard knows all this?"

"To be truthful, Matt, I haven't told anyone. It's been a hard year, and the subject is painful to me. Bernard doesn't know yet . . . even if I thought it would help for him to know, I don't see how I could tell him, now. He'd be sure to resent—"

"I don't know . . . he's pretty smitten. I bet you could tell him anything, and he'd still think you were the most wonderful person in his life. I know I do," he added.

"Thanks, Matt." She pursed her lips together thoughtfully.

"Anytime. And I mean what I said about sharing your music. When you play banjo you radiate like a

Nantucket captain's wife whose husband's just returned
home after seven years at sea. I'd sure like to see what
you look like at the piano."

He didn't say any more, and neither did Melissa. Instead they remarked on the beauty and craftsmanship
of the articles on display in the stores they walked
past.

"Come on," Matt urged, taking Melissa by the
hand. "I've seen enough of Main Street. Since you and
Bernard insist on leaving tomorrow morning, and you
probably won't come back for ages, I want to spend our
last night together listening to you play."

"Is that so?" Melissa laughed. "If you want music,
you'd better plan on playing, too."

"But of course! I'd never pass up the chance to jam
with a wizard like you. Choose your weapon: banjo or
piano?"

"What can you play on fiddle?" she asked quickly.
Last night she had wondered how her classical training
could be useful in folk music. She imagined a fiddle
and piano duet would be fun, regardless of how they
sounded.

"Any tune I can't play, Janie and Peter are sure to
know."

The five of them partied throughout the night. There
were breaks for conversation and food, but as soon as
someone picked up an instrument, enthusiasm would
spread to the others. Melissa dazzled them all, but especially Bernard, with her solo improvisations. By the end
of the evening it was she who was suggesting the key
they should play in. When it became a question of grab-

bing an hour's sleep or another few songs, Melissa
voted to continue playing.

The ferry left dock at ten o'clock that morning, and
Melissa barely had time to wash and change before the
ride home. It didn't matter that she hadn't slept more
than a few hours all weekend. She could sleep once she
was home: the company had simply been too good to
miss. She leaned her head back against the car seat and
hummed folk tunes.

"Addicting, aren't they?" Bernard remarked. Melissa
nodded, humming the refrain to "Gone, Gonna Rise
Again." "That's why it's so important that Matt's book
be published," he stressed. "Some of the songs we were
singing have never been put on paper. He's preserving a
culture." He watched her stifle a yawn with great effort.
"Tired?" he asked. She shrugged. "Sleep if you want
to," he said.

Melissa closed her eyes for a minute, but she was too
keyed up to sleep. "Bernard? About the Regal . . ."

He kept his eyes on the road. They were speeding
through lush green countryside, as they had agreed
back roads were preferable to interstate highways.

"Would I have to perform in front of a crowd?"

"Not a crowd exactly. It's a bit more civilized than
that, but the final contestants do play to a full concert
hall. Are you interested? I wouldn't be surprised if you
could win."

Melissa swallowed hard. Her thoughts whirled with
the problems she would have to face, but also the re-
wards, especially if she did win. She recalled what Matt
had said, about sharing her music. Was she selfish to
keep her ability to herself? Would a performance be

more of a betrayal to Jean-Pierre than her silence? What would he have wanted her to do?

She glanced sideways at Bernard and thought back to all the people they had met that weekend. No one had recognized her. Maybe there *was* a way for her to reenter the music world as Melissa Dennison. Without the onus of her married name, perhaps she could compete without evoking her past. She looked different now. The long hair she had worn as Jean-Pierre's wife was cut to shoulder length and it curled around her face. She was several years older . . . not so skinny. If she could establish herself as Dennison, perhaps Bernard would never have to know, and more than anything else, she wanted to be free to be with him. For herself, as much as to nourish her relationship with Bernard, she needed to be free of her past. It was important that she be someone in her own right.

"Are you thinking of ways to spend the first prize?" His question startled her reverie. "With a first prize of ten thousand dollars, you could buy yourself the farm, couldn't you?"

"I *was* thinking about 'sharing' my music," she said solemnly, "but you are right about the farm."

"I'm glad you are considering it seriously."

She was thinking too hard to answer. They drove past a field of hay rolled into huge bales. A cow hung his head over a roadside fence to chew leaves from a bush. The tires hummed on the pavement, and Melissa wondered if she could pull it off. If she did, if she were able to present herself as Dennison, she'd be free.

"Bernard?"

He rubbed the back of her neck with his fingers. "What, dear? You look serious."

"Would it be breaking the rules, to be your friend and all?"

"I'm not a judge. I have no influence, really. I'm just one of several sponsors. The judges rule."

Her brows knotted closely. "What kind of publicity is there?"

"For the winner, or for all the contestants?"

"Everyone."

"Well, the press do give the event fair coverage. . . ."

"Do they dig around in one's past, or concern themselves with only professional questions?"

Bernard smiled. "The *Post* wouldn't cover it, if that's what you mean. Are you worried about your relatives?"

Melissa nodded.

"If you win, you'll be asked for an interview, no doubt. A prize will lead to future engagements, but you don't have to accept anything you don't want. You could accept the award and disappear from sight. No one would bother you. You'd be free to spend your time, as well as the money, any way you liked."

Melissa listened, wondering if it could be true.

"On the other hand," Bernard continued, "this might be the time to get over your in-laws." Melissa shuddered. "The question is whether to act to secure your future, or continue to serve your past."

That was the issue. She wondered if she dared. "I'll need some time to think about it."

He nodded. "You'll have to decide fairly soon. I don't know the exact deadline, but it can't be far away." He watched her mouth turn downward into a frown. "As reluctant as I am to share you, dear, for your own sake, I hope you'll decide to compete."

"It sounds so simple," she said thoughtfully.

"It is simple, darling." He reached for her hand, and squeezed it reassuringly. "Try to rest, now. We'll be home soon."

Home. She liked the way it sounded when he called her house his. He was only with her on weekends, and those excursions had been sabotaged twice already by his work. It wasn't as if he spent the majority of his time with her, but the time he did spend in Richmond felt like home to them both. He hung his bathrobe beside hers on the back of the bedroom door. His shaving brush and mug sat out on the bathroom sink all week; one Thursday Melissa had used his razor to shave her legs because she couldn't wait until the weekend to see wet lather in his shaving mug. When she cooked dinner for herself alone, she spiced according to Bernard's tastes.

When he was home with her, they coexisted as effortlessly as if they had been living together for years. He studied her patterns and adapted himself to them, even when they were more idiosyncratic than logical. He was never in her way; seemed to know which cupboard she would need next to open, and moved out of her way before being asked. He kept her company while she cooked. They liked the same radio station, at the same hours. Melissa's only problem was that she couldn't bring herself to practice Arbour's works. Since she devoted most of her time to his unfinished works, she felt compromised to play something else.

In the bedroom—their bedroom—he emptied his change on top of *his* bureau, where it might well stay all week long. He was always leaving something behind in his haste on Monday mornings, and tomorrow would be no different. Melissa enjoyed the things he left behind, as though he'd be home that evening to reclaim them. It made the week during which he was away pass more quickly. He unbuckled his belt and laid it on the bureau near the change. "Are you still tired?" he asked, dropping down beside her on the bed.

"Exhausted," she admitted, snuggling into the hollow of his arm. "A perfect weekend," she mused out loud, remembering the people they had met, how relaxed she had been. "Matt was the perfect host."

Bernard rubbed her shoulders between his fingers and thumb. Melissa draped her long leg over his and leaned against him.

"I'm glad you liked him."

"He's so nice!"

"I think Matt would rather you had come alone."

His words surprised her. "Darling, I think Matt is—I think he is gay."

Bernard laughed. "Really?" He considered the possibility. "Well, not all the time."

"Oh, these artistic types."

"Real kinky, aren't they?" He kissed the top of her head. "Not like you, who after a weekend without sleep is still dying for more."

"Is that what you think? Pretty sure of yourself."

"I didn't put your hand where it is now."

Melissa looked down to discover her fingers had slid by habit over the inside of his thigh and were arousing him. "A mind of its own," she said, deferring to the evidence. Bernard pulled her back onto the bed, and with the gentlest of touches, he dismissed her need for sleep.

* * *

"I'll bring your suitcase in from the car," Bernard announced, stepping into his trousers. The sky had grown dark as they lay together.

"If you're going out anyway," Melissa said, stretching her long brown body across the length of the bed, "and if I use both ounces of my remaining strength, I might make it into the bathroom to brush my teeth."

"Don't drown. I'll be back in a minute, with your toothbrush."

"You'd better hurry," she answered, making no effort to rise from the bed. Instead, she wrapped her arms around the feather pillow for company.

Bernard sang in a loud, happy voice as he unloaded their suitcases from the car. He clamored noisily back into the house.

"I didn't know we had so much stuff," Melissa exclaimed as Bernard rounded the corner into the bedroom, his arms full of packages.

Bernard smiled mysteriously. "We didn't."

Melissa, puzzled, sat cross-legged on the bed, the pillow covering her lap. He handed her a large, bulky bag.

Tentatively, she opened the bag and peeked inside. "Oh, Bernard!" she cried excitedly, pulling a fisherman's sweater from the tissue paper. "It's exactly the one I wanted!" She knelt on the bed and pressed it against her bare chest, to peer into the mirror. Her eyes lit up. "It is beautiful!" she declared.

"Just like you," Bernard answered breathlessly, overwhelmed by Melissa's tanned lanky body kneeling up on the bed, the white wool sweater pressed close to her breast. He took the sweater from her, and it was hours later that she remembered—or cared—to inspect the contents of the other packages.

He had bought her the sheer handpainted silk dress she had swooned over in the dress-shop window, and an heirloom scrimshaw carving depicting two square-riggers at sea. She hurried from one parcel to the next, astonished to find still another of the items she had admired on her stroll with Matt.

"I didn't know I was walking with a spy," she said. "Couldn't you think of anything to buy that I didn't admire?" she bitched, too dazed to be serious.

Bernard accepted her taunt gracefully. "I prefer to buy what I *know* you will like rather than what I *think* you *might* like. However, I did manage to think of two gifts on my own." He fumbled in his jacket pocket for a tiny box.

Melissa stared at the ring box suspiciously. "You are sure I am going to like this?"

"Absolutely. But first you have to open the other present. Close your eyes, I'll bring it to you."

Melissa obeyed dutifully, until she felt cold metal pressed against her warm skin. She opened her eyes, and Bernard extended a banjo to her, a red ribbon tied through its strings. "But this is the one I played at Matt's house!" He nodded. "I can't believe it!"

"It's really a joint gift—from Matt, because he agreed to part with it—and from me because I paid a small fortune for it."

"Darling," she said, throwing her arms around his neck and covering his mouth with kisses.

"Can I have Matt's portion of gratitude, too?" he asked, when she stopped.

Melissa kissed him once lightly upon the lips. "Now that Matt's taken care of, I think I may have some appreciation left over for you."

She picked a simple tune, but stopped and put the banjo down when Bernard held out his arms. The look of love in his eyes, as well as the touch of his finger against her thigh, forged her anticipation until the teasing wasn't enough anymore, and it was hours before they satisfied their appetites for one another, before Bernard lay back with a groan of satisfaction, and Melissa curled into the protective cradle of his arm. Eventually, Bernard leaned up to reach for the small box which lay neglected—altogether forgotten—on the nightstand.

Melissa looked at it anxiously. "More?"

"Are you complaining?"

"But you've given me so much and . . ."

"Yes?" he waited for her to continue.

"And that box looks exactly like a ring box!"

"A prize for the right answer! True, it is a ring box." He held it in his open palm. "Care to take a look inside?"

"Are you sure you want to do this?" Melissa quizzed. "We've said a lot of things to each other, but we really haven't known each other very long."

"Do you have *any* doubts about the way I feel for you?"

"No," she said meekly. "But there is more to consider than just us."

"Like what?" As far as he was concerned, they were all that mattered.

"I haven't met your mother, and—and you haven't met Patrice," she said with a groping air."

"You can't come up with better arguments than that?"

Melissa took the box and weighed it in her palm. She certainly could think of better reasons! She couldn't consider marriage to Bernard without revealing her past, and she was certain he would regret his offer if he knew she'd been lying to him. "I can't give you any good reasons, but there are considerations!" she insisted.

"Unless you can tell me one, I'm afraid you're going to have to open that box."

She slid the paper off the outside. She didn't have to accept his proposal, she reminded herself. He had told her the timing was up to her, and this was much too soon. She loved Bernard and she wanted to spend her life with him, but she wasn't sure how.

Inside the sturdy white box was a smaller one: burgundy velvet rimmed with a band of gold. Melissa paused before opening it. The truth was, she wanted to accept Bernard's offer. She knew that none of it made sense logically, but nevertheless, the pounding of her heart had to be heard. Already, she loved him as if they had been courting for years. She wanted him so badly she hurt inside.

"I love you, Melissa," Bernard whispered, as she lifted the top to the box.

Lying against the royal-blue satin lining were two banjo fingerpicks. Tears welled up in Melissa's eyes.

"Oh, darling," Bernard said sadly. He had expected to have her laugh, to be relieved, anything but this. "I'm so sorry."

Melissa cried even harder, the tears ran down her cheeks onto the backs of her hands.

Bernard felt terrible. "Melissa, please," he cried, his

voice thin and scratchy. "It was a rotten trick, I admit it, but it was only a joke. I wanted to make you laugh."

Melissa dried her eyes the best she could with her wet hands. She felt ashamed and confused, but suddenly she turned angry. "You set me up . . . to be humiliated. To expect a marriage proposal! How dare you play with my emotions like that?"

Bernard hung his head penitently. "I'm sorry, darling. I made a mistake in judgment. I told a bad joke . . . you were right not to laugh. Can you forgive me, and forget it, hopefully in that order?"

The burst of anger purged Melissa. "Of course I can forgive you," she said, her anger diminishing as quickly as it came. "I'm sorry for behaving so stupidly." It was the first time she had lost her temper, and it embarrassed her, especially after he had just showered her with beautiful gifts. "I sure know how to kick a gift horse . . ."

"Does that mean you'll do it again?" he asked.

"Probably. Or something worse. Sometimes my temper runs wild." It was from holding in so much, but she couldn't explain that to him any more than she could control her temper.

"I'm really sorry, darling."

"I know. I am, too," she added. "I love you. These are beautiful presents."

"Think you can trust me again?"

"Yes," she assured him simply. There was no room for joking. The look in Bernard's eyes told her he had accepted her words as a promise to their future. As she fell back into his arms, it was a commitment she cherished making . . . for it was more important than the sleep they did without, from dark until dawn.

* * *

The next morning Bernard insisted Melissa stay in bed to sleep. She could hear him shaving, showering, opening drawers and cabinets, making his morning coffee. When he returned to the bedroom to dress, Melissa wrapped her sleepy arms around his waist and slowed his progress. When he sat on the bed to tie his shoes, he gave in to her desire for him, abandoned his hurry, indulged her whim.

"Quite a pretty hand, Melissa," he said softly, lifting her left hand into his and toying with her fingers.

For a minute Melissa didn't understand what he meant, she was so dazed by his presence, but at the same instant she felt an unfamiliar weight on her hand, she saw the ring. "Where did this come from?" she asked nervously.

"You must have wished it there," he said enigmatically.

"Bernard, *it's so beautiful!* Where did you ever find it?"

"It's part of the family jewels. The first of three rings, the last being a simple band of gold. You see, Melissa," he explained, "it's part of the Van Atman tradition to move very slowly. I, for one, have never considered taking the steps you say you fear. I've never loved anyone but *you.* It was you, not I, who married in virtual *childhood.* I've waited half my lifetime to make this commitment, and if I hadn't met you, I'm not sure I ever would have used this ring. What does it matter if we've known each other two months or ten years? I know that I want to spend my life with you. If you understand that, I'll be content, even if you remove this ring."

"What does it mean for me to wear this ring?" she asked softly. She was just beginning to understand the importance of his family tradition. Matt had, through his history and folklore, taught Melissa a lot about Bernard and his way of life. "I don't want to violate any tradition."

"If you wear the ring, you are making a commitment to our love. As long as you love me, and I you, that ring binds us."

"What about the other rings?"

"Not until you are ready. Pure and simple. Like our love. Would you consent to wear this ring, Melissa?"

His words sounded right to her. "I would be proud," she cried. "Pure and simple."

"I don't know how much chance there is of keeping our love pure, with your hand on my leg."

"I'm only following the instincts of my love . . ." she started, but before she finished, he was back with her again, his hard, powerful body pressed tightly to hers, their bodies moving to an unheard melody. She kept her left hand on his shoulder, and even with her head thrown back in ecstasy, she could see the circle of emeralds brightly lodged in gold, like the jewels of their intimacies lodged in the precious metal of their love.

CHAPTER TWELVE

"Has Manhattan been evacuated?" Melissa asked, opening the door reluctantly to greet Patrice. Bernard had just arrived unexpectedly, interrupting her work, and now here was Patrice. "What are you doing here?"

"What are *you* doing?" she returned. "I saw Bernard's car on the hill. Is he here?"

"He just got here," Melissa offered, feeling the need to explain. Patrice peered past her, into the living room. "I guess I've kept you two from meeting as long as I can. Come on in."

Bernard rose to greet the two women. "Oh, hello there," he said, and Melissa was startled at the familiarity in his voice. Bernard explained. "I passed you on the road, didn't I?"

Patrice grinned, distinctly remembering the burgundy roadster and its handsome pilot. They had exchanged an approving glance as he passed her. "I remember. . . ."

Bernard smiled through his slight embarrassment. He, too, remembered the look. "Nice to see you again."

Melissa groaned. "I knew I should never have let this happen!"

"What do you mean?" Patrice denied.

"Well, Bernard's blushing and you look positively guilty. What did you two do as you 'passed' on the road?"

Patrice laughed at the accusation. "I know better than to mess with your man."

"I don't know . . . you have good reason to worry," he warned Melissa. "She is very pretty." He tickled her until she laughed. "Where is your faith in me?"

Melissa broke away. She knew he was right. "But what are you both doing here? I'm supposed to be practicing!"

"Then why were you dancing when I drove up?" Bernard challenged.

"Dancing . . . ?" Patrice chimed in, raising her eyebrow skeptically.

"Great exercise," Melissa admitted offhandedly, and pirouetted across the room to collapse onto the living room sofa. She was feeling feisty today, and the arrival of her two friends did nothing to settle her mood.

"I think it's a good thing we came up here," Bernard said, conferring with Patrice. "The heat's made her loony."

"Bats!" Melissa shouted. The heat, combined with no sleep, had indeed made her silly.

"And lazy," Patrice added. "If we hadn't come along, she'd have spent the afternoon taking a nap in the boat."

"Which is exactly how I plan to pass the day," Bernard said. "I want to stay out of your way, dear, while you finish your work."

"Thanks a lot." She sat upright on the couch.

"I'm just here to float in your boat," Patrice assured her. "Don't let *me* interrupt your work."

Melissa pretended to fume. "How do you expect me to work with you two violating my pond?" She didn't tell them her plan to quit work early, she was so restless from the heat.

"When you finish practicing, you can join us," Bernard promised, sounding just like a parent. "Now back to work."

"Not until you tell me why you're here. You said you wouldn't be home until late tonight."

Bernard curtailed his teasing. "This afternoon's meeting was postponed until tomorrow because of the heat. I have to be back at the crack of dawn but my first thought was to come home early. The evening is never long enough as it is."

She tried to disguise her pleasure with a demand for explanation from Patrice. "And what are you doing here?"

Patrice flashed her a most insincere smile. "I thought I'd ask you to cook dinner for me." Melissa started to protest, but Patrice stopped her. "You'll find four lobsters in a crate in my car."

"Live?"

"Unless they baked in the sun. Come on, Bernard, help me bring them in."

"Let's make it fast. I'm dying to swim in the pond."

"I hope you both drown!" Melissa cried. Bernard held open the door for Patrice. "But not until after you've both sunburned and peeled!" she added.

"Wanna come with us?" Patrice invited.

"*No!* This damned competition is in ten days! Get out and let me practice!"

She could hear them talking as they walked up to the pond. As much as she did want to join them, to be out of doors to enjoy their company, she loved her solitude at the piano, the thrill that came after executing a perfect rendition of the piece she would play in the competition. For her the conflict would always be there. Maybe she'd just have to learn to live with it, to give in to the pull of loving two separate parts of her life equally. Bernard complemented her music, and her music spoke to the joy he gave her.

Laughter rippled back to the house. Melissa could hear them lowering the boat into the water, having a time of it. She was glad they were here, and through her immediate jealousy, she was pleased that they were having time to get to know each other, independent of her. She loved them so much, she wanted them to be friends, too. Maybe there was a way to bring all the parts of her life together? She doubted it, not with her luck.

Melissa groaned to herself and took her seat at the piano. She wondered if Patrice had brought a bathing suit, and if she'd keep it on. She lifted the cover to the keyboard and banged an outlandishly discordant measure, followed by another equally sour string of notes. She could hear their faint laughter as she attempted to remind herself how to concentrate.

Patrice dropped the straps to her swimsuit. She and Bernard had claimed opposite ends of the boat.

"I needed this," Bernard exclaimed. "God, Manhattan was a bitch today."

"In heat!" Patrice added. "One hundred degrees and

one hundred percent humidity. And she asks why we are here?"

"It *is* unfair of us to flaunt our leisure when she's slaving away at work."

"Who said the world is fair?" Patrice said.

Bernard pondered her words for a minute. The sun felt good here, away from the concrete of the city. He trailed his hand in the water. "Patrice," he said suddenly, "I keep thinking I recognize you from someplace."

"You look familiar, too. Who do you know?"

He ran down a list of people, but she didn't know any of them by name. "I remember!" he said suddenly. "You used to spend time with Arthur Connell?"

"How do you know Arthur?"

"He serves on my board of trustees—has for years. I've always liked him."

"Me, too," she admitted wistfully.

"You don't see him anymore?"

Patrice shook her head regretfully.

"What happened, if you don't mind me asking."

Patrice hesitated, studying Bernard's expression. He looked genuinely concerned, and suddenly Patrice felt like telling him the whole story. It *had* been an ordeal breaking off with Arthur. She'd loved him enough to make a commitment . . . to make a life with him . . . to help raise his son. The night of his party, she had agreed to marry him.

"After Melissa's husband died, she needed a lot of my time. Arthur got impatient. I sometimes thought he felt responsible for—" She caught herself. She could tell him her story but not Melissa's. "It was simply easier to stop seeing him."

"It doesn't sound like it was simple or easy."

"Arthur is one man I will always miss," she confessed. "Of course, Melissa doesn't know any of this. She had enough to think about, and she never thought to ask about him . . . probably thought he was just another passing fancy." She smiled weakly.

"I seem to recall an enviable closeness between you two. Didn't Melissa ever see you together?"

"Yes, a couple of times, but when did you?" Patrice asked, trying to jar him forward in her memory.

"Just once," he admitted, "and at a distance. Remember the party Arbour's wife played—"

Maybe it was Patrice's expression or perhaps it was the name alone that triggered his memory, but at once he felt shocked for not having guessed earlier. Hadn't he daydreamed of the young pianist for days following Connell's party? How could he have forgotten the soulful eyes of the beautiful performer? Hadn't they bored a hole straight through his soul, even then? "How could I have been so blind?" he cursed himself.

"I didn't know how much you knew," Patrice said softly.

Bernard shook his head from side to side, puzzling. "I knew there was something . . . something she wasn't telling me, but I never thought—" He paused for a moment while the pieces fell into place. "Now it all makes sense: her dread of recognition, her fear of public places, her relatives." He looked up at Patrice, an angry flash of incredulity lighting his eyes. "I never even recognized her!"

"She doesn't really look the same." Patrice offered what was the truth, but it did little to appease him. "What are you going to do?"

Bernard shrugged his shoulders, still struggling with his discovery. In an instant Melissa ceased to be merely a talented and promising pianist nervously entering her first competition. She was widow to the great Jean-Pierre Arbour; a celebrity in her own right, and something of a legend in the music world.

Just as quickly he grasped the cause of Melissa's fears, her need to hide. Even from him. He cringed at the thought of his impatience, and vowed to be more understanding.

"I would hate for anything to interfere with your feelings," she said protectively. "She really does love you."

Bernard never considered a change in *his* feelings. "I just hope she'll find a way to tell me, *before* she finds out I know."

"What if it doesn't happen that way?"

"Then I hope we've established enough trust between us to weather a confrontation." Even as he spoke, he wasn't sure they had. The press had been relentless in their coverage of her tragedy. He worried they had scarred her permanently.

The screen door slammed shut. Melissa ran toward them, waving her hands over her head. "Enough!" she hollered. "I can't stand the temptation a minute longer."

Bernard felt his heart twist at the thought of losing her. "Our secret?" he said to Patrice, his eyes beseeching her.

"Mum," Patrice agreed. She didn't want anything disrupting Melissa's romance, not the way it had been for her and Arthur.

"Here I come!" she sang, her outer clothes already

stripped and discarded by the side of the pond, the last of her tune lost to the splash of cool water.

"What's most important is that she perform again. What happens to us comes second," Bernard said quickly, in conclusion.

"Don't you have that backwards?"

Melissa burst through the water's surface to overturn the yellow life raft. Her surprise attack gave her yardage but once the Millay-Van Atman team calculated their position, they drowned her defense. The continued their plan of advance until Melissa cried for mercy. Patrice accepted Melissa's surrender and retired from the game for the night. Bernard, on the other hand, savored his advantage until morning, leaving Melissa convinced that *his* victory was to *her* advantage.

The light shifted on the score of music. Melissa's concentration broke and she missed a chord. She glanced up to inspect the flickering lamplight, but instead found the room bright with sunshine; usually she heard the bird's song before dawn, but this morning she'd been too absorbed in timing the sonata and the light had followed the birds without her supervision.

She stretched her weary body and extinguished the lamp. She knew she should work more, but she was tired. Rehearsal was exhausting, lonely work, and she wanted to feel Bernard's arms around her as she fell asleep. He'd be leaving for work in a few hours; then she would work again. Somehow she would manage to have them both.

Her clothes fell to the floor and she left them there, too tired to care. She lifted the cover and slid into bed, wrapping her arms around Bernard's warm, sleeping body. His even breathing did more to quiet her ragged nerves than a mug of warm milk. After a few minutes in his arms, her breathing became as steady as his own. Before she was fully asleep, she felt him stir, and any desire for rest was replaced by a longing to hold him tighter, closer, more deliberately.

He stirred again and pulled her into his arms, never waking completely. She felt his passion stir, and she brought him to her, sliding down to surround him, hold him, cradle him in his sleep. They held each other suspended, until the alarm went off, and Bernard woke to their union.

"Damn if I'm late," he said, dismissing the alarm with a click to the dial. "I won't fire *myself*."

"At least not the way you fire me," Melissa joked, but her burning for him was no laughing matter.

She was at the piano practically all the time now. As the days before the competition grew fewer, her meals slackened to coffee and cheese sandwiches, whenever she remembered to eat, and her sleep was measured in half-hour naps. She could do without adequate food, and even without sleep for a time, but what she missed most as the pressure increased was her time with Bernard.

Faithfully, he returned to the country each night, but she never felt free to visit for long. Sometimes he himself was too tired for more than their thirty-minute conversations, their briefer embraces, and he crawled off to bed without her.

Melissa never trusted herself to stay in his arms for long. She feared she'd never go back to work. If she had any sense, would she prefer the cold ivory keys to

Bernard's tender embrace? The struggle had increased but not because Bernard was pulling harder from his desire for her—quite the contrary, his patience with her was extraordinary—but she was giving in, letting herself be drawn over the line—or at least she feared she would be, if she relaxed for too long. Increasingly, she preferred his company to her music, but she *had* to hold out a little longer; the contest would be over in only a few more days.

Yet she could no more go to him than she could muster enthusiasm for the task before her. She suffered from the guilt of not telling him about her past life, and from the fear that once he knew, he would leave her. Melissa couldn't stand the thought of losing his love.

She returned her hands to the keyboard and tried to concentrate, but her mind kept racing back to Bernard and the life he was inviting her to join: full of love, joy, trust. But what had happened to her discipline? She forced her way through an eight-bar segment, but her mind was far away, and the music sounded as empty as her arms felt. Finally, she gave in to her distraction, and playing a familiar tune, she let her thoughts run adrift.

Without the pressure of perfecting the sonata she would perform, Melissa found herself enjoying the sensation of simply playing. Her mind relaxed, too: her love for Bernard was as melodic as the harmonies beneath her fingertips. She released a deep sigh of relief and wondered if she'd ever be able to relax with him completely. She wanted to, as badly as he said he wanted her in his life, but something kept her from him. Maybe it was just too soon? Perhaps she needed more time to learn to trust again, but even as she wondered, she knew she could never relax, not until she told him; not until she had confided her carefully guarded secret. If he didn't quit her at once, she thought she could bring her entire self to their relationship: scarred and imperfect, at times impossible; an honesty that would allow him to share his fears and flaws, too.

Was she dreaming in vain? Surely he would run from the news. How could he help but to hate her? She'd be left with *nothing,* less than she had now.

Tears spilled out of her eyes. She knew she had to tell him, but how? What could she possibly say? A thousand answers filled her head, but the result was only confusion. She was too tired to think straight. She didn't even have the energy to practice anymore, let alone consider her predicament with Bernard. She shifted her weight on the bench. After the competition . . . then she'd tell him.

Melissa straightened up, struck suddenly by an idea. She would perform Arbour's *"Le Déclaration,"* the composition she had finished out of inspiration from Bernard, as a declaration of her love for him. He would know who she was in relationship to Arbour, and how deeply she valued him in the same moment; of the same piece. She'd be admitting to her past and accepting her future in one turn.

She could explain it all to him, *after* the competition, after she had *won* the contest. Then, if he did leave her, she'd still have something of value in her life. She would have regained her integrity, her right to be Arbour's widow in public; she could stop hiding and have a normal life with Bernard. Or, without him, she could count on the concert engagements and tours to distract her from her loss. And if he did want her, despite her deception, she would have found a way to have both his love and her music.

Motivation surged through her body like water through a fountain, and Melissa was determined to win the competition. Somehow, her freedom to be with Bernard, and his understanding of her evasiveness were intrinsically tied to the first prize ribbon. With renewed determination she started practicing *"La Déclaration,"* convinced she had found the way past the problem of telling Bernard her secret.

Yet regardless of her motivation, there was no ignoring Melissa's exhaustion, and when she erred in a relatively simple passage, her spirits crashed as immediately as they had risen. How could she think Bernard would be moved by her playing? How could she think to let him into her shambled life? Hadn't she driven one man to his grave because of her selfishness? If she really loved Bernard, shouldn't she hope he'd leave her, soon, before she could really hurt him? Even Jean-Pierre's harshest criticisms, which echoed back at her now, were mild compared to what she had to say about herself. She was as worthless as she was vulnerable.

Devastated, she left her work and curled up on the sofa to escape from herself into sleep. She couldn't stand to face Bernard in bed just now. His comfort would only emphasize her hypocrisy, reinforce her feeling of worthlessness. She didn't want him to see her crying, or ask the reason for her unhappiness. She was so tired she just might tell him, and then he'd leave her for sure. Sinking into the loneliness of her dilemma, she buried her head in her arms to muffle the sound of her sobbing and cried herself to sleep.

Bernard woke to find the bed empty. Could she still be working, he wondered, scrambling out from under the covers and into the living room. Finding her asleep on the couch did something to ease his anxiety, but as he covered her with a shawl and studied her pretty face, he questioned why she hadn't come to bed. Why had she preferred the solitude of the sofa to his company?

He wanted to wake her now, as much for an answer to his question as to insist she go to bed, but he feared she would consider herself rested enough to return to work. Quietly, he stole into the bathroom to shave and shower.

Bernard understood her obsession—he knew what it was to prepare for a performance, and Melissa, he realized, had more at stake than most contestants—but he wondered if there was any sense in his bearing witness to her compulsion. He had been rationalizing the long drive twice a day because he knew she counted on his support: even if they weren't together much during their waking hours, they touched unconsciously in their sleep, embraced when half-awake. But last night he had driven two hours to spend a total of five minutes in her presence. They could *talk* over the telephone.

Maybe he should say something, he thought, rinsing the traces of lather from his face. He had been seriously neglecting his work at the office, to the concern of his coworkers. Moreover, he needed sleep, desperately. Last night he had fallen asleep at the wheel, waking just instants before he crashed his car. There was no point risking his life unnecessarily. They both needed a full night's sleep, and Melissa apparently preferred the couch to his company.

He heard Melissa in the kitchen as he toweled himself dry from his shower, and when he emerged from the steamy bathroom, he found she had fixed him breakfast. He wished he hadn't been so noisy, but as long as she was awake, he was glad for the chance to talk.

He poured cream into his coffee and carried the cup into the bedroom where Melissa had tucked herself into bed.

"I missed you last night," he said, sitting on the edge of the bed. "Are you avoiding me?"

That was exactly what she was doing, but she didn't know how to explain her reasons for hiding. Simply, she felt too vulnerable in her plan to tell him her secret, and the thought of possibly losing him made her miserable with grief. "I just need some sleep," she answered remotely.

Bernard squeezed her hand, "We could both use some sleep," he agreed, rising to dress for the office. "What would you say if I stayed in New York tonight?"

His words hurt her as much as if he had intended to leave her. She closed her eyes and turned her face away from him. "Whatever you want," she said, her words barely audible.

"If you want me to come back tonight, I will, but we aren't seeing much of each other," he reasoned.

"I know," she said sadly. He was right to stay away. She was surprised he had continued to return each night. "It's hard to enjoy your company when I know I need to work more, and hard to ignore you when I'm supposed to be working." She didn't tell him that she'd rather be with him than with her music.

"Maybe you don't need more work. Maybe you

should come to New York with me. Take a few days off before the competition."

"But the contest is this Saturday!" she said, her voice quivering. Suddenly she felt the futility of what she was attempting. She might have perfected the Beethoven sonata by Saturday, but *"La Déclaration?"* She must have been insane to think she could master it so quickly. Having found a way to tell Bernard, she hated to see it wouldn't work. "I don't think I can go through with this competition," she said unhappily, giving way to her fears. And once they surfaced, there was no stopping them. Like tears pouring from flood gates, her doubts crowded her fears for room.

"But you are doing so well!"

Melissa was so upset she could hardly speak. She rubbed her right hand with her left, searching for an excuse to quit the contest. "I can't get my hand to work right!"

"Let me see it." He knew she worried about her hand when she couldn't face her other problems. He squeezed her palm between his thumb and middle finger. "My guess is that you've worked your hand into a spasm. You need to relax."

Melissa snatched back her hand. "That's not it," she insisted. "It's these ugly scars."

Bernard reached for her hand again, hoping to calm her, but she kept it hidden. "Scars might look bad, Mel, but they don't have much to do with your performance," he said, trying to insert some logic into their conversation. "The sympton is pain and lack of mobility, but the root of your problem is an overworked hand. How did you say you hurt your hand?"

"I already told you," she said testily.

"I know, but I forgot. It was an accident, wasn't it? When your husband died?"

Melissa stared at him blankly. She had invented a story when he asked, just in time to dismiss his suspicions, but it hadn't been a very convincing story, and she had been relieved that he hadn't asked again. Now she couldn't remember what it was she had said actually. "Yes, it happened when Jean died." She pronounced it "Gene" instead of stressing the French variant. "I'm just not good enough to perform Saturday."

"That's simply not true," Bernard swore. "You play exquisitely."

"You must be tone deaf," she accused.

"Melissa, you're tired. Let's have this discussion when you are more rested."

"Stop trying to sedate me! If you want to stay in New York, fine, but don't patronize me. I sound terrible, and you know it." She glared at him. "Or you would, if you had any musical taste."

"Do you want to fight with me?" Bernard asked, trying to rally his composure to offset her unreasonable rage. "Will you feel better about yourself if I lose my temper?"

"I'm not picking a fight!" she shouted. She wished he wouldn't be so calm and reasonable. "I play the piano like a truck driver!" she said stubbornly, but her set jaw quivered. What was happening? How could she have gotten herself into this mess?

Bernard watched her anger shift from him to herself. "If you don't want to compete, you can withdraw from the contest."

Hearing the suggestion from him was more than she could stand in her present state. "Just go—leave me alone," she cried. Her words frightened her, but she'd lost control of herself. In solitude maybe she could figure things out.

"Do you mean that?" he asked, trying to disguise his hurt.

Melissa nodded yes, and burst into tears.

"Please let me help you," Bernard urged, feeling as helpless as Melissa obviously was confused.

"I just need to be alone," she managed.

"All right," he conceded. If that was what she wanted, he would give it to her.

"Please don't hate me," she pleaded, watching him dress with a speed that frightened her, though she couldn't bare to have him stay.

"I'll never hate you, Mel. You are the only one who is hating."

"Please, no lectures." Her defenses rallied.

"Don't worry. I'm going," he promised, and knotted his tie with determination. Grabbing his briefcase and car keys, he gave her a final look before closing the door.

"Drive carefully, please," she called after him, in spite of herself.

Bernard was halfway to Hillsdale before he turned the car around and returned north. He wasn't angry with her for being irrational. He knew she was under tremendous pressure, and her inability to share her misery with him did nothing to relieve her stress. He had to make her know he sympathized without backing her into a corner.

Melissa stayed in bed after Bernard was gone, but she felt too miserable to sleep. How could she have acted like that? She understood why he'd left her, and why he hadn't wanted to make the trip back to Richmond that night, but she couldn't comprehend why he insisted he loved her. She was simply unlovable.

Too restless to stay in bed, she tied her hair up and turned on the cold water to wash her face. In the mirror she saw how red her eyes were, and not just from crying. The dark circles underneath had a life of their own. Most of the tan she had acquired in the early summer had faded, and instead of leaving her skin white, she looked washed out; gray. Impatiently, she brushed her hair down around her face, to soften the gaunt lines, and slapped her face to add color.

Clearly she needed exercise more than sleep. Ever since she'd learned of the competition, she had been sitting at the piano, or pacing the room. Impulsively, she threw on her shorts and a skimpy T-shirt and ran outside.

Last night's dew still lingered on the tall grass. The moisture felt good on her feet, and the early morning's sun warmed her shoulders. Ignoring the garden and its forest of weeds, she hurried to the apple orchard where she swung herself up into one of the lower boughs.

Melissa leaned back against the trunk and frowned at her beautiful surroundings. She wanted desperately to own the farm, but she wasn't sure she could afford it, if the price was to lash out at the person she loved most. Wouldn't it make more sense to forfeit the farm, to find another place to live, than to lose Bernard? She feared his patience couldn't last much longer. Hadn't he left her in haste, anxious to regain his freedom? He had insisted he wasn't upset with her, but for how long could he tolerate her hysteria?

She swung her legs down from the branch and

hopped down to the ground. She had to get some sleep. The circle of confusion was gyrating out of control.

She hadn't even dried her feet, or removed her clothes to get back into bed when Bernard barged into the house.

"You know what our problem is?" he said, tearing off his clothes. "We haven't spent an entire day in bed for weeks. All that energy you're storing for the competition needs to be released. It's working against you."

Melissa's speechlessness didn't disturb him. He could see from the light in her eyes that she was more relieved than angry that he had returned. Both of them had felt the toll of their disagreement, and he was unwilling to perpetuate the misunderstanding; to let doubts and confusions fester unattended.

"I love you, Melissa. Even if you wish I didn't." She started to protest, but he stopped her words with his mouth. "Shhhh," he said, breaking from the kiss. "We're in this together. If you want to withdraw from the competition, I'll support your decision. And if you want to perform, I'll be there to hold your hand until curtain call."

"Scars and all?"

"Yes, Godzilla. Scars, temper tantrums, and verbal abuses, I'm with you all the way. Just don't let any of it interfere with how we feel about one another, all right?" Melissa nodded. "Now let's see if we can coax some of that tension out of you."

At noon Bernard rolled over to phone his office, but only to tell his secretary that he'd be away all day. He gave her a list of instructions and an assurance that he would be back the following day.

Melissa studied him while he talked. "Do you have a ton of work to do?"

He replaced the phone to the bedside table. "Yes, I have a great deal of work to do, but we are more important." The Regal Competitions had placed additional demands on his already heavy workload. But he didn't complain to Melissa because he wanted to spare her unnecessary worry. The truth was that he was preoccupied most of the time with worry about work. Last Monday he had installed a microphone in his car's tape player so he could dictate memos while he drove back and forth to the country. "I should go into work today, but I know you'd sneak out of bed the minute I left."

"If you want to go in, I'll be fine," she said sweetly. The tension had indeed dissolved into the aftermath of their lovemaking. "I doubt I'll freak out again," she said, stretching lazily. She felt confident about Bernard's love for her, about her ability to refine "*La Déclaration,*" if not well enough to win her the first prize, then surely enough to convey her love to Bernard. That would be enough. Later they could face the consequences of the truth, together. "Why don't you take care of business?"

"I could be back late tonight," he said, thinking he should go into the city. "But are you sure?" She nodded. He loved her resilience.

"I'll be ready for a break when you get here. We can plan to meet here at midnight," she said, indicating their bed.

"Sounds like a wonderful meeting place," he said, and before he left for the day, he held her to him for a languorous embrace.

* * *

"Hi, love. Am I interrupting your work?"

It was late afternoon, and Melissa was surprised but delighted to hear from Bernard, if only over the telephone. "I was just thinking about dinner," she said. "My hand feels a lot better—I think I might win this competition after all."

"That's what I want to hear. I love the confidence in your voice."

Melissa beamed. How far away their problems seemed. "What's up?" she asked, curious about the reason he was calling. "Or are you just checking up on me?"

He laughed. "I don't need to do that. But I left my address book on the bedroom table. Can you read me Richard Conklin's phone number?"

"Sure. Let me get it." In a minute she was back on the phone, flipping through the front pages. "Here it is. Ready?"

"Shoot."

She read off the number, admiring the bold script. "Hey, who is Arthur Connell?" she asked, her eye landing on the name above Conklin's. "Do I know him?"

"You've probably heard me mention him. He's an old drinking buddy. I knew him at school. Listen," he said, anxious to change the subject. "I'm bringing work home with me tonight so I don't have to rush into the office so early in the morning."

"Great. I could get used to spending mornings in bed with you," she teased. "I'll see you tonight," she added, anxious not to keep him from his work.

"I love you," he said, somewhat pointedly, Melissa thought.

"I know that," she answered, dismissing the urgency in his voice. "Now get to work!"

They said good-bye more quietly, and Melissa sat by the phone for a minute, relishing his words. The phone rang again, sounding very loud in her ear, jarring her meditation.

"Hi, Mel." It was Patrice. "Have you—"

Suddenly Melissa remembered. Patrice's voice had triggered her memory. "He's the guy who gave the party!" she blurted out.

"What in heaven's name are you talking about?"

"Arthur Connell!" she said, impatient for Patrice to understand what had transpired.

"You'll have to talk in full sentences if you expect me to follow you. What's this about King Arthur?"

"Do you still see him?"

"No," she answered, wondering what had happened. "What makes you ask?"

"Bernard knows him! He's friends with Arthur Connell," Melissa expounded. "He said they were old school chums."

Patrice didn't know what to say. "So?"

Melissa flipped the pages of the address book reading other names. The book was filled with what she recognized to be New York's musical society.

"Leonard Bernstein!" she read. "Right here. That means they're friends! Don't you see? He must know who I am! I'll bet he was even at that party—everything points to it! He's been lying to me all this time."

"Haven't you got that backward, sweetheart? Aren't you the one who has concealed the truth? All Bernard has done is to believe in you."

"This changes everything," she asserted unhappily. "How can we have any kind of life together when he *knows*?"

"Your logic is reversed on that point, too. How could you have a complete life together unless he knew? Your life with Arbour was instrumental in shaping you, and the loss has changed you further. How do you expect him to understand you without knowing about Arbour? He had to learn eventually. Sooner or later you'd run into someone who connected the name Dennison to the child prodigy Arbour married."

Melissa stiffened. "You knew all about this, didn't you?" she asked coldly.

"I was pretty sure Bernard knew who you were," she answered, softening her admission.

"Why didn't you say anything to me!" she demanded, feeling terribly betrayed by them both.

"Because I like Bernard," she quarreled. "And more inportantly, I like what's happened to you since you met him. There's blood in your veins again. You're happy and cheerful and full of good stories. It made me sick to watch you wasting away up there all alone."

"So you let Bernard seduce me, and trick me into performing? Whose friend are you? He would let me think I was performing as Dennison, but he'd alert the press I was Arbour's wife."

"I can't believe how twisted you have everything! Do you think the press are still interested in you? Sure, they were lousy, and you suffered a lot, but that's past. They are bothering someone else now, and you act like they're just waiting in a darkened alley to violate you. Bernard loves you as much as I do. Do you think either of us would risk hurting you?"

But Melissa hadn't heard her question. She had hung up the phone, and was searching madly for her jacket and car keys. Throwing some clothes into a suitcase, along with the stack of papers on the piano, she drove away from the house without even taking her dinner out of the oven, without even leaving the porch light on for Bernard.

Bernard responded at once to Patrice's phone call, and within ten minutes he was in his car and on to face Melissa's discovery.

In Millerton he stopped to put up the top to his car. The sky had darkened. Warm fat drops of rain hit the windshield. The kind of rain Melissa liked best, he thought, wondering if the storm had reached Richmond yet. Would he find her crouched in the hayloft, listening to the rain on the roof of the barn, safe and warm? He imagined she'd be mad at first, but he hoped she'd be willing to listen. He'd explain so that she understood that there was nothing calculated in his secrecy, except how to keep her love. Why hadn't he anticipated the problem? How could he have been so careless with his phone book?

But even as he asked the questions, he knew the time had come when he couldn't watch his every move. Either she trusted him enough now or she never would. He hoped his error would bring them closer . . . close enough to be grateful for the slip that had completed their intimacy. There was nothing left to stand in the way of their life as one.

He found the house empty. So was the barn. Melissa's car was gone, and the newest tracks in the mud belonged to Patrice's car. She had left a note tacked to

the kitchen door: FORGIVE US ALL AND GET BACK TO
WORK. YOU HAVE A COMPETITION TO WIN!

Bernard searched the house for a note addressed to
him, but found nothing. The bureau drawers were askew;
the clothes in the closet were pushed hastily to one
side. Without meaning to further invade her privacy, he
reached into the drawer, hoping for some clue to where
she might have gone. Instead, he found her picture of
Jean-Pierre, carefully hidden beneath a pile of lingerie.
At first he couldn't tell if the jolt to his nerves was from
jealousy or what, but the splash inside his stomach
might have been his heart slipping. . . . He examined
the picture more closely, and had to admit that he did
resent the bastard's good looks. But how could he be
jealous of a dead man? He felt vulnerable to her past.
Before he went back to his car, he appended to Patrice's note: DITTO!! LET ME LOVE *all* OF YOU.

CHAPTER THIRTEEN

"Will you accept a collect call from Melissa Dennison?" the operator asked.

"Of course!"

"Thanks, Trice," Melissa started, her voice restrained. "I didn't have any choice but to call collect."

"Honey, no problem. But where are you calling from? When are you coming back?" she asked. She covered the phone to inform Bernard. "It's her!"

"Who are you talking to?" Melissa asked suspiciously. "Is Bernard there?"

"Yes, he wants to talk to you," she said.

"No! I don't want to talk to him!"

"Honey, you're being irrational. Here," she said, handing the receiver to Bernard.

"Melissa?" he initiated. The line was silent, except for a distant hum. "She hung up," he told Patrice.

"What are you doing?"

"I'm trying to summon the—yes, operator, I want to know where that call was from?" He listened intently.

"What do you mean, you can't tell me?" he asked impatiently. "Then will you reconnect me?"

Patrice stood by his side, a puzzled look on her face.

Bernard slammed down the phone. "God damned country operators!"

Patrice shook her head in sympathy. "What are we going to do?"

Bernard stared angrily at the phone. "I, for one, am going to try to forget that Melissa hung up on us."

"She's upset. You've got to understand. . . ."

"I do understand! I'll even forgive her eventually, but that doesn't excuse her. Pat, we've got to stop indulging her. We've been wrong to encourage her in this need for secrecy. She's been hurt, it's true, but everyone has a scar or two. Did you stop trusting men because it didn't work out between you and Arthur?"

"No, but that's different."

"No more excuses, Patrice. We've been wrong to patronize her. I should have confronted her long ago. She has a right to be angry with my dishonesty," he granted, "but she's been dishonest, too, damn it."

"What should we do?"

He looked at her sternly. "Are you still in love with Connell?" Patrice nodded zealously. "Then I suggest you call him—tell him you've been desperate without him—"

"I couldn't say that—"

"Then tell him whatever you want—whatever you have to say to reinstate your relationship with him."

"How will that help Melissa?" she asked, not understanding his angle.

"You'll be too busy making up with Connell to help

her. She'll have to be responsible for her own life. Besides, if you make up with Arthur, maybe she'll see it as a good example and make her peace with me."

"In other words, I should let her make her own mistakes . . . while I'm making ones of my own?"

"Yes, and count me in on that mistake-making enterprise," he said.

"Bernard, what if we lose her?" Patrice asked anxiously.

"*You* don't need to worry. She'll forgive you. She called to talk to you, didn't she?"

"But what about you?"

He smiled weakly. "If I lose her love over this, I never had it."

"Melissa would call that remark 'adult.' "

"I mean it," he insisted. "I'll feel like hell if she doesn't forgive me, but I'd rather know, before we've gone any further."

"She's a very special person," Patrice said reverently, hearing the love in Bernard's words.

"Yes," he agreed. "And I'd like to tan her hide for this 'special' brand of grief she's left behind."

"I doubt she's off dancing on tabletops in delight. Do you think she'll come back tonight?"

"I don't know," he said. "But I'll be there waiting, in case she does. Do you have any idea where she could have gone?"

"None at all . . . she has no other friends. We'll just have to wait."

"I feel like the genie in a bottle . . . if she comes back tonight, I'll fall to my knees to beg forgiveness, but I can't say how I'll behave tomorrow."

* * *

"That was fast. What did she say?"

"We didn't talk. Bernard was there. I hung up," she said dejectedly.

"That wasn't very nice," he said.

"I don't feel like being nice," Melissa said hostilely. "How *dare* he go to her for comfort?"

Matt studied his new friend's belligerent expression. "You came to me for comfort, didn't you?" he asked diplomatically.

"Yes," she answered dismissively, "but that's different. We won't—"

"Ahhh, I see. You trust us to behave, but not them. Didn't you say Patrice was your best friend?"

"But you should *see* the way they look at each other."

"I've seen the way Bernard looks at you! Do you think the second you left they jumped into bed and forgot all about you?"

"I wish they *would* forget me," she said miserably. She was so confused. She didn't know what to think. "I wish *I* could forget all about me."

"Come on, let's go for that swim you refused. If I can't cool you off, maybe the Atlantic will."

They padded over the sand dunes to the empty beach. The day had been a scorcher, but the sun had set, and the sand had cooled enough for them to traverse it barefoot. They left their towels at the edge of the water.

Melissa paused for an instant before she raced after Matt and dived through the first wave.

Spent from a long swim, they collapsed onto their towels and lay quietly on the beach until it grew dark.

She was thinking about Bernard, and wondering what he was doing with Patrice, when she felt Matt's long fingers tracing a pattern through the beads of salt-water on her back. She listened to her heartbeat race amplified into the sand, and wondered if she should move his hand, but it felt so good. There was nothing flirtatious in his casual touch. For an instant she thought of Jean-Pierre, and was alarmed by the faint-ness of the memory. It had been weeks since she had last thought of him, and now she had to concentrate to focus his image.

"Why are you frowning?" Matt asked. He had seen her brows furrow. "Do you mind this?" he asked, draw-ing a circle-eight between her shoulder blades.

"No, it's not that," she offered. "I was just thinking . . ." Could she tell him? She wanted to suddenly; it would be such a relief to be honest for once. She didn't see how it could hurt. Matt wasn't going to tell anyone. "I was thinking about my late husband."

"Bernard said you were widowed recently. She nod-ded yes. "You must miss him dreadfully."

"I do," Melissa agreed, "but I was frowning because I couldn't remember exactly what he looked like. Even now, I remember a photograph, not him. I'm not sure I can stand to lose him to a faded memory. She swal-lowed the lump in her throat. "When I think about my mother—she's been dead for almost twenty years—I see her sending me off to school, as though it were yes-terday. Why should I forget Jean-Pierre?"

Matt shrugged his shoulders. "I wish I knew. Maybe you don't talk about him enough. Do you have pictures of him around your house?"

"I have one I look at sometimes," she said. She did

have a picture of Jean-Pierre hidden in her bureau drawer, but even so she worried that Bernard would find it.

"You're afraid Bernard would mind?" he asked.

"Not exactly." She took a deep breath. "You see, Bernard doesn't know——" She hesitated. She didn't see how she could explain.

"Doesn't know what? He told me himself that you'd been married and widowed."

Melissa flashed him a suspicious look. "What else did he tell you?"

"Only that you had married young, and were widowed."

Melissa considered. "That's all?"

"Yes. Do I hear the basis for your quarrel with him?"

Melissa nodded.

"Maybe you'd better start from the beginning," he instructed.

"It's a long story."

"I've got nothing planned for the evening, do you? Come on, I love folklore."

Melissa poured a handful of sand into his palm. He waited, expectantly. "I met Jean-Pierre when I was a student at Juilliard," she started, keeping her eyes on the growing pile of sand.

At first her words were hesitant, but the more she told, the more relieved she felt. By the time she revealed Arbour's identity to Matt, she was too engrossed in the story to notice the expression in his eye.

"Slow down, lady. How can you claim unhappiness when you were *married* to Jean-Pierre Arbour?"

Melissa recoiled. He hadn't understood. "Oh, I should never have told you!"

"But of course you should have! Are you kidding? I can't believe you've kept such outstanding news to yourself. Why, you're like those old sea captains who don't share their treasures until it's too late to spend the gold. You have no reason to be unhappy—you've already had more life than most people ever have. What a gift!"

Melissa turned red with anger. "You think I'm lucky? You think I've had it all?"

Matt saw the fire of contention light in Melissa's eye. "Baby, I think you've seen a lot more happiness than most people see. I can't feel very sorry for you."

"How can you be so insensitive?" she asked irately, venting her fury at herself and at the world. "After all I've told you? How dare you judge my life!" She told him about her fight with the press, about the injury to her hand, and her inability to play piano for *six months*; her loneliness. She voiced her anger at the newspapers for misrepresenting her part in Arthur Connell's party; her anger at Arbour for refusing to listen to her . . . for dying . . . for leaving her alone to face a world she was too young to fight. She shouted at Matt for not understanding how it felt to be exiled from her home—New York City—her birthplace. Her fury at Bernard surfaced for destroying her sanctuary, for offering her a life she wasn't free to accept; at Patrice for shifting her allegiance from her to Bernard; finally, she spilled her anger at herself, for not better handling the crisis, for not foreseeing the troubles, for not avoiding the problems in time to spare Jean-Pierre's life.

Matt listened to her tirade without comment, but when her words ran out and her tears began, he was there to comfort her. He held her and let her cry, rocking her gently, knowing her tears would purge her misery faster, and more thoroughly, than anything he could say. She needed to forgive herself before she could see that the rest of the world already had.

"You haven't done anything wrong. Can't you see that? This life is all trial and error. Everyone makes mistakes. People have accidents and die. There is nothing *you* can do to *stop* it. You aren't God!"

"But I don't want to go through it again!" Melissa cried, tears streaming down her face, making new tracks through the dried sea-salt.

"I know," he said tenderly. "None of us does, but we don't have a choice. If we are alive and feeling, we can't help but to hurt sometimes. Sure, fighting is lousy, but it's not the end. The end is when you don't care enough to fight, when you hang up the phone because you don't care enough to say more."

Melissa dried her eyes on his shirttail. "But I don't like it!" Her damp eyes flashed anger.

"You don't have to like it. You just have to live with it."

Melissa smiled slowly. "All right." Her anger was gone, and with it a weight of sadness. It had helped to tell Matt even if his response wasn't what she'd expected.

She told him the remaining pieces to the story she had started an hour ago. Her skin prickled from the night ocean air, but the ghosts from the sea didn't haunt her anymore.

"The world forgives a mistake, Melissa," he said softly when she finished speaking. "It takes us longer to forgive malice, however."

The frown returned to Melissa's face. "What does that mean?" she asked, her voice quivering with renewed hurt. Was he going to yell at her again? How much honesty could she stand?

"I'll be straight with you. I think you've been selfish to keep Arbour's music from his public. You were right to want to mourn his death in private. And you have no responsibility to the press and their mania. But you are wrong to keep Arbour's music for your own private use. It's like taking Van Gogh's 'Sunflower' from the Metropolitan Museum to hang in your bedroom."

Matt's candor again sobered Melissa. She looked him straight in the eye. "It's not that I want to keep Jean-Pierre's work to myself. I've been working . . ." She stopped. She wasn't willing to share that information yet. "But—"

"Then what's the problem?" he asked, more kindly.

"I'm not sure how to share his work and preserve my anonymity."

"That is a problem, but my original point still stands. *It is selfish* to keep his music for your private enjoyment. What does Bernard say about all this?"

"I never told him about Jean-Pierre," she explained, "but he *knew*," she added hotly. "And he let me think he believed me."

"Poor Bernard! That's quite a barrel you've got him over. How could he have told you he knew when you didn't trust him enough to tell him? Do you think he wanted to lose the little trust you had? You made it nearly impossible for him to tell you."

"Oh, Matt, what am I going to do?"

"You're going to forgive Bernard and—what did you say your girl friend's name is?"

"Patrice, but—"

"You're to forgive Patrice too, and —"

"No!" Melissa boomed. "She's not my friend. She lied to me! She's probably laughing with Bernard right now!"

"I doubt it. Not from what you've told me about her. But if you want to stay angry, that's up to you."

"Are you angry at me?" Melissa asked.

"No, you're a smart girl. You'll do what you think best. In fact, I think it's time everyone stopped telling you what to do."

"Thanks a lot—hey, where are you taking me?"

"Home," he said, pulling her to her feet and sweeping the sandy towels into his arm in one gesture. "For dinner."

Melissa stumbled after him, suddenly ravenous from the swim and talk.

"Thank you, Matt. You've been a good friend to me."

He pulled her closer and hurried their pace. "Only a friend?" he contested. "That sounds discouraging. I had such high hopes for our evening alone."

"I can't make love to you!" she declared frankly.

"Why not?"

"Because I love Bernard," she verified.

"That's all I wanted to hear," he said, swinging her hand down by his side. "Then it's dinnertime: would you prefer bass or swordfish?"

"I don't know," she answered, made suddenly shy by the confession he'd wrung from her. "You choose."

"Nope. Time for you to make your first decision. Come on, I'll bet you make a good one."

"Swordfish!" Melissa shouted. All at once she was as starved for the taste of fresh swordfish as she had been for truth.

CHAPTER FOURTEEN

"Do something! We're going to be late!" Melissa cried, leaning into Matt's seat and pounding on the car horn.

"It's no use, Mel. The traffic's backed up beyond Ninety-sixth Street. These cars can't move. We're going to sit here until it clears up, no matter how impatient you get."

Melissa collapsed back into her seat. "Why don't they fix this damned highway!" she complained.

"Honey, I think that's what they are doing right now, in the middle of evening rush-hour traffic," Matt pointed out.

"But today is Saturday!" Melissa argued, as if that would explain everything.

Matt shrugged. "I myself think they'd be better off letting this old highway slide into the Hudson." He looked over to Melissa for a smile, but she was instead pulling at her blouse. "Are you all right?"

"No, I'm hot!"

"I told you we should have stayed on Nantucket."

Melissa stared at him in disbelief, until she realized that he was kidding her. He had urged her to compete in the Regal, but she had only agreed when he had promised to come with her. "This is *your* home. I wish you'd show me some hospitality."

"Believe me, if I could do anything about this August heat, I would have years ago."

"Look, the traffic is breaking."

They took the Ninety-sixth Street exit and raced down West End Avenue to make up for lost time. They reached Ninth Avenue and sped south. "There's a parking spot!" Melissa screamed as they neared Carnegie Hall. Matt slammed on the brakes, threw the car into reverse, and squeezed into the tiny spot.

"Lock the door," he called, jumping out to placate the parking meter. "We've got ten minutes before they start."

Melissa ran after him down the street. "Hey, wait for me," she called. She couldn't hurry in the heels she'd worn, and she couldn't slip them off for fear of running the sheer seamed stockings necessary to the black silk dress.

Matt turned to wait, appraising her as she approached him. "For an ol' piano player, you sure do look classy!"

The auditorium was dark already and, judging from the sound of muffled voices, filled with people. Matt motioned for her to follow. They slipped back through the foyer, out the front door, then back around to the stage entrance. The guard checked them past, and Melissa and Matt disappeared into the wings of the theater.

"Is that the stage manager?" Melissa asked.

Matt tiptoed noiselessly across the backstage and spoke to a self-important-looking man. After a minute he returned. "I have bad news."

"What?"

"They scheduled you to perform last. They weren't sure you were coming," he explained.

"The piano won't stay in tune past the third contestant," she worried. "Not in this humidity."

Matt held her hand while she shifted from one foot to the other. Her tension radiated through her fingers like electricity straight up into his arm, and her lips moved imperceptibly as she counted the mistakes made by the first contestant.

By the time the third performer had finished, Melissa began to relax. Even without inspiration, she could play better than the contestants thus far. Simply, her coordination was better and her understanding of music more astute. Excitement over her selection returned, too, as she listened to the too familiar sounds of Beethoven, Bach, and Mozart. Even the last contestant's choice to play Poulenc's "Valse" sounded tired.

The more she heard, the more her confidence grew. She'd have no problem securing the first prize. And though her reason for wanting to win had changed, had more to do with herself than with Bernard, she still coveted the award. As long as she was going to reenter the world as a musician, she might as well come in at the top. It wouldn't suit her purposes to present Arbour's last works as anything less than brilliant, a testimony to the splendor of their union. She could hold her head high once again and be proud to have inspired great love in a great man. The world would hear his genius in her performance.

The audience hushed audibly when the master of ceremonies announced Melissa's change in program, but the pin-drop silence dissolved into whispers of exclamation at the mention of Arbour's name. Melissa had expected that her news would cause a stir, but most of her worry was relieved by her host's tactful disclosure, and the resounding applause when she walked out onto the stage erased the rest. The roomful of people clamored to their feet to welcome her back, and Melissa wondered how she could ever have thought things would turn out otherwise.

Alone at the piano bench, she took a moment to quiet herself and to let the room regain its composure. Before she started to play, she thought of Jean-Pierre, asked for his blessing as well as his forgiveness, then turned her thoughts to the music. Notes floated delicately out of the piano as her fingers touched the keys, but they reached the audience with a power that shortened their breath. Melissa didn't think about the audience, or the effect her music was having. She was filled with the splendor of Arbour's music.

He had given her an invaluable gift. It spoke directly to her, and she in turn, through an ability he had strengthened through instruction, conveyed it to his public.

Her hand moved as effortlessly as it had before she had smashed the windowpane at Jean-Pierre's bedside. It flew over the keyboard without any trace of stiffness, and she realized that it had healed, completely.

Yet as she neared the ending, and entered the part she had composed to finish his piece, she thought less of Arbour, more of Bernard. *He* had inspired her to finish *"La Déclaration,"* without even knowing the effect he was having. His love had given her the confidence to resume her work, and even more importantly, to reenter the world as a musician, complete, even without Jean-Pierre by her side. The sweetness of his trust, the sincerity of his love reverberated throughout the ending, and when Melissa finished playing, her only regret was that there would be no more of Bernard's love.

The audience responded as unanimously to her performance as the judges did, ushering her forth to receive the highest expression of their praise, a handsome gold trophy shaped like a scroll. Even the other contestants understood that Melissa Dennison Arbour had deserved to win. To have Arbour's music returned to them was enough of a prize for them all.

The commotion settled briefly when Melissa accepted the award from her elderly host and stepped to the microphone to voice her gratitude.

"Thank you," she started, and her voice echoed through the hall as sweetly as Arbour's music had. Shyly, she shared her plans to preserve her late husband's work, to present it all to the world. Arbour's music would receive the immortality it merited!

Yet, as she spoke, she realized the responsibility of her commitment. There would be no time for leisurely afternoons with Patrice, no swims in the pond, no nights of love with Bernard. Her decision to devote her life to Arbour's work excluded any further intimacy with Bernard. She doubted she could honor them both, and an attempt to do so would only keep Bernard from finding full-time satisfaction elsewhere.

"My late husband left a lot of work for me to do," Melissa said bittersweetly. "So, if you'll excuse me, I'll get to it now. Thank you again for your generous reception," she finished, and left the stage to renewed rounds of applause.

Backstage, Melissa was besieged on all sides by congratulations, making her plan of escape impossible. Instead, she was swept forward by the crowd's enthusiasm. She responded to it all with an effervescent smile, but there was so much noise and revelry that she could hardly distinguish individuals in a repetition of well-wishers. Unfamiliar faces greeted her like long-lost friends, and she was quite overwhelmed by her adoring public.

They welcomed her back as if they had been waiting enraptured, as if she had always been their favorite celebrity. Without Jean-Pierre present to divide the acclaim, Melissa received all the credit, for his successes as well as her own. Praise poured over her with an intoxicating effect, and when people predicted her future accomplishments with a crystal-gazer's certitude, Melissa believed them.

Patrice broke through the crowd and embraced her friend with a warmth that erased the previous day's discourse. But it was a second before Melissa recognized her face as familiar.

"I'm so proud!" Her words fell on one another. "We were afraid you weren't going to show . . . but you were the best you've ever been!"

Melissa hadn't had time to respond when Arthur Connell appeared at Patrice's side. Even before she could flinch, he was introduced anew as Patrice's fiancé.

Patrice deterred any questions extraneous to the celebration. "Just congratulate us," she prompted. "I'll give you the whole story later."

Arthur issued his own special brand of approval. "I hope you will consider Lincoln Center when you want to perform."

"Why would she even consider it when Carnegie Hall wants her?" a stout middle-aged woman asked, including herself in their conversation unashamedly.

"I'm representing Ms. Arbour," Patrice offered. "And there will be no decisions until all offers have been made, in writing."

Melissa just grinned her thanks. She wasn't used to the abundance of attention, and she appreciated the shield. More strangers promising friendship crowded toward her. Pushing in behind Patrice, Matt presented a new round of regard for her performance. Introductions were made quickly, and just as immediately the circle extended to include others.

On the whole the press were comparatively inoffensive. This time their tactic was flattery, not accusation. Their questions were decorous. They even asked permission to photograph her. And with equal grace, with a dignity befitting Jean-Pierre Arbour's protégée, Melissa smiled into the camera. Even when she spied Bernard watching her from a distance, she held that pose bravely. She'd allow no vulnerability in her new, public life. She intended to conquer her feelings for Bernard, but in the meantime, she'd just have to pretend, and hope her indifference was convincing. Her stomach churned from wanting him, but she kept on smiling, as if she enjoyed the attentions bestowed on her.

Before she reached the reception room, Bernard cornered her, and without waiting for a possible refusal, he squired her away from the madness, into the quiet of an antechamber.

"I need to talk to you," he said, but the distant look in her eyes frightened him. "I guess now you can buy the farm," he said, trying another tactic. "Congratulations—your performance was exceptional, even for you."

Melissa nodded graciously. She didn't want to talk about "*La Déclaration*," not now, not since she had censored the message she had intended for it to convey to him. "I'm not going to buy the farm," she told him, to change the subject to something less familiar. Bernard looked astonished. "Everything has changed," she continued. "Patrice is getting married, did you know?" She didn't pause for him to answer. "I'm going to move into our old apartment."

"You are moving to New York?"

"This *is* my home," she said defensively, then softened her words. "I don't need to hide anymore, Bernard. I have an enormous task ahead of me, and I can accomplish it more efficiently from the city. And I'll save money—the apartment is rent stabilized."

"I know a place you could live for free," Bernard offered weakly.

Melissa shook her head sadly. "Bernard, it won't work. I've committed myself to preserving Jean-Pierre's music."

She looked away from him, not able to bear the pained expression; it reflected too accurately her own feelings of loss. His silent agony did nothing to help her act cheerful in front of her public, and she fled him in favor of the room full of people, before he could convince her to admit the truth.

The celebration party blurred into a haze of laughter and gaiety, of handshakes and kisses from people she didn't remember meeting. She smiled until her face hurt, until Matt insisted she leave with him, and her fans regretfully let her go.

The sun had long since set by the time they reached the street, but the dark retained the day's heat. Even so, the contrast to the party's bright lights relaxed Melissa, and for the first time in hours her tense smile disappeared.

"Whew!" Melissa exclaimed. "Am I glad to be out of there!"

Matt looked at her strangely. "I thought you were having the time of your life. I was impressed with your social graces."

Melissa almost laughed. "I'm glad I looked convincing. That was the hardest part of performing again."

"But you're used to it, aren't you?"

Melissa shook her head.

"How could you not be?" he asked her.

"When I was married to Jean-Pierre, he was the star. I was only his sidekick. When there was a party, or a story, it was around him."

"What about your concerts in Paris?" he reminded her. She had looked so at ease that he wondered at her denial.

"Well, I never understood French well enough to know what they were saying. I just smiled and let Jean-Pierre do the talking."

Matt didn't answer. His eyes had focused on a figure up ahead, and Melissa was content to walk along in silence. She'd had enough talk to last months.

"Melissa?" A familiar voice sounded out of the darkness.

She spun around to answer, forgetting to disguise her

enthusiasm until too late. "Oh, hi, Bernard," she tried nonchalantly.

Matt greeted him more warmly, but Bernard hardly noticed.

"Can I talk to you for a minute?"

Melissa hesitated, but Matt accepted for her. "I'll bring the car around," he offered, and added, before disappearing down the street, "I'll be back in ten minutes or so."

Even in the darkness Melissa could feel the sadness in his eyes. She hoped he wouldn't be able to see hers. "Quite a party," she said gaily, hoping to lighten the atmosphere, but he chose to ignore the opening.

He selected his words carefully. "I know it is hard to trust people, Melissa, especially when experience tells you to do otherwise." His voice caught on his emotion but he hurried on. "I understand why you didn't want to tell me—"

"But I *did* want to," she protested, before she could stop herself. It wouldn't hurt to tell him her intention, as long as she retained her present resolve. "I realize the position I put you in. You have every right to be angry with me."

"Anger isn't what I've felt, not now or then. I love you, Mel. Can't you forgive me enough to love me again?"

"I *do* love you, Bernard."

"Then I don't understand why . . . ?" His eyes were without happiness, the blue as dark as the sea in a storm. "Why can't we pick up where we left off? It doesn't matter to me that you were married to Arbour."

"There's no time now. I have too much work to do. I have a commitment that—"

"That what?" Bernard demanded, his hurt opening into challenge. "That keeps you from being with the man you love?"

"I've made up my *mind*!"

"Why don't you listen to your *heart*?"

She tried to regain her cool. "I don't want to quarrel with you. I would like for us to remain friends."

"Why? So we can meet for lunch once a month? Is that what you expect?" He dared her to confirm his suspicions. "How do you expect me to treat you like a casual acquaintance when I want to be your lover? I will not treat you like they do," he vowed, gesturing back toward the reception room. "I refuse to admire you from afar!"

His words touched on her own feelings of emptiness but she wouldn't admit them, not to him. "Bernard, I'm sorry for my unreasonableness, and for my bad temper, but I can't love you anymore. I owe it to Jean-Pierre, and to his music."

"You feel guilty for loving me, don't you? Do you think by giving me up, you are honoring Arbour's memory?"

"It doesn't matter what you say, Bernard. I am wed to preserving his music and there is nothing you can say to change that."

"You sound like you mean what you say, but I don't buy it." He was groping for a way to convince her. "If you are serious, if you don't love me as much as I love you, why do you still wear the ring?"

Glancing down at the beautiful piece of jewelry, her heart ached, in spite of her resolve. "You can have it back right now," she said, pulling the ring from her finger.

"No. I won't take it from you now. If you decide you don't want me in your life, Melissa, mail the ring to me."

"Wouldn't it be simpler to take it now?" She wanted to be done with it.

"Yes, I think it would be too simple. I think you are being willful, and that you still want me as desperately as I want you. We *can* have it all," he stressed.

"We can't, Bernard. *I* can't."

He held up his hand to stop her denial. "Send me the ring. *Then* I'll believe you."

Melissa stopped twisting the ring. "If you insist," she said resignedly, "but it's a waste of postage."

Bernard nodded, satisfied with her concession. He was sure she would change her mind.

CHAPTER FIFTEEN

Before the exhilaration of her success wore off, and the heights of glory could spiral downward into postmortem depression, Melissa dove into her work and gave all her attention to the task at hand. She no longer wondered what should be done. She knew. It wasn't an easy chore she'd undertaken, but she could ensure Arbour's place for posterity through her hard work.

Her plan was simple. She would perform Arbour's completed works in next year's concert calendar. The rest of her time would be spent completing the remaining unfinished works so she could add them to her repertoire the following season. The proceeds would begin to establish a memorial foundation in Jean-Pierre's memory, designed to support serious musicians.

Melissa was grateful for the onslaught of work. It forestalled her loneliness, and there was no denying that she was truly alone now. Without noise and distraction it was hard to forget the sound of Bernard's tires on the gravel driveway, or his chatter first thing in the morning, or his arms around her late at night, so she pounded away furiously at the keyboard, hoping to cover the void. He would have other women to hold, but she'd just have to get used to his absence, as she had Jean-Pierre's. To her surprise Bernard was even harder to forget than Jean-Pierre had been, simply because he was within her reach, waiting for a decision that would welcome him back, hoping she would change her mind.

More than once she picked up the phone to call him. Every time she thought to return the ring, she found an excuse not to. For one thing the mails were untrustworthy. Letters were continually late, or were lost; the ring was too valuable to trust to the postal service. Perhaps she should drive into Manhattan to deliver the ring personally? Bernard's suggestion to return the ring by mail was a ploy to make her think, to give her time to reconsider, yet the more she thought, the more confused she became. And always she took her confusion back to the piano, neglecting to return the ring.

On the Wednesday following the recital she called Arthur Connell at Lincoln Center, but couldn't get past his secretary. A half an hour later Arthur was on the phone apologizing, urging Melissa to introduce herself as Arbour instead of Dennison. "I nearly strangled my secretary for not putting through the call, until I realized she couldn't have known who you were."

"I guess everyone will have to learn both names," she joked. "Arthur, is that offer still open to perform next season at Lincoln Center?"

His delight transmitted itself through the phone line. "I'd like nothing better," he assured her. "But hasn't Pat told you that she'll handle it for you?"

"She did say that, but I can't get her to talk about anything but her wedding plans."

It was true. They had been quick to reconcile their disagreement, but then Patrice wanted to talk of nothing but her upcoming marriage. Yet there was something more than just prenuptial distraction in Patrice's responses. Whenever Melissa wanted to discuss her concert plans, Patrice smiled but said nothing. Melissa missed her advice, but the effect was to make her depend on her own judgment, and finally, after a few awkward starts, she found herself relying on her intuitions.

"I don't want to cause trouble between you and your lawyer," Arthur said, "anymore than I want to create conflict with my to-be-bride. Are you sure—"

"If you don't want me—"

"I do. I do. Sign on the dotted line!"

"That's what I like. Enthusiasm."

Arthur laughed, but persisted with his questions. "Why on earth do you want to play Lincoln Center, if I may be so candid, with Carnegie Hall right around the corner?"

"Because of you, Arthur," she said simply.

"But I thought you hated me."

"No, if I ever was angry, that passed long ago. Jean-Pierre's death was no more your responsibility than it was Patrice's, or anyone else's . . . not even mine." She paused, as if to reenter the past, but the memory didn't hold her, no more than the anger had been able to. "I want to play at Lincoln Center because I'm anxious to book the dates and I know you already. I may have committed myself to a public life, but that hasn't made me less shy of people, especially booking agents."

"Consider yourself signed. I'll have a contract drafted and in the mail this afternoon. Until then, don't accept any phone calls from smart-talking agents."

"Just make sure you give me your best dates, Arthur. I plan to cost you a small fortune, and I want you to earn back your cost."

Arthur laughed at her directness. "I plan to make a profit on you, dear. Listen, I'll be in Richmond this weekend, if you want to discuss the contract."

"Making plans for the irrevocable last step?" she asked.

"I never knew a simple court appearance could require so much preparation!"

"Arthur," Melissa started, fidgeting with the cord to the phone. "Have you been seeing Patrice all along?" She knew the answer didn't matter, but she was curious and hadn't been able to ask Patrice.

Arthur's tone turned serious. "For over two years I didn't see her much at all. I got jealous of how much time she was spending with you, if you want to know the truth. I issued an ultimatum and lost."

"I'm sorry. I had no idea!"

"Everything is all right now," he said. "We both learned a lot during that separation. We had been sliding into marriage because it looked like the thing to do, but now there's a sounder reason."

"What's that?"

"Because we want to spend our lives together. We didn't know what we had until we were deprived of it." There was another subject on his mind. "Melissa, do you know that Bernard loves you?"

"No, Arthur. He loved Melissa Dennison. I'm Arbour's widow. There's a big difference."

"Have you explained that to Bernard?"

"I've tried to, sort of, but I can't expect him to understand, he's—"

"Will you stop treating him like a cardboard dummy and respect him—even his sensitivity—enough to say what you're thinking? He's human. He understands that you have complications in your life. But silence isn't fair."

Melissa sighed dramatically. "There isn't any point."

"Don't give all your love to the grave. You'll be a pretty dull interpreter of Arbour's work if you stop living. I'd rather see you give up exclusive rights to his work than give up love."

The other end of the line was silent. He wondered if she had heard anything he had said.

"So, save your questions for the weekend," he prompted. "I'll be up early Friday night."

Just like Bernard, in the old days, Melissa thought, as she hung up the phone.

No matter how busy Bernard was in the following week, he always managed to leave the office at noon to check the mail at home personally. On Thursday nothing had arrived in the mail, and Bernard's hopes rode high. Still, he didn't want to assume too fast—New York's mail delivery was notoriously slow, or she might have taken a day or two to decide. One way or another, he wanted to know her answer before he spoke to her again. If she returned his ring, as she had promised she would, there was little point in pursuing the matter. There would be no satisfaction in banging his head against that particular brick wall.

Friday's mail brought nothing from Melissa, and he was tempted to break his vow to wait. Only a thread of doubt kept him from celebrating her silent acceptance.

On Saturday Tommy brought the mail up to his study, and Bernard's heart wrenched at the sight of the tiny brown parcel. He waited until the houseboy left before examining the package. Postmarked in Richmond, it was the same size box he had given her. Without even bothering to unwrap it, he dropped it into his jacket pocket.

Bernard canceled his plans for the afternoon. He wasn't in the mood to see anyone. All he wanted was to find a way to pass time, until his heart healed. He buttoned his coat, and without telling Tommy his plans, left the house in a hurry. At the corner of Sutton Square he caught a cab downtown. Fifteen minutes later he boarded the Staten Island Ferry.

He needed to be out of the city just then, and the place he wanted to go was closed to him. He had lost her. He had loved her more than he had ever loved anyone, or anything, but it hadn't been enough to keep her. She was married to her art, and too blind to see there was room in her life for him, too.

Battery Park disappeared from sight; the Twin Towers shrank as they approached the Statue of Liberty, Manhattan's proud lady, America's gift from France. He fingered the box inside his pocket and wondered if she would think him relentless if he sent it back. She should wear it—if not as his lover, then in memory of the love. Certainly he'd never use it again. If he couldn't have her, he didn't want anyone.

He was tempted to throw the damned ring overboard, but he couldn't even bring himself to open the box. Instead he shoved it more deeply into his pocket. There was no point in destroying beauty. The was what Melissa was doing. He would send the ring back to her, with a note that he accepted her decision, but wanted her to wear the ring nonetheless. If only in a small way he wanted to remain in her life.

Suddenly Bernard was furious with Melissa and he could hardly wait until the boat docked. She'd just have to find a way to have him *and* her art in her life. He was willing to make concessions to her, except one: he would not live his life without her.

On the drive north he grew even more determined, and pressed the accelerator to the floor. The speedometer pushed eighty: at this rate he'd be there in another hour.

Around a blind curve a deer bolted into the road. Bernard swerved to miss the animal, momentarily losing control of the car, and ran up over the shoulder onto the grass embankment.

"Jesus," he muttered aloud, but his first thought was of Melissa. If he had been killed in an auto accident, he might just as well have killed her, too, for the guilt she would suffer. Carefully he returned to the road, keeping his speed within the limit.

When he reached Melissa's house, he found her piling boxes into the trunk of her car.

"What do you think you are doing?" he asked forcefully. He feared she had packed all his belongings in her determination to clear him out of her life.

"What do you think?" she answered.

"This is no time to be enigmatic," he warned. Didn't she know how much pain she was causing him? He wondered how she could be so insensitive.

Melissa frowned. "Didn't you get my package?"

"Yes," he said. "Why do you think I'm here?"

"To help me pack?"

"How can you be so calm? Can't you see how upset I am?"

She did see but she didn't understand. "Can't you take a joke?"

"This is hardly a joke!" His exasperation took over. "If you want to lock yourself away to spend every day of your life brooding over Arbour's music, that's fine with me, just as long as you are in my bed every night, do you hear?"

Melissa nodded calmly.

"And if you think—" He interrupted himself to stare at her. "You are agreeing?"

"Of course. Do you think I'd marry you to sleep in someone else's bed at night?"

"What are you talking about? Didn't you send back the ring to call the whole thing off?"

An impulse to laugh caught in her throat. "Did you receive my package?"

"I told you I did," he said, his patience wearing thin. "I have it right here," he added, retrieving the box from his pocket.

Melissa stared at the unopened box. "But you didn't open it?"

"I *know* what the ring looks like."

"Bernard," she started firmly. "I think you'd better open the box."

He released a deep sigh, as if to indulge her queer behavior, and began to unwrap the box. Blood rushed to his face as he examined the contents. Inside lay two finger-picks, the very ones he had given her.

"Now we can continue this discussion," she said, flashing her adorned finger for him to see.

Bernard's eyes filled. "Didn't you know what you were doing to me?" he cried, his voice shaky with pent-up emotion.

Immediately Melissa regretted her gag. "I assumed you would open the package. Why didn't you?"

"I was too hurt, too scared—"

She took his hand reassuringly. "I'm sorry, Bernard. I meant it as a joke."

"But I don't understand. What are you trying to tell me?"

"That you were right. I can't spend all my time at the piano. I kept going to the banjo, for relaxation, I thought, until I realized it was just an attempt to be close to you." She smiled, remembering. "As much as I like the banjo, I knew I'd never go back to the piano unless I had you." He stared at her, not knowing what to say, and she continued. "I hardly heard what I played . . . but I'd sit for hours, pretending you were beside me."

"Oh, Melissa—"

She stopped him mid-sentence and took a pick from the box and slid it onto his left ring finger. "Bernard—" She paused to gather her words. "I'm not frightened anymore—at least not of you. I think we *can* have it all."

And they did.

Bestsellers

- [ ] **NOBLE HOUSE** by James Clavell..............$5.95 (16483-4)
- [ ] **PAPER MONEY** by Adam Smith..................$3.95 (16891-0)
- [ ] **CATHEDRAL** by Nelson De Mille.................$3.95 (11620-1)
- [ ] **YANKEE** by Dana Fuller Ross $3.50 (19841-0)
- [ ] **LOVE, DAD** by Evan Hunter..........................$3.95 (14998-3)
- [ ] **WILD WIND WESTWARD**
  by Vanessa Royal...$3.50 (19363-X)
- [ ] **A PERFECT STRANGER**
  by Danielle Steel $3.50 (17221-7)
- [ ] **FEED YOUR KIDS RIGHT**
  by Lendon Smith, M.D. $3.50 (12706-8)
- [ ] **THE FOUNDING**
  by Cynthia Harrod-Eagles..................................$3.50 (12677-0)
- [ ] **GOODBYE, DARKNESS**
  by William Manchester..$3.95 (13110-3)
- [ ] **GENESIS** by W.A. Harbinson.........................$3.50 (12832-3)
- [ ] **FAULT LINES** by James Carroll $3.50 (12436-0)
- [ ] **MORTAL FRIENDS** by James Carroll.........$3.95 (15790-0)
- [ ] **THE SOLID GOLD CIRCLE**
  by Sheila Schwartz $3.50 (18156-9)
- [ ] **AMERICAN CAESAR**
  by William Manchester.......................................$4.50 (10424-6)

At your local bookstore or use this handy coupon for ordering:

Dell DELL BOOKS
P.O. BOX 1000, PINE BROOK, N.J. 07058-1000

Please send me the books I have checked above. I am enclosing $_____ (please add 75c per copy to cover postage and handling). Send check or money order—no cash or C.O.D.'s. Please allow up to 8 weeks for shipment.

Mr./Mrs./Miss_____

Address_____

City_____ State/Zip_____